Unwrapping Mr. Darcy

L.L. Diamond

Unwrapping Mr. Darcy
By L.L. Diamond
Published by L.L. Diamond

Cover and internal design © 2018 L.L. Diamond
Cover design by L.L. Diamond/Diamondback Covers
Cover Art by Lana Lesiuk and Naddya via Shutterstock

ISBN-13: 978-0-9967891-7-2

Facebook: https://www.facebook.com/LLDiamond
Instagram: @l.l.diamond
Twitter: @LLDiamond2
Blog: http://lldiamondwrites.com/
Austen Variations: http://austenvariations.com/

Other works by L.L. Diamond include:

Rain and Retribution	*Particular Attachments*
A Matter of Chance	*Unwrapping Mr. Darcy*
An Unwavering Trust	
The Earl's Conquest	
Particular Intentions	

For Cindy Hinkle and Erika Hoemke,
Thank you so much for your amazing donations
for hurricane relief!
It was a wonderful gift to those who needed it.

Prologue

Elizabeth startled and groaned. No! Turn that ear-splitting noise off! Without opening her eyes, she reached one arm from the warm cocoon of the covers and began slapping at her bedside table. The beeping had to go! Eventually, she'd hit that stupid alarm clock, then she could sink back into oblivion for a little while longer.

Slap! Her hand landed flat on the end table. Slap! Her palm smacked the side of the bed. She missed! Consciousness was returning more and more with each passing second. She had to turn it off! On the next downswing, her hand struck the corner of something that made a loud crack before it dropped out of reach. After a crash, the annoying noise stopped, and she burrowed back inside the cozy pocket of warmth under the blankets.

Her body relaxed, and she began to sink into the mattress, losing more and more of her surroundings when another round of loud beeping made her sit up and throw the covers from her. She flinched at the sting of cold air that hit her after being ensconced under the comfortable quilt. "Oh, shut up!"

Bleary eyes scanned the bedroom and ended up on Grunt, her long-haired black cat, sitting on the pillow next to where she slept. "I know this means you get breakfast, but you don't have to look so pleased with yourself." After a chirrup, he trotted across the bed, jumped down, and ran from the room.

She inhaled sharply when her feet touched the cold wood floor. It shouldn't be this cool. It was October in New York, for goodness' sakes. She needed to check the thermostat. Now that she'd been out of the covers for a minute or so, the room was still colder than she liked.

She rose, stepped forward, and at a sharp stab to the instep of her foot, yanked her leg back and dropped back down to the bed. "Shit!"

She shook her leg, trying to distract from the lingering pain, while she brushed the hair out of her eyes. What the heck was that? When she glared at the floor, shards of plastic and the no longer blinking face of her two-week-old Bluetooth alarm clock stared back at her. She slumped. She needed to stop breaking those.

With a sigh, she unplugged the offending machine and tossed it in the trash can by her bed, then trudged to her dresser and stopped the alarm she'd set the night before on her cell phone. She jumped when the cursed object rang, touched the screen to answer, and put it to her ear. "I'm up!"

"Don't yell at me." Jane's voice wasn't angry, but it sounded slightly lower than usual. "You're the one who asked me to call and make sure you were awake, remember?"

"I was drunk."

Jane laughed. "You were stone cold sober. Now, go put on that new sheath dress we found at Saks this weekend and knock 'em dead."

"You sound like I'm about to compete for World Heavyweight Champion." Jane was always Elizabeth's biggest cheerleader, and she liked to joke that her eldest sister was too good—the perfect sister.

"You better replace that alarm clock before tomorrow. I only agreed to do this for your first day. After that, you're on your own."

Elizabeth glanced over her shoulder at the trash can. "How did you know I broke my alarm clock?"

"How many of those have you smashed since we were little? You always refuse to put it across the room when you know you should."

Elizabeth shuffled into the kitchen and filled the bottom of her stovetop espresso maker with water. "Yeah, yeah. I'll manage. Today is different, though. You know I don't want to be late for the appointment with personnel."

"Oh! Charlie said he'd meet you there at nine. He wants to show you around and introduce you to Darcy."

Elizabeth's ears pricked up like Grunt's when he spotted a bird passing by the apartment window. She finished spooning grounds into the coffee maker and fit it back together. "Have you ever met him?"

"Darcy?"

She put the little pink Bialetti on the burner and turned it on. "No, the Pope."

"You're always such a crab in the morning."

"Well, have you?"

"A few times. Charlie usually goes over to his house to watch football on Sundays."

She bit her lip. The magazine articles she'd read claimed he was stiff and formal, but was he different in real life? "What's he like?"

"When we did meet, we didn't speak much, but he seemed nice enough." Nice? Jane thought nearly everyone was nice. She even believed Charlie's bitchy sisters were the sweetest ladies on Earth. Unfortunately, Elizabeth couldn't always put much stock in her older sister's judgment of people.

"Okay, I better get ready if I'm going to make it."

"I love you, Lizzy. You'll be amazing. I know it."

She couldn't help but let one side of her lips turn up. "I'll do my best."

"Call me when you get home tonight?"

"Okay, but I need to go. Love you too. Bye." She pressed "end" and took a small pot and her giant mug out of the cabinet as Grunt jumped on the island.

"No! No milk for you. You don't drink all of it, and it's not good for you anyway." When she took the carton from the fridge and began to pour some in the pot, the black fur ball pressed forward like it belonged to him. "I said no." She pushed him back. "Don't give me that pouty, innocent look. You forget that I know you. You're trouble wrapped up in a cute package. All you need is a bow and no one could say no to you."

While the milk heated on the stove, she took out a can of cat food and dished it into a small bowl on the counter. "There, maybe that will earn me some forgiveness?"

Grunt chirruped a thank you and dove in while she finished making her latte. When she had her steaming mug prepared, she took it with her to the bathroom to get ready.

After a sizeable sip, she stared with a sigh at the mess of long waves falling around her shoulders. She should've combed it after her shower last night. "Ugh! It's going to frizz the moment I start brushing." She plugged in her hair straightener and set to work. When her hair lay in smooth layers, she applied a little mascara and lip gloss. She never wore much make-up and today was no different, first day or not. She wasn't there to impress anyone with her looks.

Grunt came casually walking into her room as she took her dress out of the closet. He plopped himself on her pillow and began to partake of his after-meal bath. "I'm not putting this on the bed. You'll decide it's an ideal place to settle, and I refuse to wear your fur to work." Her voice was firm, but he didn't seem to care and continued to clean his face as thoroughly as possible.

She traced the contours of the new dress. Jane swore the conservative midnight blue dress would be perfect. She'd better be right. Elizabeth often wore suits, so this was a bit of a departure from the norm. Once she put it on, she turned to the side, ran her hand down her stomach, and adjusted the tie at her waist.

As she took her last sip of coffee, Elizabeth glanced at her phone for the time. "Crap!" She wasn't late, but she needed to be walking out the door. Her hair had taken too much time. Once she slipped into her matching pumps, she took one last look in the full-length mirror. "I can do this."

Enough of that! She had to go! After one last scratch behind Grunt's ears, she grabbed her purse and briefcase and hurried to the subway. As usual for rush hour, people on their way to work were packed into the train like sardines. Fortunately, the ride wasn't long.

A half-hour later, she stood in front of the Darcy Holdings building with a brick resting in her stomach. This was not the time to let her nerves take control! She blew out a long breath, breathed one in, and stepped inside.

At the counter, a man dressed in a black blazer looked up from a computer screen, the Darcy Holdings logo emblazoned on the wall behind him. "Good morning."

She smiled. "Good morning. My name is Elizabeth Bennet. I have an appointment with Cindy Hinkle for eight o'clock."

"May I see some ID?"

Elizabeth pulled out her driver's license and set it on the counter.

He clicked around on his keyboard. "Yes, Miss Bennet. I see you're a new employee, so we should get you set up with your office ID." He motioned toward a place to the side of the counter. "If you could stand on the taped 'x' on the floor, I'll take a picture. While I get the ID set up, I'll notify Ms. Hinkle of your arrival."

She nodded. "Thank you." After placing her briefcase, purse, and coat on a nearby chair, she stood where he directed, and he cued her to smile for the photo.

"If you'll take a seat, I'll only be a few minutes."

Elizabeth sat in one of the chairs but had barely pulled up something to read on her phone when he called her back to the counter and handed her a lanyard. "If you'll scan into the inner doors, the elevator is to the left. Take it to the second floor, and Ms. Hinkle should be at reception waiting for you."

She thanked him and checked out her Darcy Holdings identification while she walked to the doors. Scanning in was a cinch and the elevator was exactly where he told her it would be. Two floors passed quickly, and when she exited the elevator, a brunette woman approached with a wide grin.

"Welcome to Darcy Holdings, Miss Bennet. I'm Cindy. I see security got you all set up with your ID, so let's get to the rest of the paperwork so you can get started." Cindy had a warm, genuine smile that helped relieve some of the weight resting in Elizabeth's stomach.

At least her shoulders relaxed. Her neck had started to ache, she was so tight.

She shook Cindy's hand. "It's nice to meet you."

Elizabeth took a moment to hang her new identification around her neck before she accompanied Cindy to the personnel office where the two of them sat down to a stack of documents already laid out on Cindy's desk. Why did it always feel like you were signing your life away merely to earn a paycheck?

Numerous forms later, she stopped for a moment to stretch her fingers. She'd shifted her pen down to sign the last of the tax forms when a sound came from behind her, so she turned her head to see who it was.

"Am I too early?" asked Charlie. His head peeked through the slightly open door, a wide grin across his face.

Elizabeth pushed the last bit back to Cindy. "I hope not. I believe I've promised the company my first-born child."

Cindy laughed. "No, we're done. Miss Lucas had her orientation last week and is already at your office. I can show you, if you like." Elizabeth had breathed a sigh of relief when personnel had an opening for an assistant at the same time she was hired. Her long-time assistant and friend was able to move jobs with her. She'd have more than just Charlie for a friendly face on her first day.

"No worries," said Charlie with a smile. "I'll make sure Miss Bennet finds her way. I believe Miss Lucas has everything ready and waiting for her."

Cindy picked up the stack of papers and tapped them against her desk. "Sounds like you're all set. If you have any questions, you know where to find me. I'll be happy to help."

Elizabeth grabbed up her belongings and shook Cindy's hand again. "Thank you."

After she followed Charlie out of the office, he leaned a hair closer. "How do you really feel?"

She wiped her free hand down her hip while they headed towards the elevators. "I'm nervous."

He pressed the up button and leaned back against the wall. "It's understandable why you would be."

"This isn't my first job."

"It's something new, Lizzy. Every company is going to have differences and similarities. Relax. We won't snatch up that first born right away. You can't presume to know everything off the bat, and no one expects you to."

She grinned and lifted her eyebrows as the doors closed behind them. "Maybe not, but I can sure try."

The sound of his chuckles filled the small space. One thing about Charlie, he was always so cheerful. His friendly personality complemented Jane, who always thought the best of everyone, but tended to be quiet and reserved. They'd only been going out for six months, but Jane had moved into Charlie's spacious Upper West Side apartment a couple of weeks ago. He was family; he just hadn't made it official yet.

"We'll start at your office." They stepped off the elevator, and he turned to the left. "You can stow your briefcase and purse before I introduce you around."

When she saw Elizabeth, Charlotte bounced up from her desk and led the way into the office. "Did everything go well at security and personnel? I prepped the documents for Cindy on Friday, so you should've been all set."

"Everything was completed except for the parts of the forms I had to fill out myself. Thanks." She looked around her new office. It was slightly larger than her last and needed some decoration, but that wouldn't take long. She tucked her purse under the desk and put her briefcase on her chair. "Mr. Bingley wants to show me around and introduce me to Mr. Darcy. Do you have anything set up for me yet?"

"You have an eleven o'clock with Mr. Hurst. It's on the schedule on your computer, just click the icon on the desktop. Do you have anything for me to do while you're gone? I've been bored to tears since I arrived this morning." She glanced at Charlie. "Sorry."

He shook his head, his strawberry-blond curls shifting with the motion. "No, I understand. Until Miss Bennet has work to do, you have very little to keep busy."

Elizabeth lifted her briefcase to the desk. "I have some personal belongings you can take out and organize if you want. You know where I usually keep things. You said I should bring a framed photo of Grunt for my desk. There's one in there. You decide where it should go." She looked up at Charlie. "Are you ready?"

He waved her to follow. "Let's go. We'll start by introducing you to Darcy." Charlie glanced at his watch. "He should be getting out of a meeting right about now, so it's probably the best time to catch him."

They took the elevator up two floors while Elizabeth tried not to shake in her pumps. William Darcy was no little fish in the business world. He was the third generation to inherit Darcy Holdings, each son in the line making it larger than it was before; however, William Darcy hadn't made the company bigger so much as increased its worth substantially. His business acumen was well-known, and people coveted the opportunity to work for him. He wasn't difficult to look at either! His handsome face certainly spiced up the cover of a business journal from time to time. Now, she was to meet him. She tugged the sides of her skirt. With her luck, she'd stumble over her words or accidentally spit on his tie.

"You're very quiet all of a sudden."

She jumped at Charlie's voice interrupting the low hum emanating from the offices around them. "I'm fine."

"We've discussed business before, Lizzy. I know you admire Darcy."

With a hand to his arm, she stopped him from continuing. "From a purely professional standpoint, yes, but forgive me, I'm not like your sister. I don't stalk him in the society pages or scheme ways to be thrown into his presence." The last thing she wanted was for Charlie to think of her like she was a little girl with a crush.

"Relax," he said. "I never meant anything more. I know you're nothing like Caroline. I love my sister, but I know she tries Darcy's patience. He can't stand her."

When they entered Darcy's outer office, his assistant looked up from her computer. "He's not back yet, Mr. Bingley, but he should return any minute." She smiled and stood. "You must be Miss Bennet. I'm Meghan Reynolds, Mr. Darcy's assistant."

"It's nice to meet you." Elizabeth shook the hand the older lady offered. Most of the executives at her last job had young assistants with legs that went on for days. In contrast, Meghan Reynolds was probably in her mid-fifties with sandy-grey hair and a pair of vintage looking horn-rimmed glasses.

Both of them turned at the sound of steadily louder voices coming from the hall. Elizabeth pulled herself as tall as she could when Darcy emerged followed by a much shorter man, who walked quickly in order to keep up and talked with his hands as well as his voice. "But Mr. Darcy!"

"I said no and I meant it. I don't like the proposal, and no rework is going to change that fact. Scrap it and move on, Mr. Wickham. I mean it."

The man stopped in his tracks. "You simply can't handle that I'm right. You know this is a great project, but you hate it because it didn't come from you."

Elizabeth stepped back as Darcy approached and handed several items to his assistant. "Mrs. Reynolds, please call security. Have someone show Mr. Wickham to his office so he can pack up his belongings and be escorted from the building. Then call personnel.

They will need to find a qualified candidate to replace him."
Elizabeth's eyes almost burst from their sockets.

"Yes, sir." Mrs. Reynolds picked up her phone and dialed several numbers.

"You can't do that!" Mr. Wickham sputtered as he spoke, spit spraying from his lips. "Your father hired me."

"It's done. If you'll excuse me, I have work to do." Darcy's tone was stern and resolute.

Mr. Wickham continued to yell, but Darcy ignored him and entered his office with Charlie following close behind. Mr. Wickham started to trail after the two, but Mrs. Reynolds held an arm out in front of him. "May I remind you, Mr. Wickham, that there are security personnel assigned to every floor."

The man opened his mouth, his face contorted into an ugly sneer, when two burly men in Darcy Holdings coats rounded the corner. They were polite and didn't force matters, but Mr. Wickham had little choice but to do as they asked.

With the show over, Elizabeth stepped toward the open office door, pausing in the doorway. Charlie stood at Darcy's side, leaning on a small boardroom table while Darcy sorted papers. "What do you expect me to tell her? She knows you're in here."

"I don't care what you tell her." He had a deep voice—one that was low and rich, like melted chocolate poured over gooey caramel. It made something inside her flutter. "I'll meet her eventually. It doesn't have to be today."

Charlie exhaled, sounding a lot like a growl. "You always make a point of meeting new employees. Why are you being so stubborn about this one?"

Darcy slapped the papers in his hand on the work surface. "I'm busy, Bingley. If you haven't noticed, I have a mountain of paperwork on my desk. I can't be expected to take the time to welcome a new company attorney—especially one who required her sister's boyfriend to get her the job. You hired her, Bingley. You make her feel welcome."

What? She gasped, and they both looked up, but she backed away from the door. She couldn't stay—not in his office and certainly not at this job! She walked as fast as she could to the elevator, which thankfully opened as soon as she touched the down button.

Charlotte wasn't around when Elizabeth returned, so she went into the office and opened her briefcase, which still remained sitting on the desk. She reached up over the computer, pulled down her calendar, and threw it inside.

She certainly wasn't staying where she wasn't wanted. Charlie had sworn they needed someone with her skills. Why would he lie? She hadn't been looking for a new job. She'd been happy where she was, but working for Darcy Holdings was a move up she couldn't ignore. The company was larger than the law firm, and the position held more room for advancement.

"Don't you dare put another thing back in that case."

"I don't need this, Charlie. I won't stay where I'm not needed. I'll go back to Longbourn, or I'll find another job. Fortunately, I have some savings put aside. Don't worry, I'll be fine."

With two strides forward, he closed her briefcase and leaned over her desk. "You're staying right here at Darcy Holdings, and I'm going to tell you why."

Two hours later. . .

At the slam of his office door, Darcy's pen skittered across the paper. He lifted his gaze from his desk to Bingley and glared. "Was that really necessary?"

"Yes, yes it was." Bingley's normally cheerful voice was more of a growl, and his face was so red, it looked like he'd swallowed a dollop of wasabi, which wasn't good. It took a lot for Bingley to get that worked up.

"You aren't still upset about what happened earlier?"

"You're damned right I'm still upset. I just spent the better part of an hour convincing Lizzy to stay. I even went with her to her meeting with Hurst to make sure she didn't change her mind. Why would you be such a colossal ass?"

"If Hurst retires in March, like he's been telling us for the last five years, we won't need another corporate attorney for almost five months, but you insisted on hiring and paying for one now." Bingley made that strange, guttural growling noise under his breath that Darcy only heard every once in a blue moon. Uh oh, he'd really pissed him off this time.

"She finished Harvard Law at the top of her class—"

"So did I—"

"That doesn't make it something that happens every day! Do you think I decided to hire her on a whim or merely because she's Jane's sister? She left a good job at Longbourn, Netherfield, and Haye because I offered her this one." Bingley pressed his hands against the desk and leaned closer. "She interned for several prominent corporate firms during her undergrad and law school summer vacations. She's also been recognized as one of the up and coming female attorneys by two of the three major women's groups in this city, but she's really just made it into people's radar in the last couple of years, especially since she made the "Top Women to Watch" list in Business Quarterly Magazine. Heck, for the last six months, Longbourn, Netherfield, and Haye have been arguing over whether to give her a big pay raise, and Haye was pushing for her to be partner. He knew if they didn't act, they would lose her. She hasn't even been practicing ten years yet. I'm telling you, it was only a matter of time before someone grabbed her, and I thought it should be us."

He sat back, threw his pen down, and scrubbed his hands over his face. "Okay! I'm sorry. I was in a foul mood after that meeting and the run-in with Wickham. I know it's no excuse for what I said, but she could've started closer to Hurst's retirement."

Bingley plopped into one of the chairs. "Didn't I say she might be offered another job or a sizeable raise by then?"

Darcy tilted his head. "Who told you that? Her?"

"No, I mentioned her to Hurst. He's been friends with Grant Haye since they interned together in college. When Hurst found out I knew Lizzy, he even said I should make her an offer before Longbourn made their decision. It took me two months to convince her to come to Darcy Holdings, and you almost sabotaged it all today."

"Fine! I'll apologize."

"You better," said Bingley, his voice insistent.

Darcy dropped his head back and closed his eyes. That dull throbbing behind them was becoming a distraction. The entire mess was giving him a headache and it wasn't even one o'clock yet. Was noon too early for a scotch? A double with no ice? He pressed the heels of his hands to his eyes. He had a meeting this afternoon. Instead, he'd be settling for ibuprofen and water.

Chapter 1

Six weeks later . . .

Darcy sat at the head of the long boardroom table and trained his sight on James Hurst, head of the legal department. If he continued to look precisely in that direction, he wouldn't be distracted by *her*. Instead of obeying his wishes, though, his eyes started to shift, pulling in the same direction they always did. No! He wasn't going to do it. He couldn't look at her again. She'd taunted him for the last six weeks with her teasing grins and her brilliant green eyes. Those eyes grew fiery when she was angry or determined to convince someone of her opinion, and he couldn't look away.

Six weeks now, and the chance to apologize hadn't happened. He'd simply never had the opportunity. She wasn't head of the legal department, so he never met with her one-on-one, and she always seemed to be chatting to one person or another before group meetings or while she walked around the building. Her assistant or Ms. Hinkle from personnel, or both, accompanied her most of the time. Miss Elizabeth Bennet had become friendly with a number of his employees since she began working at Darcy Holdings, but he wasn't one of them.

He tried to maintain his gaze on Hurst, but Elizabeth Bennet was like a freaking magnet and her pull was overwhelming. He could never avoid looking at her for long. When had that started? He honestly couldn't remember. One day he acknowledged she was an attractive woman, the next he fought to prevent her from discovering any hint of his interest—and he was definitely interested! What part of him didn't react when she tucked a lock of that long chestnut hair around her ear or moistened her lips, offering a slight peek of her delicate pink tongue? He shifted in his chair while his gaze traced the graceful line of her neck.

His eyes wrenched from that spot under her earlobe back to Hurst. He had to stop this! She worked for him, for Pete's sake. What did he expect could happen? He'd never dated an employee, and he had no intention of starting with her. Even the idea of it was completely inappropriate.

Who was he kidding? It was unlikely she'd agree to even a cup of coffee with him unless he used work as an excuse. He'd never had the opportunity to apologize for his inane comments on her first day, and when he did try to speak to her, her eyes widened like he was some hideous creature out of a horror movie. Yes, he'd been a prick, but why did he come across as frightening?

Hurst asked Elizabeth to take over, and Darcy's resolve crumbled. His attention drawn to the way her hair spilled in waves over her shoulder. His eyes traced up the curve of her neck to the set of full lips that turned up a tiny bit on each side, like she held a secret no one else knew, but he wanted to know desperately. She never wore much make-up, but she didn't need it. The slight sheen to her lips set them off perfectly, and whatever she did to her eyes was subtle but made them stand out. He followed the straight line of her nose to those vivid forest green eyes framed by long, thick eyelashes. He could get lost in those for hours.

"Darcy!"

He started and glanced around the table. "I can hear, Bingley. You don't have to yell." Had anyone else noticed him staring? Hurst's shoulders shook, but his head was down. Darcy couldn't see his face.

When he turned, Bingley's eyebrows rose on his forehead. "I said Miss Bennet seems to have the proper documentation under control. I think we can put off meeting on this topic again until we're closer to making our move. What do you think?"

"I agree. Unless we have further business for today, we can adjourn. I have a conference call with San Francisco in an hour, and I'd like to double check my figures first." After an almost-collective nod from his employees, he forced a smile and checked around the table while everyone organized their notepads and files. A few people spoke to one another, but no one watched him or Elizabeth. The more important question: did she know he'd been drawn to her? He cleared his throat and pushed his seat back. He needed to get out of there.

When he rose, Bingley and Mrs. Reynolds followed. He waited until they entered his outer office before he turned to Bingley. "Was there something you needed?"

"A quick word, if you don't mind."

Mrs. Reynolds sat at her desk. "I'll order you a sandwich. With the conference call, you won't be able to go yourself. Would you like anything, Mr. Bingley?"

Bingley gave that smile that never failed to charm the ladies. "No, thank you, Mrs. Reynolds. I'm meeting Jane for lunch in an hour."

"Chicken and avocado on whole wheat?" she asked Darcy.

"Yes, that would be great, thank you."

When the door closed behind them, Bingley sat in his usual seat in front of Darcy's desk. "I think it's time to start talking about a Secret Santa." Darcy had no chance to say a word since Bingley held up a hand. "I don't mean the entire company, only this building. We could even split it up by floors to keep it from being too large."

"Sounds like a pain in the ass." Great! Now, he sounded like the Grinch!

"Don't worry about it. We all know you're the company's biggest Grinch. I'll coordinate our floor, and I already have volunteers lined up for the other sections." One side of Bingley's lips curved upward in what was for him a rather mischievous expression. "I don't suppose you'd want anyone in particular?"

"What ridiculous idea has gotten into your head, Bingley?" He woke up his computer and clicked one of the folders on the desktop. He needed to review those figures for the San Francisco office. It was so like Bingley to become nosy at the worst time.

"Only that you've been staring at Lizzy a lot. Did you ever apologize to her?"

He scratched the back of his neck. "I've never had the opportunity. Usually, I speak to Hurst involving anything in the legal department, so it's not like Miss Bennet and I are ever alone."

"You could've gone down to her office. It's not like she works in the San Francisco or London offices. Have you ever simply tried saying hello?"

"No," he said weakly. The longer he'd put off the apology, the more difficult it had become.

Bingley laughed. "Why don't you admit that you like her?"

"What makes you think I like her?" He opened a file on his desk. He couldn't look Bingley in the eye. The two of them had been friends since kindergarten, and Darcy had always had a hard time hiding anything from Bingley.

"Oh, come on. Are you really going to deny it? Give me some credit."

Darcy groaned and leaned back in his seat. "How long have you known?"

"Since about a week or so after she started here. Don't worry. I don't think anyone has figured it out, but I've known you a lot longer than everyone else. I also remember that pining expression you used to give that little brunette sophomore year. The way you look at Lizzy is different, but that was how I recognized it. You know, if you would only apologize, she might stop avoiding you at meetings."

Darcy shook his head. "What good would that do? It's not like I can ask her out. She's an employee, for God's sakes. Do you know how inappropriate it would be? With my luck, I'd get slapped with a sexual harassment suit."

"So, become friends with her first. For what it's worth, Lizzy wouldn't jump to a lawsuit for something as little as an invitation to dinner. She's not like that. You could start with a lunch meeting. Use one of the company projects she's working on as an excuse. You wouldn't have to talk about work the entire time. Bring up Ana. Your sister is a subject you can talk about easily, and Lizzy can relate to it since she and Jane are so close."

A strange almost bark came from Darcy before he could stop it. "That's dishonest and manipulative."

"So, you're going to stare at her for the rest of your life."

"No!"

Bingley crossed his arms over his chest. "Really? Because it doesn't sound like you're going to do anything about it."

"Eventually this *thing* will go away, and I can move on. I'm working on it."

His friend rolled his eyes. "You aren't built that way, Darcy. You hardly ever find yourself really attracted to someone, but when you do, it never just goes away. You've either had to have a relationship with the person that ends as a tremendous failure, or you avoid them until you get over it—like when you had that crush on Mary King when you were at Harvard. For some reason, you never told her, and you became a hermit, avoiding her until you graduated."

"Okay, and your point is?"

"My point is Lizzy isn't going anywhere, and neither are you. You can try to pretend she doesn't exist, but Hurst told me that he's having second thoughts on recommending Denny as his replacement. He's leaning towards Lizzy, and if she gets that promotion, you'll be working much more closely with her than you are now. You can't avoid her."

This was going nowhere, and he had work to do. "I'll try to talk to her."

"What about the Secret Santa?"

He waved his hand in a dismissive way. "Fine. As long as I don't have to organize it."

"Not a problem," said Bingley. "I already have everything prepped, but I'm going to wait until the week before Thanksgiving. That way, people can shop for their gift on Black Friday if they want."

Darcy detested Secret Santa! What was it about buying a gift for someone you hardly knew that was so much fun? He was more likely to get a raging ulcer from the stress of it all. Of course, that was why he had Mrs. Reynolds. She bought the presents, and he filled out the card, which worked for him. If only he could buy a present for someone he knew, then it might be more fun. If only he could buy a gift for . . .

"Bingley?"

"Yeah?"

"Were you serious when you asked if I wanted someone in particular for Secret Santa?"

His friend's head tilted a fraction to the side. "It was a joke."

"I want you to do something for me."

Bingley shook his head. "Why don't I like the sound of this?"

"Relax, I'm not asking for anything illegal. I only want you to rig the Secret Santa."

A knock sounded on the door before Mrs. Reynolds hurried in and set a bag and a bottle of mineral water on the side of his desk.

"You want me to rig the Secret Santa." Bingley's tone was flat and his jaw slightly slack. "I can't believe you just said that."

Darcy glanced to the side to find Mrs. Reynolds looking back and forth between the two of them. Her eyebrows rose. "Forgive me for intruding."

He waved off her apology. "You know everything that pertains to the company, and I've never required you to wait for permission when I've met with Bingley in the past."

Bingley shifted, so he rested on the arm of the chair. "Exactly *how* do you want me to do that?"

"Rig the Secret Santa?" asked Mrs. Reynolds.

"Yes."

"It's simple." Darcy picked up his pen and began doodling on his post-it notes. "I want to have a certain individual. You can separate that name out and have the rest of our section pick from the remaining names."

Mrs. Reynolds chuckled. "You don't even purchase your own Secret Santa gift. I do that every year."

His eyes met hers. "You won't this year. I'll shop and find the gift myself."

"I'll believe that when I see it," she said, her voice light.

Bingley narrowed his eyes. "No, you participate by the rules, just like everyone else."

"Then count me out." Darcy rose, walked to the window, and watched the people on the sidewalk below. He was bluffing but would Bingley realize?

After a minute, a loud breath was blown out. "Who do you want?"

His hands clenched and released. He could do this. He'd have to apologize at some point, but by the end of the year, he'd hopefully be able to speak to her. "Elizabeth Bennet." The gift would have to be good, no ridiculous impersonal pen or tear off calendar would do.

"This is a bad idea," muttered Bingley.

Darcy turned and rested his shoulders against the window. "Why? It's only a Christmas gift."

Mrs. Reynolds sat in the chair at the end of the table. "Because you've been interested in the girl since you first took a good look at her. What was that, about a week or two after she started? —after you were such a horse's ass. You need to talk to her, not buy her gifts."

Bingley pinched the bridge of his nose, something he usually did when he was stuck for an argument. "You forget that I've gotten to know Lizzy since I started dating Jane, by speaking to her and by what Jane has said of her. She's more likely to think you were trying to impress her with money."

Darcy shoved his hands in his pockets. "Isn't there a spending limit?"

A small chuckle came from Mrs. Reynolds. "Since when would you let that stop you?"

She was probably right. He never looked at the price when he bought gifts for his sister, Ana. He would do the same when it came to Elizabeth as well. He loved spoiling those he cared for.

Bingley rubbed his eyes and dropped his hands to his lap. "Okay, I'll do it, but you better not make me regret it. If you hurt Lizzy in any way, Jane will have my balls in a vise."

"Why would you think I'm going to hurt her?"

"My condition on this is that you have to try to talk to her. You can't simply drop a gift on her before Christmas and expect her to forgive you. She doesn't like you, but she also doesn't know you. You're going to have to change that."

His assistant stood and leveled a hard almost glare at him. "I agree. You're a kind and generous man, but she's not a business deal. She's independent and stubborn. She won't simply bend to your will because you drop an expensive trinket in her lap." She brushed her hands together. "On that note, I have some calls to return and a few memos to write. I suggest, Mr. Darcy, that you get to those figures and your lunch before San Francisco has you tied to the phone for the next few hours."

Bingley stood. "She's right. I hadn't meant to take up this much time. I thought Secret Santa would be a quick meeting. I would ask, you would moan and groan, and I'd insist. Normally, it would take ten minutes max. Teasing you about Lizzy would only add another five minutes before you'd lose your temper." A big grin lit Bingley's face. "I'll let you know when I have the draw for the Secret Santa. I was thinking the Monday before Thanksgiving. That seems as good a time as any."

He followed Mrs. Reynolds out, leaving Darcy to turn back to the window and stare, not really seeing anything in front of him. He could do this. He would apologize and let her get to know him and maybe . . . maybe she might give him a chance.

Maybe? How could that word be so hopeful and so depressing at the same time?

Chapter 2

December 1st

 Elizabeth strode through the automatic glass doors of the Darcy building, scanned her identification at the inner employee entrance, and hurried to the elevator. Don't break a heel! Don't break a heel! That would be just her luck if she did!

 She'd broken another alarm clock this morning and had forgotten to set her freaking cell phone alarm. Forty-five minutes ago, she'd woken to the sound of the same cell ringing furiously. Thank God for Charlotte, or she'd still be in bed, sleeping the day away—not that Charlotte did anything more than yell, "Get up! You're late!" at the top of her lungs and hang up.

 After dumping some food in Grunt's bowl, she skipped her morning coffee, threw on the same dress she'd worn her first day, and pulled her hair into a quick, high ponytail. It was raining, so there was no point in a curling iron or straightening it. It would frizz the moment she walked onto the sidewalk anyway. She applied her mascara and lip gloss on the subway, somehow managing to avoid being elbowed or jostled in the process. At least instead of being really late for the morning meeting, she would only miss the beginning by a few minutes—if the elevator cooperated.

 Her foot tapped a quick, even staccato while she waited and periodically glanced back at the door to the stairs. She was not climbing forty-eight floors! She would be sweating and disheveled by the time she got into the meeting, and the elevator would still beat her up there.

 A ding preceded the doors opening, and as soon as the people on board filtered out, she darted inside and pressed the button for the forty-eighth floor, her foot tapping again as the doors closed in front of her. Come on! Hurry up! Why did it always seem like elevators slowed to a crawl when she was in a rush?

She could've screeched when it stopped at two floors on the way up to let others on, but instead, she gripped the handle of her briefcase tighter and tapped her foot a little faster. When they reached her floor, she shot down the hall until right before her office when she broke into that awkward jog that could only be accomplished in heels.

Charlotte rose and followed her inside. "You broke your alarm clock again, didn't you?"

She yanked off her gloves and unwrapped her scarf, tossing them in her chair. "I forgot to set my phone as a back-up."

"Do you want me to order you another?"

"Please, same model. I'll have to figure out somewhere else to put it."

Her assistant rolled her eyes. "Jane and I have been telling you that for years." Charlotte handed her a lint roller. "Leave everything where it is. I'll hang your coat after I bring your coffee."

Elizabeth nodded. "Okay." She reached for a pen but her hand froze over her pen cup. "Charlotte, what is this?" Why was there what looked like a Christmas present on her desk?

"I don't know. It was there when I came in this morning." Charlotte reached into a cabinet behind the desk and shoved a notepad and a file into her hands. "I'm dying to know what's in there, but you need to get to the meeting. You're two minutes late as it is."

"Shit!" She grabbed the pen, pad, and file from Charlotte and rushed back to the elevator. By the numbers lit up over the doors, none of the elevators were even close to her floor, so she hurried to the stairwell, took off her heels, and ran up two floors. Once she put her pumps back on, she walked as fast as she could to the main boardroom. She paused when she reached the door, took a deep breath, smoothed her hair to the band, and entered with her shoulders back. "I'm sorry I'm late." Of course, everyone looked up when she entered! She needed to keep her chin up and act like everything was perfectly normal.

She took her usual seat next to Mr. Hurst, who patted her hand. "Don't worry. We were just getting started."

"Thanks," she whispered. She leaned back in her chair and listened. What were the odds that the man she saw fired on her first day would become her primary assignment? She peeked over at the man she hadn't laid eyes on in months while his attorneys spoke of his case, bandying about terms like wrongful termination and compensation like it was all so simple.

Her pen moved smoothly along the paper as she took notes until a prickly sensation on her neck and arms made her glance around the room. When her eyes met those of the CEO, he cleared his throat softly and turned back to Mr. Wickham's lawyers on the other side of the table. Since when had he decided to attend? Hadn't Mr. Hurst recommended against it? She'd been in such a hurry she hadn't even noticed him when she'd entered, and why was he looking at her? Did she have something hanging from her nose? She casually brushed right above her top lip with her finger.

Charlotte entered and placed her pink, oversized mug of coffee in front of her. Hurst chuckled under his breath. The first time he saw her cup, he'd had a field day with how someone so little could drink so much coffee without bouncing off the walls. He had no idea what a night owl she was. After a sip, she turned her attention back to the lead attorney for Mr. Wickham, a Mrs. Younge.

Mr. Wickham wore a smug smile when Mrs. Younge finished speaking. Mr. Hurst flipped through some documents they'd handed over, then passed them to her, but that strange sort of feeling she had before returned, so she looked up. Why was Mr. Darcy staring at her? What the heck! Those hazel eyes did something strange when their eyes met, or maybe that strange zing was from the coffee. She glanced down at her cup. Did Charlotte use the usual blend or had she swapped it for something else? When she looked back, their eyes held for a moment before he turned down to his notepad and began writing.

"Elizabeth?"

She jumped at the sound of Mr. Hurst's voice. "Forgive me." She stood, opened the folder, and passed copies of her paperwork to Mr. Hurst and Mr. Darcy. "During the six years Mr. Wickham has worked for Darcy Holdings, he has undergone eight performance reviews." She placed each one separately on the table in front of her. "Those from his initial two years were predominantly favorable. He made some mistakes, but his supervisor believed he would improve. He felt Mr. Wickham showed promise. However, the performance reviews from the years following tell a different story. Mr. Wickham had a habit of arriving to work late."

Mrs. Younge opened her mouth, but Elizabeth pushed another set of papers across the table. "Extremely late. At first, it might have been ten to twenty minutes once or twice a week, but by the end of his employment, Mr. Wickham was entering the building several hours late two to three days a week as evidenced by his identification card login downstairs. His supervisor also noted when he gave Mr. Wickham a verbal warning as well as the written notes he included in his file upon the subsequent warnings." The entire time she spoke, the urge to squirm in her spot was overwhelming. What was that pull from right below her ribs? He was watching her again, and it was distracting!

Mr. Darcy glanced over the documents and made a few brief notes, but whenever she was speaking, that piercing gaze never failed to return to her. What had she done to displease him? He didn't smile. He didn't nod. He just stared at her—hard. She must've done something wrong, but for the life of her, she couldn't think of what it could be.

"Mr. Wickham also became increasingly frustrated and even lost his temper with executives when he was overruled. He became belligerent with Mr. Darcy on the day he was terminated, which was witnessed by our vice president Charles Bingley, Mr. Darcy's assistant Meghan Reynolds, and myself. Any of those Darcy Holdings employees in attendance can also verify that Mr. Darcy did not lose his temper, he did not insult Mr. Wickham, and he did not strike Mr. Wickham as Mr. Wickham alleges." Elizabeth drew a disc from the folder. "We also have the video footage from the outer office where the confrontation took place, proving Mr. Darcy never struck Mr. Wickham."

She pulled out another set of documents and set them on the table in front of her. "After Mr. Wickham's termination, our IT department came in to ensure nothing personal remained of Mr. Wickham on his computer. This initial document was discovered first, divulging the identities of acquisitions and mergers Darcy Holdings intended to make as he learned of them. As a result, our security staff sorted through his emails and discovered these." She pushed copies of more messages across the table. "The Securities and Exchange Commission has been notified. I imagine they will be contacting Mr. Wickham in the due course of their investigation, particularly if he or any person in these emails purchased or sold stock in any of the companies mentioned at strategic times."

A sudden pallor suffused Mrs. Younge's complexion as Elizabeth took her seat. When Mr. Hurst took over, she clasped her hands in her lap. Mr. Wickham and his attorneys had made it clear they expected a profitable deal when Charlotte had called to arrange the meeting. From his lawyer's agape mouth, Mr. Wickham had obviously not been too forthcoming with Mrs. Younge.

Goosebumps broke out down her arms, and she pressed her lips together. Not again! Her eyes darted in Mr. Darcy's direction. He was definitely watching her, that is, until Mrs. Reynolds entered and whispered something in his ear.

Elizabeth relaxed back into her seat while Mr. Hurst continued. At least she didn't have to sit next to Darcy today. At a couple of meetings, she sat at his side. She needed an ibuprofen after each of those meetings. Her neck was in knots within an hour.

Mr. Wickham's legal team was quiet when Mr. Hurst concluded matters. They packed up their belongings and their copies of the documentation Elizabeth provided and began to file through the door, but Mr. Wickham stood, his chair rolling back with the quickness of his movement.

"That's it? You're quitting?" His hands clenched at his sides while Mrs. Younge turned to face him.

"Mr. Wickham, if you will accompany us back to our office, we need to discuss the information Ms. Bennet has disclosed and plan from there. There's nothing more we can say or do at this time. If we find any proof contrary to what has been presented today, we can schedule another meeting."

"I don't want another meeting! I want matters settled today!" The words came out of Wickham's mouth snarled and at a high volume.

"Mr. Wickham." Mr. Darcy drew the phone on the table closer. "Do I need to call security and have you removed from the building again?"

At Mr. Darcy's threat, the idiot turned abruptly and followed his attorneys, but not without a glare back before he disappeared down the hall.

Elizabeth paused a moment, long enough to ensure they'd cleared the hall before she made to return to her office, but at, "Miss Bennet," she stiffened. She knew that rich, low tone and it was all she could do to keep her shoulders from slumping.

Instead, she pulled herself as tall as possible and faced him head-on. "Yes, sir."

"I hoped to discuss with you the Wickham case and any further issues we might need to resolve before concluding matters. You've handled all of the legal paperwork, research, and planning, so it makes no sense to speak to Hurst. I know it's last-minute, but perhaps over lunch?"

Lunch? With Darcy? With William Darcy, her boss? No! She'd have to max out on pain relievers by the time they were done to deal with the back cramps from the stress. How bad would it look to pop half a bottle of ibuprofen during a two-hour meal? She opened and closed her mouth. What was she supposed to say? She didn't want to have lunch with him. "I . . ." Could she claim she had plans with Jane and not offend him, or would he expect her to cancel? Who was she kidding? He was her boss. Not merely the head of the department, but the head of the company. She couldn't say no. "Yes, of course."

"Excellent. I'll have Mrs. Reynolds set a time with Miss Lucas." Someone called his name and he glanced around her to a man standing in the door holding a file. "Forgive me. I need to speak with Chamberlayne for a moment."

"Okay."

He stepped around her, while she stood stock still. What just happened? She snapped out of it long enough to start walking toward the elevators but took the stairs for the quiet. She had to get out of this lunch somehow! Talk about awkward! After all, it wasn't like he wanted her working for the company. He'd made that clear her first day. He'd also never said anything to indicate he'd changed his mind either. He did nothing but stare at her, like he couldn't stand the sight of her.

When Charlotte saw her, she jumped from her seat and followed Elizabeth inside the office, shutting the door behind her. "Mr. Darcy asked you to lunch?"

Her head whipped around and she gawked at her assistant. "How do you know that already?"

"Mrs. Reynolds called down right before you got here."

She dropped her supplies on the desk. "He only wants to discuss business. It's not like he asked me on a date, but I need to find some way to get out of it. I *don't* want to go to lunch with him."

Charlotte's chin gave a slight jerk back. "He's the boss, Lizzy. You're going to end up having some kind of work lunch or private meeting at some point. You may as well get the initial awkwardness over with now rather than later. Besides, everyone here says he's an amazing employer."

Elizabeth plopped into her chair and put her head in her hands, lifting it only to speak. "Probably because he wants them here. He didn't want to hire me and is only putting up with me because of Charlie."

"You didn't have to take the job." Charlotte's flat tone and lifted eyebrow irked her.

"If you remember, Charlie begged me to stay. He swore that I wouldn't regret it, and I felt obligated because he stuck his neck out for me." She smoothed her hair. "What am I going to do about lunch? I tried to think of anything I could to get out of it, but my mind drew a blank."

"Maybe you should give him a chance. You haven't given the man much of a break since you began working here."

She straightened and glared at Charlotte. "He hasn't exactly been the poster child for polite and warm bosses."

Her assistant crossed her arms over her chest. "And how would you know? Maybe he was having a bad day when Mr. Bingley took you to meet him."

"You sound like Jane. You know how she always believes the best of everyone?"

The muffled sound of Charlotte's phone ringing prevented her from saying whatever she'd planned. With a quick punch of a couple of buttons, Charlotte answered it from within Elizabeth's office while Elizabeth once again put her face in her hands. Excuse! She needed an excuse.

Charlotte hung up the phone. "Well, you're off the hook it seems."
Elizabeth's head jolted up. "What?"

"That was Mrs. Reynolds. She called earlier to let me know that he'd forgotten a previous meeting, but she hadn't checked to see if he wanted to cancel your lunch or the appointment. He wanted to come down himself and apologize, but his ten o'clock was waiting for him when he returned."

The world suddenly appeared a little lighter and brighter. She was free from spending an hour or two in the lone company of her boss. That deserved some sort of celebration. "Maybe Jane will want to go to lunch or we could all go. I haven't treated you since we started here."

Before she could dig her cell phone out of her purse, she scanned the room. Something was missing. The gift! "What happened to the present that was here earlier?"

"Oh, I put it in the cabinet behind you in case someone returned with you from the meeting. I didn't think it would be appropriate to leave it in the middle of your desk." Charlotte placed the box in front of her, and Elizabeth pulled it forward.

The box was simply wrapped in an almost grey-blue paper adorned with a holiday snow scene. She angled it to get a better look. Elaborate horse-drawn carriages and people in old-fashioned winter clothes walked along or rode on the tops of the coaches. It was like something out of a period drama. On the top, offset by the fairly dark paper, was a large glittery number one. Who could've left it here?

"Don't sit there staring at it. Open it. I want to see what's inside."

"Why do you think it belongs to me? I'm not expecting anything like this. Maybe someone put it in the wrong office. Besides, shouldn't I wait for Christmas?"

Charlotte's finger pointed to a small tag on the side that said, "To Elizabeth. Please open me now." However, there was no indication who it was from. She should really find out who left it before she opened it, but she did love gifts.

With a smile, she tore the top of the paper in strips until an unadorned white box inside stood in its place. She lifted the lid, removed a sheet or two of tissue paper, and drew the box into her lap, looking inside. "Bath supplies?" She lifted a pretty bottle with a purple gel inside. The label claimed it was lavender scented bath bubbles, and a pink bath sponge lay beside it, nestled in the paper. Along the side of the box was a card.

I hope you like Advent Calendars because this is mine to you.
Hoping to make your holiday a little brighter,

Your Secret Santa

Her eyes widened. "There's no way it would stay under the spending limit."

Greedy fingers snatched the card from her hand. "Lucky bitch," said Charlotte. "Why do you always have all the luck?"

"How many days are on an Advent Calendar?"

"I think it's twenty-four." Charlotte picked up the bottle and took a closer look at the label. "The last day is usually on Christmas Eve, isn't it?"

Elizabeth grabbed the card back. The design on it matched the snow scene on the wrapping paper, but as she studied it, she noticed numbers randomly placed in the scene. "Charlotte, look."

"What?"

"The card is an Advent Calendar."

Charlotte leaned closer and ran her finger along the top. "It doesn't look like the numbers are doors that open."

"No, I think it's more to go along with the theme." As Elizabeth counted along with the numbers, she pointed to one set on top of a carriage door. "There's a twenty-five."

"Maybe they liked the idea of it going until Christmas?" Charlotte shrugged. "Or maybe they made a mistake." Both of them jumped at the sound of a knock.

Elizabeth gathered up the wrapping paper and wedged it between her leg and the side of her chair. "Come in!"

Charlie walked through the door, and they both relaxed. Why was that? They weren't doing anything wrong. Why did the idea of the entire office finding out make her uneasy?

"A little birdy told me Darcy asked you to lunch." He wore a wide grin as he dropped into the seat in front of her desk. Charlotte promptly excused herself and closed the door behind her.

"Does no one have anything better to do in this office but gossip about others?" Why did she sound like a petulant child?

He laughed and shrugged. "Honestly, I overheard him. I could also tell you were searching for some excuse to say no." She opened her mouth. "Don't. I know what happened on your first day, but he's been pleased with your work. I know he's told you in sort of a generic way in meetings, but he means it. He would tell you to your face if you'd let him. You should really give him a chance."

"Well, he was saved from eating crow. He forgot he had an important meeting."

Charlie clapped his hands together. "Then you can have lunch with me and Jane. We're meeting at that little bistro around the corner at noon."

She smiled and nodded. "I'd like that."

He sat forward and pointed toward her lap. "By the way, what is that?"

She almost flinched. She'd forgotten about the box in her lap. "I'm not sure." She put her hands on each side and tilted it so she could see inside. "It says it's my Secret Santa gift."

His eyebrows drew down a bit in the middle. "Really? Isn't it a bit early?"

"Okay, this is the odd part." The box was set to one side of her desk, and she scooted her chair forward until she was leaning on the work surface. "The outside had a number one on it, and when I opened it, this was inside." She handed Charlie the card and waited while he read it.

"An Advent Calendar? Your Secret Santa intends to give you a gift every day until Christmas?"

She motioned toward the card. "There's a twenty-five. I think there's a present on that day as well."

He waggled his eyebrows. "Well, what was in it?"

"Some lavender scented bath bubbles and a pink bath sponge."

He peered inside the box. "They will definitely go over the limit if they continue. You might want to keep most of it to yourself. Just in case someone makes more of this than it really is."

She put the lid on the box, placed the gift under her desk by her purse, and put the wrapping paper in the small trash can. "I thought of that. Maybe I can discover who it is and stop them. It's definitely more than the norm for a Secret Santa."

Charlie shrugged. "It might only be someone who enjoys giving gifts and wanted it to be special. If you do find out who it is, don't be stubborn."

With a gasp, she pulled some crumpled paper from the bin and chucked it at him. "I'm not stubborn."

Laughing, he tossed it back at her. "Yes, you are. You can ask your sister if you don't believe me."

She dropped it back into the trash can. "Jane loves me."

"She does," he said. "And I'm sure she's not the only one."

Elizabeth gave him a sidelong glance. What in the world did that mean?

He didn't say anything else but stood and went to the door, turning before he opened it. "I'll meet you at the elevators at eleven forty-five."

"Charlie?"

"Sorry, I have to go light a fire under the ass of someone in public relations. I'll see you later."

She sat and watched the door for a while after he left. Did he know something she didn't? Well, that was something she'd definitely have to figure out.

Darcy slid his laptop into his bag with several folders before scanning his office. What was he forgetting? He strode over to the board table and touched each stack of folders, double-checking, going over each project in his mind. Would he need any of them this evening? He had no plans, and it was rare that anything on television sparked his interest these days. Most nights he worked until an hour or so before bed when he would read. Sometimes his reading material was even business related.

As he walked back to his desk, Bingley strode in and leaned against the door after it closed. "An Advent Calendar? Really? You won't be able to stay under the spending limit."

He wasn't surprised at Bingley's appearance in his office or that he wanted to interrogate him. He knew the minute Bingley discovered how he was giving Elizabeth the Secret Santa gift, Bingley would have something to say about it. "Ana and I were shopping last weekend, and I bought her the chocolate Advent Calendar she loves so much. I buy her one every year." Darcy smiled at the memory of her opening it when she was younger. Every day she would show him the different holiday shaped chocolates. "Anyway, it gave me an idea. I thought it would be fun, and Elizabeth will have a little something to look forward to each day."

With a chuckle, Bingley walked to his usual chair. "Expensive bath bubbles and a bath sponge go way beyond a chocolate a day. I've bought that brand of bath supplies for Jane. I know how much it costs." He cocked his head to one side. "Have you apologized yet?"

"I wanted to today, but you should've seen her face when I asked her to a business lunch—a business lunch. I swear she looked like a deer caught in the headlights. She can't stand me. Not that I blame her after what I said, but I've told her in meetings that she's done well. I'd hoped that would help some to get me out of the dog house."

Bingley sighed. "You might need to build up to lunch. She's wary of you, and for someone who's usually quite forgiving, she's holding one heck of a grudge."

As Darcy lifted his bag, he paused, resting it on the top of his desk. "You aren't going to tell her it's me, are you?"

"No, I'm not. I told her I had to light a fire under someone's ass in public relations to get away before she could ask me too many questions." Bingley rubbed his hands up and down his legs and stood. "But please be careful. I'm worried you could make things worse than they already are."

When the two of them headed out toward the elevator, Darcy looked over at Bingley. "Worse than her hating my guts?"

Bingley pressed the down button. "Thing is, I don't think she hates you—not really. You insulted her and belittled her. I think you injured her vanity more than anything. Isn't it something like you have to say five positive comments for every negative one? Well, your negative comment was probably ten times worse than most in her book. You may as well have insulted her looks. I think it's going to take a lot to overcome it."

Great! Just what he wanted to hear. The doors in front of him opened with a ding. He stepped inside and turned.

"Darcy?" Bingley put his hand over the edge of the elevator door. "The Advent Calendar is a good idea, but how are you going to give her gifts on the weekend?"

Darcy smiled. "Give me some credit. That's not as difficult to figure out as you might think."

Chapter 3

With a moan, Elizabeth stretched her arms over her head and pressed her feet toward the foot of the bed, luxuriating in the delicious pull of her muscles. Lord, she loved Saturdays. No alarm clocks, no early mornings, and best of all, no rush-hour commute! She did love her job, but she didn't adore waking at six or seven, dressing in a hurry—and cramming herself into the subway. That was the worst part of her morning. Who could love it? Inevitably, someone pressed themselves much closer than she would like, and they never failed to have a bad case of body odor.

She rolled to her side and grinned at Grunt, who sat perched on the pillow beside her, levelling her with an unwavering stare. "Let me guess. You want your breakfast?" She reached out, and he purred when her fingers found that sweet spot under his chin. After a few scratches, she threw her legs over the side of the bed, grabbed her pajama bottoms from the foot, and slid them on while Grunt made a little chirp and ran to the door where he rubbed back and forth against the frame. He continued to watch her like a hawk as he waited, scratching his sides.

Once he had a half can of his favorite tuna meal in his bowl, she fixed herself a cup of coffee, sat on the barstool at the island, and opened her laptop to begin checking her emails. She had a little work she needed to do, but that could wait until later. It wasn't eleven yet, and she had most of the day all to herself.

Her satchel sat in the seat next to her along with the white box she received yesterday. Over the last week, she'd become quite familiar with those small white boxes. One appeared each day filled with more and more bath supplies. Of course, she'd had the bath bubbles and sponge the first day. On the second, she'd received another containing two bars of French milled lavender soap, and the third day was lavender bath salts. She placed the newest box on the pink granite worktop and lifted out the latest gift, the one for Friday, the fourth day.

One at a time, she pulled out two bath bombs. They were such a pretty pale purple color and had real lavender blooms embedded in them. She brought one to her nose and inhaled the delicate floral fragrance. The last item was a pretty etched glass bottle of lavender scented bath oil. She definitely didn't have to worry about being stinky. Her Secret Santa had taken care of that. She'd be smelling of lavender for the next six months!

Grunt came over and sniffed a bath bomb, pulling back quickly.

"What's the matter? You don't like it?"

She picked up her gift and carried it into the bathroom, arranging it in a basket on the small table next to her claw foot bathtub.

Question was, if her Secret Santa intended to give her a gift a day, would she get gifts on Saturday or Sunday? If it was necessary, she occasionally worked weekends, but nothing was pressing at the moment. Would she find multiple gifts on her desk when she went to work on Monday or would they skip the weekends altogether? Even though the numbers showed on the card, hopefully, they wouldn't go to that much trouble!

Her coffee! She hurried back into the kitchen and returned to her emails. After deleting another ridiculous sales ad, the buzzing of her phone drew her eyes to the screen, but her mother's name on the display made her flinch. "Sorry, Mom. Not in the mood."

Not even five minutes after she ignored the call, the messages started, and she resisted the urge to bang her head against the countertop. She loved her mother, but the woman had the ability to drive her bat shit crazy. There were definite reasons why Elizabeth remained in New York when her parents moved to Florida, and her mother was numbers one through ten on the list.

"I can't believe you still sleep until noon! You're not a teenager anymore, Miss Lizzy! You need to behave more like an adult!"

Hopefully, that was the end of her mother's usual lecture, which was an exaggeration as usual. At least, it had nothing to do with how she needed to be more like Jane. Elizabeth logged into her work account before the phone vibrated again.

"I have so much to tell you!"

She groaned. No! She didn't want to do this. Please no!

"You should've seen the horrendous suit Mrs. Long wore to her husband's mayoral inauguration. It was the ugliest thing I've ever seen in my life!"

Yup, she was going there. Her parents had moved to the Sunshine State three months after Elizabeth graduated from law school. Her youngest sister, born ten years after Elizabeth, was a wild child. Now that the eldest two were both done with college, her parents felt it best to get Lydia away from the city. Her mother was a perpetual gossip, so instead of getting all of the gossip from New Jersey, where Elizabeth was born and raised, she had all of it from Florida and people she'd only met in passing. The phone buzzed.

"Where that woman finds her clothes is beyond me. I wouldn't be caught dead in that color or that style! No one has worn either since nineteen-sixty-five."

"Exaggeration," she said in a sing-song voice. "Come on, Mom. It's Saturday morning. Can't I enjoy it?" The phone rattled against the granite again. "Apparently not."

"New neighbors moved in down the street. The man is quite handsome, but the wife! She thinks she's all that, but she's really not. If I had those ankles . . ."

Elizabeth turned on the do not disturb, flipped the phone over so the face wasn't visible, and got up to pull out a pan to make eggs. She'd just turned on the burner when the doorbell rang, causing Grunt to look up from his food and make a little trilling noise that made her laugh.

"Looks like I'm not going to have a moment's peace. Who do you think it is, boy?"

45

She peered through the peephole but didn't recognize the pimply-faced teenager standing there. "Who is it?"

"Delivery," he called.

She cracked the door and peeked through. He had a beautiful, vivid pink Christmas cactus in his hands. "Oh, hold on." She unhooked the chain and opened the door. "Are you sure this is for me?"

The boy, who wore a shirt that said Kympton Florists, glanced at the number on her door. "Three-eleven, right?"

"Yes, that's me."

"Then it's definitely for you." He held it out by the matching pink ceramic pot.

"Thank you. If you give me a moment, I'll get you a tip."

Once she had the plant in her arms, he waved his hand as he turned in the direction of the stairs. "It's already taken care of. Happy holidays!"

"Oh, happy holidays!" She kicked the door closed, looking at the beautiful blooms. She'd always loved Christmas cacti. Her grandmother had several when she was a little girl, but she'd never bought one of her own. With her work schedule and now Grunt, it was unlikely the poor plant would make it a week.

She set it on the island and Grunt abandoned his food for the lure of something new, trotting over to inspect it. "Oh, no! I don't know if it's poisonous or not." He made a tiny "umph" when she gently lifted him and set him on the floor.

A click of a few buttons on her laptop confirmed it wasn't toxic, but could be irritating to the stomach, which meant it should be put somewhere Grunt couldn't attempt to eat it. Crap! She had very few hiding places from the curious feline because he constantly proved that she couldn't hide anything from him. He scaled cabinets and bookshelves. Maybe if she put a hook in the beam near the window and let it hang where he couldn't reach it? That might work, but it was possible Grunt might try his best impression of a flying squirrel. She certainly wouldn't put it past him.

Grunt came up to investigate, so she let him satisfy his need to know what invaded his space while she pulled the card from inside. Luckily, he must've found the plant boring because after sniffing it intently for a moment or two, he went back to his food. When she opened the card, she gasped at the familiar snow scene and a small glittery five on the outside. Santa had clearly realized that she liked pink. Her mug at work was a bubblegum color, some of her clothing was in various shades, and her fingernails were also often pink. But how did her Secret Santa know where she lived?

She grabbed her phone, ignoring the barrage of texts lining her screen, and clicked on Jane's number. With the phone to her ear, she began rapping her toe against the wood floor.

"Hi, Lizzy! What time are you coming over?"

"I need to talk to Charlie. Is he around?"

"I love you too, sis," she said dryly. "Hold on."

Charlie's usual chuckle greeted her before his voice. "What's up?"

She pulled the phone back a little, stared at it, and put it back to her ear. "What are you? Bugs Bunny?"

"You're in a good mood."

"Ha, ha! I received a delivery a few minutes ago."

"I didn't send you anything."

She put her hand to her forehead, propping her elbow on the worktop. "It has a card with a silver number five on it."

"Oh, it was delivered to your apartment?"

"Yup."

"I don't see why it's big deal."

She huffed. "Charlie, does everyone at Darcy Holdings have access to employee addresses and contact information?"

"Look, all your information at Darcy Holdings is in personnel files. Access is limited to those who work in personnel or the accountants in finance because they prepare your tax statements. It just depends on the person's job and the reason for access, but we keep a tight rein on personal information." His tone had changed to one she'd heard often for business, when he had to state facts. "I'm inclined to think they found it somewhere else."

"Like where?"

"Have you ever looked yourself up on the internet? It doesn't take a rocket scientist to find most people's address online."

"Do you truly believe they found my address online? There's also the possibility that they followed me home one night."

He mumbled something, probably to Jane. "Did this gift just show up on your doorstep?"

She scrunched her forehead. "No, it was hand delivered by a kid in a uniform. Why?"

"Because whoever it is probably didn't even step foot in your building. Think about it. They had someone else deliver it. Doesn't sound like a stalker to me."

"Charlie—"

"I don't see any reason to worry unless they sent you a knife or a gun or one of those creepy notes made out of letters from different magazines. Did they?"

"No!" Was he serious? "It was a Christmas cactus."

"A plant? So, a florist showed up at your door with a flowering plant. Hardly threatening."

"Charlie—"

"Lizzy, I promise, if I thought you had reason to worry, I'd find out who it is, but I think your Secret Santa just wants to do something nice for you. Probably an overdue welcome to the company."

"Would you say the same thing if it were Jane?"

He chuckled. "That would depend on who the individual was, and whether it was a young, single man or not. I would definitely have a huge problem if he was better looking than me."

Elizabeth burst into giggles. "You can be so ridiculous."

"But I got you to laugh." When her laughter subsided, he continued, "Seriously, I'm certain everything is okay, or I would be all over it. I promise. I'd be more thorough for you than I would Caroline."

"Caroline would enjoy this."

"You're right, she would. I hate to tell anyone to emulate Caroline, but in this instance, why not?"

"I don't know, Charlie." She said the words sort of long and drawn out. "Are you sure you don't know who it is? I feel like you're dismissing this rather easily."

"I get why you feel this is strange, but I think a lot of people would say it's a great idea and have some fun with it, which you should definitely do." He paused for a second. "Look, Jane wants to know when you're coming over this evening and whether you're bringing your drunken pecan pie."

"Tell Jane I'll be there at four to help her cook and ask her what dessert she wants. I know you're the one who wants the pecan pie."

He laughed. "Busted. Here, let me hand you over to Jane."

"Lizzy?" Jane asked after a minute. "I heard most of what Charlie said, and I agree with him. If this person was creepy, they wouldn't hire a florist to deliver you a plant. They'd have to give their name and credit card information for the delivery. It's not like it couldn't be traced if they were up to something illegal."

She exhaled heavily. "Okay, okay! I must be overreacting. I get it. Who knew I had one of Mom's most annoying traits?" Jane laughed. "Anyway, I told Charlie I plan to be there at four to help cook. He's put in a request for a drunken pecan pie. What do you want me to bring?"

"It's just the four of us. A pecan pie is plenty. I have a few pounds I need to get off before Christmas. I can't afford to have a bunch of dessert in the kitchen. It calls to me, you know. I'm so weak. I can't say no."

Elizabeth rolled her eyes. Jane's few pounds were all in her head. The woman had been a cheerleader and volleyball player in high school and played on just about every intramural team in college. She'd never had to worry about weight a day in her life. Charlie even had a home gym at his apartment that Jane used almost daily.

"Do you want me to make anything else?"

"Do you know what I've been craving for the last week?"

She bit her lip. That was how Jane asked whenever she wanted something time-consuming. "What have you been craving?"

"That homemade olive oil and rosemary bread you make. Would you mind?"

At least it was cold enough outside that the radiators were warm, because she'd have to put the bowl near one for it to rise. It was doable. "Yes, I can make some bread."

"Thank you! You're the best. We'll see you at four. Don't worry about bringing any wine. As we speak, Charlie is gearing up to go to the liquor shop around the corner."

"Sounds good. I'll see you at four." Elizabeth pressed end. She'd better get the bread going. She'd have to make breakfast once she got the dough rising or it would never be done in time. So much for a relaxing afternoon!

After ringing the doorbell, Darcy waited for a moment or two before Bingley's voice grew steadily louder and more understandable, his friend's huge grin greeting him when the door opened. How did he always stay so happy? There was no way Darcy could conjure that much cheer and energy. He'd probably collapse with the effort after ten minutes.

"Darcy! I'm so glad you could make it!" Bingley took his coat and his gloves, put them in the coat closet, and motioned for him to follow.

"Jane and Lizzy are cooking in the kitchen. Lizzy brought her drunken pecan pie, so make sure you save some room for dessert. It's killer."

"What makes it drunken?"

Bingley shrugged and chuckled. "I honestly don't know. Lizzy won't even tell Jane. It's some recipe she stumbled across I guess." He patted his stomach. "I don't really care what's in it as long as I get to eat it."

"What would you like me to do with the wine?"

"I told you to just bring yourself." He took both bottles of wine and raised his eyebrows at the labels. "Nice selection. They should go well with the prime rib. Jane went all out when she found out you'd agreed to come. She even had Lizzy make her famous olive oil and rosemary bread."

One side of Darcy's lips tugged upward. "More famous than her pecan pie?"

An amused bark came from Bingley as he turned toward the kitchen. "As far as I'm concerned, nothing is more famous than her pecan pie, but others may disagree."

After Bingley disappeared through a swinging door, Jane hurried out. "I'm so glad you could make it. Caroline had to go out of town for some spa retreat or another, some sort of an emergency about flaking skin on her feet. She spoke so quickly, I didn't hear all of it. Don't worry, she won't be dropping in on you out of the blue."

He laughed as she hugged him. "Thanks for letting me know, but I would've come anyway. I hope you know that." Most of the time, hugs from women who weren't family made him uncomfortable, but Jane was different. He'd been a little stand-offish at first, but he'd always been that way with people he didn't know. In the end, Jane proved to be genuine and extremely kind. Even though they hadn't been in company a lot, he'd grown quite fond of Charlie's girlfriend over the past months.

"The wine is lovely, but you know you never have to bring anything when you come for dinner here."

"Did your sister have to bring something?"

She waved dismissively. "That's completely different. I can cook almost any recipe you put in front of me, but I cannot bake to save my life. My pie crusts taste like cardboard, my cakes are never fully cooked through or they're dry, and my bread never rises. Lizzy's tried to teach me, but I've proven myself woefully inept. I could buy a dessert at the bakery, but Lizzy's are so much better. You'll see." She took his hand and pulled him toward the kitchen. "You can't just sit in here with Charlie when all the fun is in the kitchen."

When he stepped from the carpet in the hall to the ceramic tile of the kitchen, his eyes honed in on Elizabeth. "Good evening."

Her eyes widened, and at that moment, it became apparent that she had no idea he was coming. He was going to kill Bingley!

Chapter 4

He stood frozen while Elizabeth stared, her mouth slightly open. All of a sudden, she started, glanced at Jane and Bingley, and cleared her throat.

"Mr. Darcy," she said softly and a little slowly.

His insides clenched. She definitely hadn't known he was coming. Well, this could be terrible or it could give him an opportunity to redeem himself—if he could find that ever elusive opportunity to speak with her.

Now that they weren't in the office, should he call her Elizabeth? He thought of her as Elizabeth even though he called her Miss Bennet at work. He never referred to any of his female employees by their first names. He meant it as a show of respect, but did that mean she would object to the use of her first name now? Good Lord! Why did he have to make everything so difficult and awkward? Well, he could solve part of that dilemma.

"We're not at work. You don't have to call me Mr. Darcy."

She wiped her hands on a towel and picked up a glass of red wine. "Then how do people who don't work for you, address you?"

He tried to keep his gaze on her eyes, but his line of sight drifted lower as she brought the wine to her lips. "Um . . ." He cleared his throat as his collar cut off the air to his lungs. "A lot of people call me Darcy."

"Or you could call him William like I do," said Jane. She opened the oven and pulled out a rack.

Elizabeth's right eyebrow arched at her sister. "I didn't think the two of you knew each other very well."

While Jane checked the temperature on the meat, she continued, "Oh, that was only at first. We've become better acquainted over the last couple of months. I used to call him Darcy, but a few weeks ago, he invited me to call him William."

Bingley pulled four plates from the cabinet, and Darcy stepped forward. "Let me help you set the table."

Jane put her hands up and shook her head. "No, you're a guest. I'm not going to make you work for your food." Before Darcy could insist, Jane pulled another wine glass from a rack over the counter, set it in front of him, and filled it almost to the rim. "Lizzy and I have already had a glass while we cooked. You need to catch up."

At a barrage of coughing and the clink of a glass against the counter, he looked over to Elizabeth, who was as red as a firetruck and had covered her mouth with her hand.

"Are you okay?" He stepped around the counter to help, but Jane lifted her sister's arms over her head.

"Arms up!" Jane bent down a bit to meet her sister's eye. "Wine went down the wrong way?"

Elizabeth nodded and inhaled a shaky breath. "Yes, thank you." She coughed a few more times into her elbow and wiped her eyes, which had teared a little.

Jane returned to pull the meat out of the oven. "I'm going to bring this out to the table. I'll be right back."

Elizabeth's mouth opened while she looked between him and Jane, then again at him, and back to Jane as she stepped through the door. She grabbed her glass and took a sizeable sip. "Excuse me." Before he could say a word, she all but dove from the room. Wonderful! How was he ever supposed to talk to her if she wouldn't even be alone with him for more than a few seconds?

Unfortunately, her retreat became the theme of the meal. He needed to apologize, but he couldn't if she didn't allow him one moment alone with her. For the entire evening, she spoke freely with Jane and Bingley, but she looked at him only if necessary and talked to him even less. It was almost as if she played some sort of game where she pretended he wasn't in the room.

Once they'd eaten, cleaned up the kitchen, and finished off several bottles of wine, Elizabeth hugged Jane. "I'm heading out. I want to get to bed. I'm tired."

Jane peered back at the clock and narrowed her eyes, crossing her arms over her chest. "Why don't you stay? I'd feel much better if you weren't walking home on such a cold night, especially after all those glasses of wine." She swatted Bingley's arm with the back of her hand. "Charlie, tell her she should stay."

Bingley grinned and winked. "You should stay."

Elizabeth lifted that one eyebrow, and Darcy took a deep breath. That eyebrow made him want to grab her and kiss her senseless— something he definitely couldn't do. "Jane, those glasses of wine were drunk over several hours. I'm fine. I don't need to stay. I'd rather sleep in my own apartment and in my own bed." Elizabeth embraced her sister again, and after a quick kiss to Bingley's cheek, headed toward the front hall. Jane started after her, but Darcy placed his hand on her shoulder.

"I don't mind making sure she gets home safely."

Jane's eyes lit. "Would you? I never like it when she walks home by herself, but with the cold snap, it's freezing outside. I'd much prefer if she at least had someone make sure she made it home. Thank you so much." After he gave her a quick hug and shook Bingley's hand, he followed Elizabeth to the front hall where she was fitting her hands into her gloves.

He pulled his own outerwear from the closet and began putting on his coat. "Would you care for a ride?"

"No, thank you," she said. "I live across the park. It's a quick walk."

He frowned while he wrapped his scarf around his neck. "Forgive me, but the park isn't the safest place to walk at night."

"I walk through the park all of the time. I've yet to be mugged or put upon by ruffians." She said the last few words with a bit of sass. She was teasing him.

Before he was ready, she started out the door, and he hurried to trail behind, pulling on his gloves as he caught up. "My car and driver are waiting downstairs. It's really no bother to drop you at home."

"I like to walk, Mr. Darcy. I walk around this part of town all of the time."

"William."

Her quick stride halted and she turned. "Pardon?"

"You can call me William."

She shook her head, and instead of taking the elevator, began jogging down the stairs, requiring him to use his longer legs to keep up. "Mr. Darcy is less complicated. I don't have to worry about calling you the wrong name at work."

"Do you have that problem with Bingley? You call him Charlie when you aren't in a public work setting."

"That's different."

"Why?"

"Because it is. He's family—or as good as."

Something inside him flinched. What he wouldn't give to be more comfortable with her, more able to speak what was in his head. But she treated him with such hesitancy and avoidance that he clammed up and couldn't speak for some reason.

When she reached the front doors, he pressed his hand to the door to prevent it from opening and she stopped like she was about to hit a brick wall. "See the Mercedes parked there?"

"Yes."

"I texted my driver when we began cleaning up. The car will be warm, you'll be home in a matter of minutes, and Jane will be relieved you aren't walking through the park in sub-zero temperatures. It's a win-win for everyone."

She turned so she looked at him. "Jane is a worry wart."

"I can sympathize with her. I'd be the same way. So, will you put her mind at ease and let me give you a ride?"

Her shoulders dropped. "I appreciate the offer, but it's really not necessary."

"It's frigid out tonight. The wind chill is supposed to be almost ten below. I can't have my new company attorney losing her fingers and toes to frostbite. If you want, I can even wait here while my driver drops you off. He can return for me once you're home."

Her head gave a slight hitch back, she shoved her hands in her pockets, and watched him for a moment, her eyes shifting back and forth like she was studying him. "I suppose when you put it that way I have to accept, but I would never ask you to wait here while your car and driver took me home." When he opened the door, she looked him in the eye. "I apologize if I seemed ungrateful. I do appreciate the offer."

"I'm not offended. I know you'd much rather walk, but I would prefer to know you're home safe." He ushered her to the car and to get her into the warmth of the inside before his driver noticed their approach. "What's your address?"

"Five-ninety West End Avenue," she said as she climbed in. When he looked in the rearview mirror, Carson nodded to him, put the car in gear, and pulled from the curb.

While Darcy leaned back into the plush seats, Elizabeth sat on the opposite side of the backseat, her hands clenched in her lap. They needed to have some kind of conversation. He couldn't sit there with her in silence, even for the short drive to her building.

"I enjoyed the bread and the pie you brought tonight. Bingley called it a 'drunken pecan pie,' but it didn't have as much alcohol as I expected with the name."

Her lips curved a little on the ends. "I've told him it only has two tablespoons of alcohol, but he loves calling it that."

While they rounded the block, silence fell between them, and she gazed out the other window as the trees of the park passed by in the darkness. He should apologize and do it now. She'd made it nearly impossible to get a moment alone and here they were finally by themselves—well, almost. Carson always had a headphone in one ear anyway, so he could listen to classic rock.

After shifting in his seat and then shifting again, he opened his mouth to speak, but the words got stuck in his throat. He coughed to clear it. "I'm sorry." His voice came out hoarse. What the heck? He took in a big breath. "I wanted to say that I'm sorry for what I said on your first day."

She turned with her mouth slightly open. After blinking once or twice, she pivoted towards him just a little more. "You didn't want to hire me and Charlie did. You're entitled to your opinion."

He shook his head. "But I don't feel that way. I was frustrated after what happened with Wickham, and I'd wanted to wait to hire you until Hurst was closer to retirement. I should've asked why Bingley was in such a hurry, but I didn't. I was wrong and I'm sorry."

The car slowed and Elizabeth glanced out of the window as her building came closer. "Thank you for saying that. I do appreciate it." She awkwardly pointed at her building. "Thank you for the ride. Have a good night." She gave a tight smile and hurried from the car. She couldn't even wait for him to open the door for her? Darcy slid across the seat and stepped out behind her.

When he approached her from behind and pushed open the door, she whirled around. "What are you doing?"

"I'm seeing you to your apartment. I promised Jane I would ensure you made it safely home."

"I don't think she meant inside the building." She laughed while she spoke. As she strode across the small entry, she pulled off her hat and began to climb the stairs like she was on a mission—one to lose him before she reached her apartment. By the time they reached the third floor, she'd also removed her gloves and tucked them into her pockets. She headed down the corridor and lifted her coat to get at her jeans pocket, removing her keys as she slowed to a stop before apartment three-eleven.

She put the key in the lock and turned it as a loud crash came from inside and her head jerked up. "Grunt!" Before he could stop her, she pushed the door wide, and a little dark furry face popped out about a third of the way up the frame.

She must have left on a lamp before she departed because there was a soft light coming from inside. He glanced back down to the fluffy black cat, who sat on a small hall table set just inside the door, watching Darcy. Shards of blue glass littered the floor.

"Oh, no! Grunt, what did you do?"

The little monster made a chirp while he stood and arched his back, rubbing against the wall. Darcy stuck his hand inside, letting the cat sniff him, before he scratched under his chin.

"Do you have something to clean this up? I'll help you before I go."

Her shoulders slumped as she looked at the shards of cobalt-colored glass all over the oak floors. "It's not necessary. I can manage."

Grunt bent his legs like he was going to jump down, but Darcy grabbed him. "I don't think you want him cutting his paw. Why don't you go get a broom and dustpan, and while I sweep it up, you can get your vacuum to make sure all the little pieces get picked up."

She hesitated for just a moment, but hurried off, only returning when she had a broom and a dustpan. He handed the cat to her, and while she went to get the vacuum, he swept up as many of the sharp slivers as he could. He was trying to be polite and helpful. Hopefully, between the apology and his help, she would see that he wasn't an ogre, but that he possessed a few redeeming qualities. Maybe?

This was not happening! Mr. Darcy, her boss, was not, at this moment, on his hands and knees in her doorway sweeping up glass.

She knew better than to put that bowl on the hall table. Once Grunt learned how to jump on that table, he always greeted her in the same way. It would've broken sooner or later.

She'd found the piece at a thrift shop on her way to the grocery store two blocks down, but she'd loved it. That little store always had the cutest things in the window, and one evening, right before they closed, she'd noticed it. It was simple but reminded her of one that belonged to her grandmother. Now, the darned thing was in pieces, and Mr. William Darcy was sweeping it up.

She shoved Grunt into the bathroom, and before he could run between her legs, she shut him in. "There, that will keep you from cutting yourself." The only vacuum she owned was an old relic she kept in the small laundry room off the hall, so she pulled it out and rushed back to the door. Mr. Darcy wasn't there. Had he gone home?

"I hope you don't mind."

She jumped at the voice behind her and whirled around. "What are you doing?"

"I dumped the broken glass into the kitchen trash can." He motioned around him. "This is a nice apartment. Have you lived here long?"

Really? Small talk? "It belonged to my grandparents. My uncle and aunt own it, but I've been updating it since I moved in after law school." She set the vacuum on the floor and put her hands on her hips. "I appreciate the help, but I can get it from here. It's getting late and your driver is waiting for you. I'm sure you'd much rather be at home, doing . . . whatever it is you do . . . than helping me clean this mess."

He stared, just like he had before dinner, during dinner, and in the car on the way here. Why did it always give her this weird sensation like he could read her thoughts? Something inside her flared at his intent gaze. It must've been his looks. After all, he was handsome enough to be called eye candy. It was still unnerving how she couldn't control this reaction to him.

His mouth opened and closed, but he didn't speak. He merely nodded and leaned the broom and dustpan against the wall. "Good night, Miss Bennet."

"Good night, and thank you for the ride." After she shut and locked the door behind him, she let out a long exhale. Thank goodness that was over with! She switched on the vacuum and tugged at the hose to clean the entire entry area, which was a good idea since several pieces of what could only be remnants of the bowl rattled through the machine before she was done.

Once she'd stowed the cleaning supplies back where they belonged, she released the fuzzy black troublemaker from his incarceration. He chirruped and trotted from the bathroom as if he'd been a perfect angel all evening long.

"You could drive a person to drink. Do you know that?" His golden eyes flicked in her direction, but he didn't come to her or even offer a meow of apology. Instead, he took off down the hall. When she caught up to him, he was sniffing the floor here and there, then he rubbed along the legs of the hall table. He always ran and jumped onto that table like something was chasing him, sliding across the top while he skidded to a stop. No doubt, he'd slid right into her pretty new bowl and sent it flying off the edge.

She picked him up and cuddled him to her chest. "Did you wreck anything else while I was gone? Should I go look?"

A quick survey of every room revealed that other than her new bowl, he hadn't been incredibly busy in her absence. The Christmas cactus sat exactly where she'd left it with all the leaves and soil intact, and nothing else appeared disturbed. The biggest change was the move of his little catnip mouse from the kitchen to the living room, so the glass dish must have been his sole victim.

Grunt struggled to get down, so she set him on the back of the sofa. "Do you plan on playing for a while? I'm tired. I want to go to bed."

While she walked to her bedroom, she pulled out her phone and called Jane. "You could've told me Mr. Darcy was coming tonight."

"Firstly, I did say it would be the four of us when you called this morning, but you never asked and I didn't spell it out. Honestly, Charlie was afraid you wouldn't come if you realized, and after seeing the two of you together, I can see why. You were so abrupt with him that your behavior bordered on rude. He's a good guy, Lizzy. You need to cut him some slack."

"I was not rude to him! He makes me uncomfortable. He's always glowering at me and I don't think he likes me at all."

"Why do you say that?"

"Well, he apologized tonight for what he said on my first day, but he hasn't made it a secret that he didn't want to hire me. He always glares at me as though I've done something wrong."

"Oh, Lizzy," she said on a sigh. "I'm certain he likes you. You're always so dead set in your first impressions and your opinions. One day, it's going to come back to bite you in the ass."

That was unlikely! "We'll see. By the way, I'm going to get my Christmas tree tomorrow. Did you want to come along? You and Charlie could get yours."

"Call me when you get up in the morning. We'll plan it out then. Night, Lizzy."

"Night." She hit "end" and tossed her phone on the bed. Cut Mr. Darcy some slack. As usual, Jane saw the situation through rose-colored glasses instead of the clear lens of reality. Nothing was as cut and dried as she claimed, especially Mr. Darcy. No, he disliked her. There was no other explanation for the way he kept eyeing her all day at work or even tonight at Jane's. Sure, he apologized, but would he stay the same stuck-up prick he'd been since she started at Darcy Holdings or would he be different? Only time would tell, but until he proved her otherwise, William Darcy was a grade "A" asshole, and only he could change her mind.

Once he was back in the car heading home, Darcy's head dropped back onto the seat, and he suppressed a groan. The night couldn't have gone any worse than it had. Elizabeth practically ran from the room whenever threatened with being alone with him. He might've made some progress with his apology, but he wasn't certain. She'd been eager for him to leave, but she could've also been embarrassed to have him cleaning up her cat's mess.

His phone dinged, and he glanced down to the illuminated screen. He'd texted Jane on his way out of Elizabeth's building to let her know her sister arrived home safely and she'd texted back, *"Thank you!"*

Little did Jane know how much her sister disliked him. What if Elizabeth never gave him a chance? He dropped his head back once more and pinched the bridge of his nose. His temples were beginning to throb. Why couldn't he just apologize and have everything become all unicorns and rainbows? Lord, that sounded like something Ana would've said when she was a little girl!

Chapter 5

Light began to permeate the crack in his eyelids, burning a trail along the nerves to his brain. Darcy squeezed them tight and pulled a pillow over his head. Why did it feel like someone was pounding his cranium with a sledgehammer?

A knock vibrated through his skull, and he squeezed the pillow tighter over his ear with a moan.

"William? Are you decent?"

He shifted the pillow so his mouth peeked out the edge. "William isn't here."

His sister giggled, and the bed dipped on one side. "Come on, sleepyhead. You promised we'd go Christmas tree shopping today."

"You were imagining things."

"No, I wasn't. You promised, and I'm holding you to it." Something rattled on his bedside table. "How much scotch did you drink last night?"

"I went to dinner at Bingley and Jane's. Had several glasses of wine."

"And then you came home and drank scotch? No wonder you're such an Oscar the Grouch this morning. You never sleep this late." The bed shifted. "I'll get you some Tylenol and a glass of water. Then I want you to get your behind out of that bed, and shower. You owe me some Christmas shopping today, mister."

He exposed part of his face and squinted in an attempt to lessen the piercing pain caused by the light in the room. Why had he forgotten to pull the curtains before he went to bed? Oh, that's right. He downed half a bottle of scotch and stumbled to bed without thinking of much. He pushed himself up to a seated position and rubbed his eyes.

Ana returned a few minutes later and handed him two pills, followed by a large glass of water. He swallowed the medicine and drank down the contents of the entire glass before handing it back to her empty.

"Thank you."

"Don't thank me yet. Go get in the shower. It's almost time for lunch, and we have some serious decorating to do today."

He scanned around the bed, looked down, and frowned. He wasn't wearing a shirt. Had he gotten naked before he crawled under the covers or had he left on his underwear? Four glasses of wine and that half bottle of scotch rendered his memory a little hazy. He pulled the sheet back just enough to take a peek. "Um, Ana?"

"Yep," she said as she picked up the empty liquor bottle from beside the bed.

"I'm not getting out of this bed with you in the room."

Her eyebrows furrowed as she gave him a sidelong look before she flinched. "Oh! I'm going!" Without any hesitation whatsoever, she was out of the door, and he suddenly had all the privacy he could desire. What he wouldn't give to sink back into the plush mattress. But he couldn't. Ana would only come back to wake him again.

With a yawn, a stretch, and a scratch to the back of his thigh, he shuffled into the shower and turned the knobs until a stream of hot water flowed over his head. He leaned his forehead against the grey slate and gave a long, satisfied exhale when the hot water ran in rivulets down his back. The slight sting and the intense heat were heaven and helped ease a lot of the tension from his head and his shoulders.

Forty minutes later, showered and dressed, but not shaved, he walked into the kitchen. His headache had diminished some with the medication and the heat of the shower, but he needed one last thing to bring him back to the land of the living.

"Coffee, Mr. Darcy?" Mrs. Hill held out his favorite mug, filled to the brim with black, steaming goodness.

"You're an angel of mercy."

The older lady tittered. "Oh, Mr. Darcy. You sound like Mr. Bingley when you say that." A plate of toast was set before him when he sat at the table. "I saw that empty bottle Miss Ana brought down, so I didn't make you eggs."

A burp escaped before he could stop it. "Excuse me." He moved the plate closer. "This is perfect, thank you." She patted him on the back and hurried out of the kitchen, passing Ana as she came in.

"Hey, you're alive."

"Ha, ha!" He leaned back and glanced over what she was wearing. When she hit her teens, Ana went through a major change, shifting from her old pink frills and rainbow unicorns to some of the most interesting combinations of clothes he'd ever seen—and today's ensemble was no different. The red tartan plaid skirt she wore had an asymmetrical hem and a leather lace-up waistband. She paired it with thick black leggings, a black turtleneck, and her favorite Dr. Martens, which had red roses embroidered up the sides. She topped off the outfit with a ruby red stud that glittered from the side of her nose.

She grinned and pivoted in a circle. "Do you like it?"

"What happened to the little girl with pigtails and braces?"

"Ew! She gained some style. Thank goodness!" She plopped into the chair next to him and took a bite of his toast. "So what made you finish off a bottle of scotch?"

He snatched his toast back. "I don't want to talk about it."

"Must be a woman to have you *this* moody."

He stuck his tongue out at her.

"That's mature." She laughed and rolled her eyes. "You might scare your employees, but you forget that I have access to your baby photos. I'm not afraid of you."

"Who would you show them to? Your boyfriend or some of your friends from school? I believe I'm safe."

A wicked gleam lit her eye. "Not if I post them as public on social media. One click on Instagram or Twitter and I could ensure the entire world has access."

"I could say the same to you, little sister."

"You could, but you'd have to know how to post something first." Her elbow landed on the table and she leaned her chin in her palm. "So, what drove you to drink last night?"

"How's Jacob?"

"My boyfriend is fine. He has to finish his piece for composition class or he would've come with me. No changing the subject."

"Perhaps I don't want to answer." He took a large bite of toast and started to chew.

"I could just ask Charlie."

He dropped his hand to the table with a thud. "Why do you *have* to know?"

"Because usually you won't talk to anyone when you're upset. You can't keep everything buried inside that way. It's not healthy." She tilted her head a fraction to one side. "Is it a woman?"

He nodded. This was humiliating.

"Is she a Caroline?"

He grimaced. "No."

Ana lifted her head just enough to bite her thumbnail while her eyes remained on him. Suddenly, those same hazel eyes widened, and she straightened. "Oh my God! You like her, but she isn't interested!"

His stomach tightened. "It's a little worse than that. She can't stand me."

"Then she doesn't know you. You should make more of an effort. You're so reserved and quiet. She needs to know what a great guy you are."

"It's not that simple." He tapped his toast on the plate. "Bingley hired her a few months ago for the legal department. I wanted to wait until Hurst was ready to retire, but Bingley insisted on hiring her then and there. On her first day, he brought her to my office to meet me, but I didn't want to at that moment. I . . ."

"You were an imbecile and said something stupid." She sat up straight and crossed her arms over her chest. "Exactly, how much of an imbecile were you?"

He rested his forehead in his hand. "She's Jane's sister."

"Charlie's girlfriend?" she asked.

"Yes, but Elizabeth and Jane are very different. Where Jane is quiet and serene, Elizabeth is fiery and likes to tease."

"So, what did you say?"

He dropped the toast onto the dish and dropped back in his seat. "I more or less said I didn't have time. I also might have implied she got the job because he was dating Jane. She overheard."

Ana gasped and a sharp pain in the back of his head whipped his head forward while his brain rattled back and forth against his skull. The Tylenol had kicked in, but it was still a painful shock.

"You hit me!"

"Someone ought to! Mom and Dad would be ashamed of you. I can't believe you said that. How long have you known Charlie?"

"Ana." He drew out her name.

"No, how long have you known Charlie?"

"Since kindergarten."

"Dad told me all of the time how he first hired Charlie at Darcy Holdings when he was sixteen, and how the two of you worked together there each summer, learning your way around every department. When he graduated from Columbia's business program, Dad brought him in as an assistant department head and ensured he finished learning the company inside and out, remember?"

Darcy nodded and rubbed the back of his head.

"Dad wasn't an idiot."

He glared at her. "I know that."

"So why say Charlie hired her for such a stupid reason? You know I once overheard Dad telling Mom why he trained Charlie and hired him into the company like he did."

"You never told me about that."

"I suppose it never occurred to me until now. I think they must've been revising their wills so the topic came up. The point is, Dad knew that if something happened to him, you'd need someone in your corner; someone you could trust to help you run Darcy Holdings. You and I would hold most of the shares of the company and while I was underage, you held mine in trust. Your place as CEO was secure, but he worried about the older executives. He wanted you to have an ally. Fortunately, Charlie never took advantage of Dad and always did an excellent job. Charlie loved Dad and he loves Darcy Holdings. You should know that. You didn't just insult Elizabeth, you were incredibly insulting to Charlie, too."

He slumped in his chair. She was right.

"When Mom and Dad were killed, Charlie did exactly what he was hired to do. Dad's last instructions gave him a promotion and a substantial pay increase so he was in precisely the position Dad wanted. Your best friend helped keep you and Darcy Holdings going while you adjusted to the responsibility of CEO *and* the responsibility of being a single parent to a despondent teenager. He would never do anything to jeopardize the company. If he insisted on hiring Elizabeth at that moment, then he had a damned good reason."

"He did. He never explained why though until after he spent over an hour talking her into staying."

One side of Ana's lips curved. "She tried to quit on her first day? I like her. She won't take your crap."

"Thanks a lot."

She grinned. "Don't mention it." After a moment, she wagged a finger at him. "I think I can guess what happened after that. You passed her in the hallways, finally got a good look at her, and found yourself attracted to her. She's definitely no slouch at her job or you wouldn't care how hot she is, you would've dismissed her at the first sign of laziness or incompetence. Now, she probably won't interact with you above the barest civilities outside of work, and you don't know how to fix things."

He swallowed hard. "Am I that predictable?"

His little sister laughed softly. "Probably only to me and Charlie. So, what happened last night?"

"Charlie and Jane invited me to dinner. Elizabeth was there. I wanted a moment alone with her to apologize, but anytime she realized she would be left without a buffer, she ran for it. Because of the cold weather, I gave her a ride home, and I finally managed to get in that apology."

"How'd she take it?"

"Alright, I suppose. She thanked me."

Ana put her hand over his. "You're probably going to have to prove yourself to make her believe it. I hope you know that."

He nodded. "I walked her to her door despite her protests that it wasn't necessary. I even helped her clean up the broken glass from her cat until she insisted she could do it herself. I didn't want to force my presence on her."

"No, I think that's the last thing you should do. Just keep trying to speak to her. Make her see who you are."

"Wow." He tugged at the end of the long auburn braid she had resting over her shoulder. "When did you grow up?"

"Who says I'll ever grow up? Now, eat the last of your breakfast. I want a Christmas tree."

He picked up what was left of his toast, put his plate in the dishwasher, and waved her to follow. "Let's go. I can eat this while we walk. The tree lot isn't that far."

She gave a girlish squeal and tore from the kitchen. When he met her in the huge foyer, she was decked out in her heavy coat with a tartan cap and scarf.

The moment they were walking in the direction of the tree lot, he nudged her with his elbow. "So, how's school going?"

"The same as always. You know I live for it. My cello professor has me learning a Bach piece that I absolutely love."

He took a half-step to the side and looked at her. "You've never been a huge fan of Bach."

"I know!" Her eyes sparkled, and her voice sounded a little breathless. He was familiar with that look and the slight tremor in her voice. "I adore this one, though. It's difficult technically, but so much fun to play, and I like the melody as well. I can't wait for you to hear it." She wouldn't just master this piece, she'd perfect it, just as she'd done to the all of the pieces she became infatuated with.

"Whenever you're ready for an audience, I look forward to hearing it."

She skipped a few paces ahead and turned to walk backward. "We're getting a big tree, aren't we? I know you said it wasn't necessary, but it wouldn't be the same. Besides, how would we choose which ornaments to leave in the boxes and which to put on?"

"You're going to Maine with Jacob, so it will be just me and Mr. and Mrs. Hill. Charlie invited me to spend Christmas Day with them, so I don't need a huge tree. If you didn't want to decorate one so badly, I'd probably not even bother this year." They rounded the corner and crossed the street.

"Then I'm glad I made you come out to buy one. Everyone should have a Christmas tree."

"What if someone is Jewish?"

Ana gave a slight snort. "You know what I mean."

He smiled and took her hand. "Come on, let's pick out a tree."

When they reached the small corner of the park cordoned off as a tree lot, they walked through the rows of fir and spruce trees, all different shapes and sizes. Of course, Ana chose the biggest Noble Fir they had with a tremendous toothy grin. He didn't need such an extravagant Christmas tree, but he couldn't say no when it made her so happy. At Christmas, she behaved with some of the mannerisms she had when she was a little girl. The glimpse of that child made every penny he spent worth it.

She bounced up to him. "Tree taken care of. You just need to go pay."

"And set it up for delivery."

"We could carry it home."

He glanced over her shoulder at what had to be a fourteen-foot tree. "Not on your life. You'd be complaining by the end of the first block." Before she could make a sarcastic comment, he pinched her side and walked by to go talk to the lot manager.

Five minutes later, he was the proud owner of a Christmas tree. Fortunately for them, most people carried their trees home, so the man was willing, for a hefty price, of course, to load theirs up and deliver it. He slid his credit card back into his wallet and glanced around for Ana, who was next to the wreaths.

After a quick text to Mr. and Mrs. Hill to warn them of the tree's impending invasion. He returned to Ana and tugged her braid. "What are you doing, Squirt?"

She pointed ahead of them. "Look, it's Charlie and Jane. I've never met her, but he posts a lot of pictures of her on Instagram. She's very pretty."

He glanced over, his gaze not landing on Bingley or Jane, but on the brunette a few trees down. Her eyes glowed, and a small smile tugged at her lips as she touched a branch, stroking the needles.

"Is that Elizabeth?"

He started. Ana's cheek was right next to his shoulder. "Yes, that's her."

"She's pretty. Not in the usual way, though. I think it's her eyes. They're very expressive."

"Darcy!" He turned as Bingley approached and kissed Ana on the cheek. "How are you, Squirt?"

She crossed her arms over her chest and huffed. "Not you, too."

Bingley chuckled as Jane walked up and hugged Darcy. "Thank you for seeing my sister home last night. I know she was probably a big grump over it, but I can't thank you enough."

"Really, it was no bother." He put a hand to Ana's back. "Ana, I'd like you to meet Jane Bennet."

Jane beamed as she shook Ana's hand with both of hers. "I've heard so much about you from Charlie and your brother."

"I've heard a lot about you as well."

"Did the two of you pick out a tree?" asked Bingley.

"Ana selected one. I'm just the poor sod with the credit card."

"Lizzy wanted to pick out a tree today, so we all came out together." Jane glanced over both shoulders. "I wonder where she went?"

"We'll let you get back to her." Darcy put a hand to Ana's elbow, starting to steer her forward. "I promised Ana some hot chocolate from Goulding's, and we still have to make a stop to buy her a new ornament."

Jane's eyebrows raised slightly.

"When she was born, my mother started the tradition of buying her a special ornament every year, so when she has her own family, she has a collection for her own tree."

"What a wonderful idea! Well, we won't keep you. It was nice to meet you, Ana."

His sister nodded. "It was nice to meet you, too. See you later, Charlie."

After Ana and Jane both gave a quick wave, he led Ana across the street to Goulding's coffee shop and straight to the counter.

"You don't want me to meet Elizabeth?" She looked up to him with a sly smile on her lips.

"You know better than that. You agreed I shouldn't push, and after last night, she was probably hiding from me."

"William," she said, drawing out his name.

"No, I'll see her tomorrow at the Monday morning planning session. I'm not giving up. I'm just giving her a break."

"Don't give her too much of a break. She might find someone else."

Elizabeth wandered through the trees touching the lush needles and breathing in the smell. She loved that scent! It meant Christmas was here. She pulled a tag from the tree she wanted and glanced around. Where had Jane and Charlie gone? When she backtracked through the trees, she stopped when she found them standing on the other side of the lot talking to Mr. Darcy, who had a woman on his arm.

Something about seeing the lady touch his arm made her want to slap him. What was up with that? Who was the woman and why would she want to hit him for being with her? Elizabeth squinted. The girl was graceful and attractive, but seemed . . . young, very young compared to him. No one ever mentioned a girlfriend, but who else could she be?

Elizabeth started over to say hello, but he and the girl walked off while Jane and Charlie started back towards her. "Sorry, were you looking for us? The trees are nice this year, don't you think?" Her sister ran her fingers along the needles of a nearby branch. "Did you see William? He was just here buying a tree, too."

"I saw him when I came looking for you." They started to walk further into the trees while Charlie followed behind. "Who was the girl?" Why did she ask that? Why did it peeve her that he was there with a woman? She didn't even like him. "I don't think I've ever heard of him dating anyone." Oh, good grief! Why hadn't she stopped before that came out?

Jane's eyes narrowed a bit. "That girl wasn't his date, but even if she was, what difference would it make?"

"Okay, his *friend*." Elizabeth attempted to walk around Jane, but her sister stepped in front of her.

"Ana is William's little sister. She's quite a bit younger than he is and attends college here in the city. He brought her out to buy a Christmas tree."

"He did?"

"Yes, Charlie has told me they're very close. They've had to be since William raised Ana after their parents were killed by a drunk driver."

"Oh, I vaguely remember the headlines after the accident, but I didn't remember that he had a younger sister."

"I think she was about sixteen, which would've made him about thirty. It couldn't have been easy." Jane peered back over her shoulder toward Goulding's. "Could you imagine having to suddenly take over raising Lydia for Mom and Dad?"

Elizabeth shuddered. "Mom and Dad better not go anywhere until Lydia can take care of herself. She couldn't live with me. I'd throw her out the window before the first week was out."

Jane giggled and shook her head. "Lizzy!"

"Well, it's true! Not everyone is as patient as you are. Now, you and Charlie need to pick out a tree." Elizabeth held up her ticket. "I found one right over there. I'm going to go pay for mine, so we can carry them back." She made her way through the trees until she found the man to pay. While she waited for him to run her card, she watched the people around her—the children's happy faces as they ran through the maze of trees, the people walking by with shopping bags, and the customers leaving Goulding's with steaming cups cradled in both of their hands.

She froze. That wasn't some random person, it was Mr. Darcy. He spoke with the woman she'd seen him with earlier, his sister, pointing down one way then the other. She couldn't stop herself from staring. He was wearing jeans. She'd never seen him wear anything but suits, but William Darcy actually owned jeans—and was that stubble on his cheeks? He hadn't shaved?

Despite the cold day this warm sensation began to spread from her stomach through her body. She shifted to get a look at his sister, but instead, met the girl's eyes and immediately turned away, her cheeks hot. What was that?

Chapter 6

At the familiar prickling sensation, Elizabeth tensed. Why did he spend every meeting staring at her? It was unnerving. That was it! She wasn't simply going to sit still while he glared at her. She abruptly turned and lifted her eyebrow, but he did no more than blink and turn his attention back to Charlie.

The prickling returned when Mr. Hurst asked her opinion about the legal aspects of their newest acquisition, but she couldn't challenge Mr. Darcy at that point. It was one of the few times he should be watching her, even though she wanted to jump out of her skin.

Lately, Mr. Hurst had arranged for her to join him at almost every company-centered meeting he attended, and, much to her dismay, that meant more contact with Mr. Darcy. Mr. Hurst indicated that she could benefit from an understanding of how each part of their legal department worked. That meant she now went home and reviewed books she'd only used for reference since she'd passed the bar exam rather than reading for her own enjoyment.

When she concluded her input on the discussion, Mr. Darcy took over, but she resisted the pull to look at him. Instead, she doodled on her notepad while he outlined his expectations. Once he was finished, Charlie chimed in, and that familiar goosebumpy feeling returned. She turned her head around in Mr. Darcy's direction, but a sudden crash on the marbled floor startled her. She paused, covering her mouth at the mess. What an idiot! Her arm had followed her head and sent her favorite pink mug to floor.

"Shit!" A few of the men in the room chuckled. "Sorry, it scared me." She dropped to her knees and began picking up chunks of ceramic, but a hand to her wrist made her pull back, her eyes darting up for a moment to meet Mr. Darcy's hazel ones. He frowned but somehow, he didn't look angry.

"Mrs. Reynolds is calling down to janitorial. Let them handle it. You might cut yourself."

Charlie brought her the trashcan and she dumped what was in her hand inside.

"I can't just leave this mess."

Mr. Hurst waved it off. "We're almost done, and someone is on their way to clean up. Let's wrap up. You'll just have to find yourself a new whale of a mug before tomorrow."

"Ha, ha. Tomorrow, I'm hand-delivering some paperwork so we can finally conclude the Wickham case. I can always grab coffee later. I won't need a mug."

She hesitated before she stood. She couldn't leave the mess for someone else. Charlie held out his hand. "Come on. Let someone who doesn't have to pick up the pieces with their hands do it. Darcy is right, you might cut yourself."

Mr. Darcy stood in front of her when she rose. "Why are you delivering paperwork? We can hire a courier to do that. It isn't necessary for you to make the trip yourself."

"Since Wickham only tried to file a civil suit, I told Mrs. Younge I wanted a no prosecution form so he couldn't try to have you charged criminally. I also emailed them a gag order for Wickham to sign. I'm probably being overcautious, but I'd like all of this wrapped up and put away. I'm going by Younge's office to gather that part of the paperwork. It's too critical to trust to a courier."

His brows drew down in the middle. "I appreciate your thoroughness. I admit it'll be a relief to be free of him."

She nodded and returned to her chair, so they could finish the meeting. Charlie began speaking again, but Elizabeth stared at her wrist. When Mr. Darcy touched her, it almost seemed to have left an imprint—not in the physical sense but in that it still felt like he was touching her. It left her unsettled, her entire body stiff.

The annoying sensation of her hair standing on end returned, but this time, she didn't look at him. Instead, when Mr. Darcy adjourned the meeting, she shot out of her chair, hurried down to her office, and grabbed her purse.

"Where are you going?" asked Charlotte. Her assistant leaned against the door frame with her arms crossed over her chest.

"I broke my coffee cup. I want more coffee, so I'm going to that coffee shop a few doors down."

"Don't forget you have a conference call in," she looked at her watch, "thirty minutes."

"As long as the line isn't too long, I'll make it."

Charlotte laughed. "A short line at Lava Java? Good luck with that!" she called out as Elizabeth powerwalked down the hall. The gods must have been on her side because the elevator arrived promptly and, without any hassle, she made it to the coffee shop in under ten minutes. While she waited in line, she checked her email and messages on her phone. There were only two people ahead of her. That wasn't too bad.

"Replacing your coffee?"

Her eyes closed at the familiar voice. Why would he be here? She opened her eyes and lifted her head from her phone. Mr. Darcy was really and truly standing behind her.

"Yes, I'd barely drank any of it."

"Your work on the Lambton merger was excellent."

She stood stiff, gaping at him. "Thank you." What was with that tiny voice? She cleared her throat.

"Miss!"

She almost fell she pivoted so fast to face the woman at the register. "Oh! I'm sorry. I'll have an extra-large, non-fat, hazelnut latte, please?"

The girl plugged it into the computer, but before she could give Elizabeth a price, a long arm reached by and held out a card. "And I'll have a flat white."

"No!" Elizabeth turned. He wasn't paying. Besides, why did he even want to? She shook her head. "Thank you, but I don't expect you to buy me coffee."

"I've been known to buy coffee for employees now and then. You also appear to be in a rush."

"I have to be at Mr. Hurst's office for a conference call in fifteen minutes."

He bent forward just a hair and held her eye. "Then let me pay while you grab your coffee and go. I wouldn't want you to be deprived of caffeine for the rest of the day because of me."

Her head gave a slight jolt. Was that a joke? "Okay," she said softly. "Thank you."

"I'm happy to do it."

She glanced over her shoulder while she walked to the end of the counter, but he was busy talking to the barista. While she waited, she concentrated on her phone, but more than once, somehow found herself watching him. "Stop it, Elizabeth." Even though she whispered it, the kid behind the counter looked at her as if she might start running around the coffee shop screaming and waving her arms. He shoved her coffee to the front of the counter, and without pause, she scooped it up. She lifted it a little when she passed Mr. Darcy. "Thanks again."

His lips barely curved on the end. Maybe that was all he could manage for a smile? Did the man ever really do more than barely lift a side of his lips? If he did, she'd never seen it. How sad was that?

Three hours later, the interminable conference call finally ended. If she hadn't been in her supervisor's office, she would've jumped up and down and danced, and he would've thought her certifiable. No, it wasn't the longest conference call ever—at least not from what she'd been told, but why was it so difficult for some people to understand the simplest of concepts? She and Mr. Hurst had explained the procedure they wanted implemented multiple times until both of them wanted to pull their hair out—not that Mr. Hurst had much to lose!

Her stomach growled, and she pressed her hand to her belly. "Excuse me."

Mr. Hurst chuckled and set a paper to one side of his desk. "Don't worry about it. I'm hungry too. What's left isn't going anywhere. We can go over it later. Go get something to eat."

"I don't mind waiting." Not that she really wanted to. She needed to find food, and soon!

He leaned against his desk. "Go get some lunch, Bennet. I won't have you getting grumpy while we work."

She sat forward in her seat. "Do you want anything? I don't mind picking something up for you."

He lifted his pen and began to write. "I wish I could take you up on that offer, but my wife has decided I need to lose some weight. She sent me with some cardboard tasting frozen dinner, a small salad, and an apple." He glanced up from his work and pointed his pen at her. "I know she has spies here on the inside, because the last time I cheated, she knew. I'm certain my assistant tells her. The two of them are thick as thieves."

Elizabeth laughed. "What time do you want me back?"

"I don't have any meetings this afternoon, so surprise me."

"Yes, sir." She gave a tiny salute and headed down the hall. Lord, she needed to eat! If she didn't eat soon, her stomach would begin to digest itself! A quick bite would have to do. It wasn't what she really wanted, but after the coffee earlier, she'd start to get sick to her stomach if something didn't make its way in there soon to satiate it. Mr. Hurst also wanted to go over the upcoming projects and the documentation that would be needed. She didn't like him waiting on her.

When she reached her office, Charlotte stood in front of her desk, arguing with a delivery boy. "Lizzy, I'm so glad you're back. This guy claims to have your lunch? Did you order something because I haven't?"

She slowed to a stop. "I didn't order anything yet."

The guy held out a ticket. "I have an order of spaghetti carbonara for Elizabeth Bennet, forty-eighth floor, Darcy Building. Is that you?"

"Yes, that's me, but—" A card, with the design from the Advent Calendar, caught her eye when he lifted the bag from his side.

"Then this is for you."

Any argument she had died in her throat. "Thank you."

Charlotte's head jerked back and forth. "I don't get it."

Elizabeth gave a slight shake of her head. "Can you tip him? I'll pay you back."

He held his hands in front of him. "It's already taken care of. Have a good day."

"What was that?" Charlotte pointed to the delivery boy, but Elizabeth motioned for her assistant to follow her into the office.

She set the bag on her desk and turned it around. "Charlotte, look."

Her assistant's eyes bugged when they landed on the card. "Seriously? How did he know you would need lunch?"

"I suppose it depends on when they ordered it. Who says they didn't somehow find out how long the conference call was running or know how time-consuming it would be." Elizabeth opened the bag and looked inside. "There's more in here than just spaghetti carbonara." One at a time, she pulled three containers from the bag followed by a bottle of sparkling water.

"Holy cow," said Charlotte. "Is that tiramisu? I'm jealous. How do I swap for your Secret Santa?"

Elizabeth removed the lids from the small Caesar salad and the spaghetti, pulled out a fork, and sat down. "Are you hungry? I don't mind sharing."

"I already ate, but I wouldn't mind tasting the carbonara. I've never seen a sauce that golden before." She handed Charlotte the extra fork from the bag, and they both took a little sample of the dish, her assistant moaning when she put it in her mouth. "Is it possible to orgasm from food?"

"I know," said Elizabeth with her mouth full. "This is amazing."

"Seriously! How did you get all the luck?" Charlotte leaned against Elizabeth's desk. "I mean, first he buys you all those bath products, then the plant and those treats for your cat delivered to your door. This week, he's sent a candle, a certificate for a Snow Leopard adopted in your name, and now lunch."

"Why do you think it's a he? How many men would go to so much trouble to discover the favorites of a woman they aren't dating or married to?"

Charlotte wagged a finger. "But what if he *wants* to date you? What if he's had a thing for you and somehow managed to draw your name? Then wouldn't he be motivated to do something a little over the top to try to impress you?"

"Money and gifts don't impress me. If this is a man and that's his belief, then we have a problem."

Her assistant rolled her eyes. "Maybe he's deeper than that, but you just go on and continue believing the worst."

"I never said I believe this person is terrible, but this is rather extravagant, don't you think?"

"A little." Charlotte shrugged. "But if you count the executives on the two to three floors involved, there's a pretty good pool of people who can afford it. Besides, I hear the Christmas bonus is going to be pretty sweet this year."

Elizabeth chewed and swallowed her bite. "We haven't even been with the company six months. We won't be getting the Christmas bonus."

"That's not what your future bro-in-law told me."

She lifted her eyebrows. "Really? Charlie said that?"

"Yes, everyone gets the same bonus, regardless of when they started with the company. Mr. Darcy believes it helps foster loyalty."

"So, he buys his employees." Elizabeth stabbed at her salad. "Why doesn't that surprise me?"

"Wow! First your Secret Santa and now the big boss man. Why do you always look for the worst in people?"

"I don't think the worst of people. I believe the motivations of my Secret Santa are suspect, and you know why I dislike Mr. Darcy. Why do you think so highly of *the big boss man* anyway?"

Charlotte sighed. "You thought quite a bit of him at one time."

"That was only when I knew him by reputation."

"Have you ever considered that your first impression of him is not who he really is? That maybe he was having a bad day? Maybe someone tried his last nerve? You should know all about that. Your mother is famous for blaming people about her last nerve."

"Yes, he had a bad day. That was when the entire mess with Wickham happened, but did he really need to say what he did? Shouldn't he have more faith in Charlie?"

Charlotte stood. "At least he apologized."

"That's true," she agreed. "Did I tell you he showed up in line behind me at Lava Java?"

"No, you didn't. Did he say anything?"

After a sip of her drink, Elizabeth sort of shrugged. "He said I did excellent work on the Lambton merger, and when I ordered, he insisted on paying for my coffee."

"See, you've proven to be an asset. I don't think he dislikes you as much as you think."

Her hand with the fork rested on her desk. "Then why does he stare at me like he does?"

"Maybe you happen to be in his line of sight. Maybe you have a hair out of place. Maybe . . ." One side of Charlotte's lips quirked upwards. "Maybe he likes you."

"Likes me?" Elizabeth took another sip of her drink. "I don't think he loathes me, but I don't think he's harboring some secret crush."

"You could be right, but I think you should consider that he isn't staring at you because he has some problem with you." Charlotte now stood with her hands on her hips. "I also don't believe he's as disagreeable as you make him out to be."

"That's because you listen to Charlie. You don't realize how similar to Jane that man really is."

Charlotte rolled her eyes. "Enjoy your lunch. I have work to do. I'll hold your calls until you're finished."

"Thanks, Charlotte."

When the door closed, Elizabeth pulled the card off the bag and studied the snow scene. The people on the card all looked happy and joyful. Their lives were so much simpler. They didn't have difficult bosses and deadlines to meet for work. They also didn't have crazy Secret Santas.

Why did her life have to be so complicated?

The next morning . . .

Elizabeth scanned her employee identification and limped to the elevators. Of course, she would break a heel on one of the busiest days of her work week! When the elevator doors closed in front of her, she leaned against the wall and pulled both shoes from her feet. Stupid storm drain! At least she got the paperwork filed!

The elevator car dinged, and the doors opened on the forty-eighth floor. When she reached her office, Charlotte wasn't at her desk, so Elizabeth continued inside, throwing her broken pumps in the trash.

"Miss Bennet?" She whirled around to find Mrs. Reynolds in the doorway. "I'm sorry for startling you." She pointed to the trash. "Did you have a problem with your shoes this morning?"

Elizabeth put her palm on her forehead. "My foot slid over a storm drain when I was rushing to get to the subway station before the next train. The heel didn't make it. I don't suppose you know where Charlotte is?"

"Miss Lucas called in sick this morning."

She picked up her phone to find three missed calls and four texts. "She must have called when I was on the subway." After a breath in and out to settle herself, she put her purse under her desk. "Do you know of anyone else I could send out? I have to meet with Mr. Hurst in fifteen minutes, and I can't get out of the office before the meeting with the Lambton board this afternoon. I can't exactly show up barefoot."

"No, you can't." She stepped forward, picked up the phone, and began to dial. "What size do you wear?"

"Um, seven."

"Yes, Lindsey Grantley please?"

"Hi, Lindsey. It's Meghan Reynolds at Darcy Holdings." She smiled for a moment and held up a finger. "Yes, well, I have a problem I need solved quick and was hoping you'd be able to help me. One of our corporate attorneys broke a heel on a work errand this morning and we desperately need it replaced. She wears a size seven." She nodded a couple of times. "Of course, give me a number and I'll text a photo over as soon as I hang up."

When the number was written down, Mrs. Reynolds winked at Elizabeth. "Yes, it goes on the Darcy account, and we'll need those couriered over pronto. Thanks so much, Lindsey!"

Before Elizabeth could argue, Mrs. Reynolds hung up the phone and pointed to the wall. "Stand there and I'll take the photo."

"I don't want Mr. Darcy buying me shoes."

Mrs. Reynolds' phone made that electronic shutter noise, and the older woman immediately started pressing away at the screen. "Oh, Mr. Darcy isn't paying for them, dear. The company is. Do you think we don't have issues like this crop up from time to time? I've replaced shirts for just about every executive here, one or two pairs of shoes, and I've even replaced one of Mr. Hurst's ties." She cupped her hand like she was telling a secret. "Major problem with some lasagna." She patted Elizabeth's hand. "Don't worry. I've got it sorted."

For the first time since she walked in the door, her neck and shoulders relaxed. "Thank you so much, Mrs. Reynolds."

Mrs. Reynolds opened her mouth to respond, but one of the girls from the front desk appeared. "I'm sorry to interrupt, Miss Bennet, but someone left this for you at reception." She held out a pressboard container made to hold a paper coffee cup on one side with a lid on the other. The name "Lava Java" was emblazoned on the outside with the coffee shop's volcano logo.

"Looks like you have breakfast sorted." Mrs. Reynolds grinned. "I'll send down those shoes when they arrive."

Elizabeth took the container, and the girl handed her an envelope. "This was with it."

She set it on her desk and turned the envelope over in her fingers. She was willing to bet it was one of those Advent Calendar cards she'd become so familiar with the last week and a half. Her fingers shook a little as she opened the seal, revealing a glimpse of the scene she knew so well. She'd called it! It was the Advent Calendar just like she'd thought it would be.

That mystery sorted, she took a tiny sip of the coffee and grimaced—an unsweetened latte. That was easily solved. The breakroom had all sorts of sugar and sweetener packets. She held her breath when she opened the lid to the side compartment but let it all out when it was only a pumpkin cheesecake muffin and a couple of little containers. On closer inspection, those turned out to be flavored syrup. She wouldn't need to go to the break room after all.

After mixing some of the syrup into her coffee, she stashed the rest in her desk drawer for later, pulled out the muffin, and popped a piece into her mouth.

Who was her Secret Santa? Up until now, she'd considered a few people in the office, but not truly sought to identify the person. Maybe she should start. If she could figure out this person's identity, she could disabuse them of the notion they should be buying her so much—not that she didn't enjoy the gifts, but they simply weren't necessary. A part of her felt guilty, too. No one else had such a generous Secret Santa, so why should she?

She also needed to become accustomed to some of the eccentricities of Darcy Holdings. She'd never heard of other companies purchasing replacement clothes for employees, but if Mrs. Reynolds could be believed, it wasn't exactly a rarity.

She laughed softly. "Lizzy, you're definitely not in Kansas anymore."

Chapter 7

"I'm coming!" Elizabeth hurried out of her bathroom and was rushing down the hall when the doorbell rang a second time. "Sheesh, impatient much?" When she opened the door, Jane stood on the doorstep.

"I only rang once. The second was her." She pointed to her left where a girl stood with two boxes in front of her.

"Elizabeth Bennet?"

"Yes, that's me."

The girl bent over and picked up one of the packages. "Delivery."

Elizabeth took the first, and Jane helped with the second. "I'm going inside. I'll carry it for her."

Before the girl could rush off, Elizabeth grabbed a couple of dollars from the hall table and held it out. "Thank you."

The delivery girl waved it off. "It's taken care of. Thanks! Have a good weekend!"

Jane's eyebrows lifted almost to her hairline, and she laughed. "Seriously?" As the girl headed down the building's corridor, Jane came inside, kicking the door closed behind her.

Elizabeth shrugged and headed to the kitchen. "Happens every time." She placed the box on a stool at the island so she could peel back the tape. "None of the Secret Santa deliveries will take a tip."

Her sister set the box she carried on the counter. "That's so weird."

The first thing out of the box was the card, which she handed to Jane. "It's the same one each time, an Advent Calendar with a snow scene." While Jane peeled back the flap on the envelope, Elizabeth pulled the packing from the box, dropping it on the floor, until she reached what was inside and carefully removed it. "Jane, look."

She cleared what could've been a huge ceramic jar from the paper, but it wasn't a jar. It had a metal wire handle at the top and a design was cut out of it. Part of the pattern looked like an owl, and she stared at it for a moment. What was it?

"Oh, it's a lantern!" With a delicate finger, Jane traced the cutouts. "It's beautiful."

After Elizabeth dropped the empty box to the floor, she handed it to her sister while she opened the other box and pulled out some packing. "I thought it might be candles, but it's a smaller version."

Jane hugged the larger to her chest. "Where do you want them? I think they'd be really pretty just about anywhere."

"I don't know. Maybe I should pack them back up. This is getting crazy. I mean, who does this? A gift a day for twenty-five days?"

"It sounds like fun to me," said Jane. She propped the bottom of the lantern against herself and studied it. "I actually think they'd be pretty next to the tub in the bathroom once we have the walls painted."

They both startled at a thud from the floor. When Elizabeth glanced down, Grunt sat inside one of the boxes while he watched her over the flap. She closed it over him, and he ducked inside.

When Jane took a piece of the packing paper and trailed it along the opening, one of his paws shot through the crack, claws extended. "He's so much fun," she giggled.

"Except when I have to clean up his damage."

"Oh, I can't imagine he does it on purpose." Leave it to Jane to think the best of even a cat.

"No, it's all in the spirit of play, but he doesn't show one hint of remorse. He almost seems to enjoy watching me clean it, like I'm his human servant."

"What are you going to do with him while we paint?"

"He'll run loose. We'll just have the door of the bathroom closed. I hope you brought an old sweatshirt because it's chilly in there. I have the fan on and the window open for ventilation."

A shudder wracked her sister's body. "Seriously? You couldn't wait until summer for this?"

"No, I couldn't. Uncle Andrew put in my new vanity yesterday while I was at work, and he's coming tomorrow to change out the lovely olive-green toilet. I love the black and white ceramic tile that's already in there, though it does need some freshening up. Uncle Andrew is going to check into re-glazing it. *That* will be done this summer."

They took the gifts with them to her bedroom, leaving Grunt to play in the boxes and packing paper that he'd, no doubt, have strewn all over the room in pieces by the time they finished. After they placed the lanterns to one side of her dresser, Elizabeth led the way into the bathroom.

Her sister scanned the room. "Oh, you already taped everything up."

"All you need to do is help me paint."

Elizabeth poured the paint into the tray while Jane fixed up the roller. "So, if you'll paint, I'll come behind with this," she held up a brush, "and do the stippling."

"Oh, fun," said Jane. She loaded up the roller, and they started, soon developing a rhythm to how it needed to work. "What gifts did your Secret Santa give you Thursday and Friday?"

With a quick glance to her sister, Elizabeth paused for only a second before she continued with her part. "What gifts did I tell you about?"

"The candle, the Snow Leopard adoption, and Charlotte *may* have told me about the amazing lunch on Wednesday."

She shook her head and chuckled. "That doesn't surprise me. She's my Secret Santa's biggest fan."

"So, what else was there?" Jane's excited voice made her smile. Her sister enjoyed the gifts as much as she and Charlotte did.

"Well, Thursday, I had to file some paperwork early, so I didn't get into the office until almost ten. I don't know how they knew, but I had a coffee and muffin from Lava Java delivered within ten minutes of getting to the office."

She paused and turned to Elizabeth with her eyebrows raised. "That's impressive."

"Just wait until I tell you about the shoes!"

"He bought you shoes?"

"No, the company did."

Jane stopped and put her free hand on her hip. "The company bought you shoes?"

"Yes, ask Charlie about it. According to Mrs. Reynolds, he's had a shirt or two replaced at the company's expense. Charlotte called in sick Thursday, and I'd broken my heel on my way to the office. I had no one to send out and I had meetings the rest of the day, so Mrs. Reynolds called a stylist at Bergdorf's and had a pair of shoes sent over."

Her sister put the roller back on the wall. "What if they didn't match?"

"Mrs. Reynolds took a picture of me in my pink suit."

"The one that you wear the black top with?"

"Yup, anyway, they sent over a pair of effing Jimmy Choos."

Jane dropped the roller. "Shit!" She hurried to pick it up from the drop cloth and gaped at Elizabeth. "Jimmy Choos?"

She nodded.

"Real Jimmy Choos? Not like the ones they sell online or on discount sites where you can't tell if they're authentic or not?"

"Seriously. Mrs. Reynolds said the stylist usually sends over designer shirts and ties for the men. Apparently, Mr. Darcy doesn't mind since they courier everything over quickly, and it saves the company from sending out someone to shop."

Jane pointed the roller at Elizabeth. "When we're done, you're letting me try them on." She loaded the roller and started painting again. "What color are they?"

"Pink and black snakeskin."

"A stylist sent those over for an executive?"

Elizabeth shrugged and continued working. "I thought it was strange, but Mrs. Reynolds insisted I try them on. She said that Lindsey has never steered her wrong."

Her sister paused the up and down motion of the roller. "That's so cool. You'd never buy those for yourself. You're too practical."

"I know. I really wasn't too sure of them when I took them out of the box, but I fell in love with them on. I did have to get used to the heel though. I don't usually buy shoes quite that high."

"And I never wear pink, so you don't have to worry about me borrowing them." For a minute or two, the only sound was that of the paint roller running up and down the wall. "Wait! You changed the subject! Those shoes have nothing to do with your Secret Santa, and you didn't tell me about your gift from Friday?"

Why was she not surprised Jane would realize? "It was an oversized mug with a bag of gourmet espresso beans. The cup says, 'In front of every strong woman is a strong cup of coffee.' Oh, and it's bright pink with black writing."

Her sister giggled. "Sounds perfect for you."

"Where's Charlie today?"

"He's at William's researching college football statistics. According to Charlie, the two of them get involved in this football pool every year. It's one hundred dollars to enter, and you put up your predictions for who wins each and every bowl game. The person with the most correct guesses wins the pot. Charlie said last year's winnings were between five and six thousand dollars."

Elizabeth stopped and turned to her sister. "How is that legal?"

Jane grinned. "I don't care if it is or not. I'm not turning him in—especially if he wins."

"Who are you picking to win, Notre Dame or Louisiana State University?" Darcy looked up from his laptop at Bingley. They did this every year—trying to increase the odds of one of them winning by making sure their picks weren't identical.

"Louisiana State University." Bingley didn't even glance up from his notebook. "Have you ever seen how big those boys are on their defensive line? One of them could snap me in half like a twig."

Darcy scrutinized the spreadsheet in front of him then clicked over to a few articles on the teams and the games. "I think I'm going with Notre Dame."

His friend did no more than shrug. "It's your money." He glanced up and looked back to the screen. "Did you decide your point spread for the championship game?"

"Alabama by twenty."

A grimace formed on Bingley's face. "Do you think anyone other than Alabama will ever win?" He'd never been a fan of Alabama. Bingley mentioned on more than one occasion, over the last few years, how their winning streak rubbed him the wrong way.

"Just for a change, I hope so, but it doesn't look like it's going to happen anytime soon."

Bingley closed his notebook with a snap and rubbed his neck. "I'm finished with mine. How about you?"

"Done." Darcy folded down the screen on his laptop and stood. "It's almost five. Do you want a beer?"

"Sure," said Bingley following him to the kitchen. "You know your gifts to Lizzy have become quite popular with Jane. Lizzy has texted photos of some of them to her. I don't think you've failed to surprise Lizzy once."

He smiled while pulling two bottles of Guinness from the refrigerator. "I just hope she's liked them." Once he removed the caps, he handed Bingley one of the bottles. "It's taken some time and thought for some of them. Since I don't know her very well, she hasn't been the easiest person to buy for without resorting to jewelry, but I've enjoyed the challenge."

"I still can't believe Mrs. Reynolds hasn't done any of it."

"She's made sure the deliveries made it past security downstairs. Other than that, she picked up the coffee and muffin for me the other day, but I told her what to order. I simply couldn't get out of the office and Lava Java doesn't have delivery."

Bingley swallowed his beer and tipped his bottle toward him. "They should. They'd make a killing in our building alone." The enthusiasm in Bingley's voice made Darcy smile. "Well, what do you have planned next?"

"When Ana and I were out last weekend, I found some lanterns at this vintage store where my sister loves to shop."

"Sounds expensive."

He laughed. "That's the thing. The clothes are, but the lanterns belonged to the owner. She'd redecorated her apartment and really wanted to get rid of them, so she put them up in the store. I don't think she'd even burnt a candle in them. They looked brand new. Mrs. Reynolds offered to have her niece play delivery girl. You know she lives only a few buildings down from Elizabeth."

After a gulp of his beer, Bingley shoved his free hand in his pocket. "By the way, you owe me big time. I didn't get a chance to mention it at work this week, but Lizzy called last weekend completely freaked out that you had something delivered to her door. I had to talk her down. She figured you got her information from the Darcy mainframe and was not pleased in the slightest about it. Oh, and Jane knows."

Darcy's hand holding his beer became a lead weight and dropped to his side. Jane would tell Elizabeth! "What? Why?"

"She heard me trying to reassure Lizzy, and I had to tell her. She knew I was hiding something."

"Because you suck at lying."

Bingley lifted a shoulder. "That's what you and Jane tell me." He rested his bottle on the counter. "For what it's worth, Jane wants to help. She thinks you would be good for her sister and knows Lizzy still holds her first day against you."

"About that," said Darcy. "I owe you an apology. I should've trusted your instincts more. I'm sorry." Bingley stared at him for a moment. "Well, are you going to say something?"

"Sorry, you don't apologize often. I was just letting it sink in. Thank you." He wore a huge grin, but pointed at Darcy. "One thing Jane wanted me to make clear—you have to try to repair things with Lizzy by talking to her. All the money and gifts in the world won't impress her."

"I know that. I hoped creativity and proving that there's more to me than the self-absorbed ogre she first met might help. If anything, I thought it might get her talking to me. I can work on things from there. I just can't seem to get past the deer in the headlights look she gets whenever I speak to her."

"She and Jane are painting her bathroom today. We could go help."

"But would she even let me in the door?"

Bingley drained his bottle and tilted his head as he set it on the counter. "You know, there's this little thrift store not far from Elizabeth's apartment. She adores the place. She doesn't buy things often since she's been paying to renovate her apartment, but she can walk through the antiques for an hour just looking at what they have. You should give it a shot."

He put his bottle next to Bingley's. "Let's go."

"What?" The high-pitched squeak made Darcy chuckle.

"I need some gifts for next week, and you know where this place is."

With a growl, Bingley pushed away from the counter. "Fine, but if we get busted, it's not my fault."

"How would we get busted? You said yourself that Jane and Elizabeth are painting."

"I don't know." Lord, his voice was whiny. "But I don't want Jane upset with me."

Darcy threw Bingley his coat. "Put it on. We're going. We'll just have to keep an eye out for them when we get close, but if they're both busy, we shouldn't have any issues." Once Darcy managed to shove Bingley out to the sidewalk, the shop wasn't too far past Elizabeth's building, which was a little over a mile away. The front of the place looked like most other stores in the area and was decorated for Christmas. Darcy had to give Bingley some credit for the idea. He would've never thought to try a thrift shop without Bingley mentioning it.

The lady behind the counter greeted them when they entered but let them walk around undisturbed until Bingley walked over and started talking to her. Darcy suppressed a smile. Bingley could charm the pants off a nun, and by the glint in his eye, he was definitely turning on the charm with the redheaded sales clerk. Darcy picked up a figurine, but when he looked up, Bingley was waving him over.

"This is Erika. She has an idea you might like."

Erika leaned onto the counter in front of her. "I just told your friend that Lizzy was in here either Monday or Tuesday. She walks through about once a week mostly looking at our stock, keeping up with any new merchandise. She's a sweet girl, always talks to me while she browses. A few weeks ago, she purchased a pretty blue Depression glass bowl."

Blue glass? Could that have been the blue glass piece that shattered the night of Bingley and Jane's dinner?

"Do you have something you know she'd like, but that maybe she hasn't seen yet?"

97

With a tilt of her head and a smile, the woman led them to a shelf and pulled out two pink wine glasses with flowers etched in a pattern around the body. "Wine glasses?"

"Technically, they're water goblets, but antique. We got them in yesterday, so Lizzy hasn't seen them yet. My grandmother had some that were similar to these that she bought in the nineteen-twenties." She nudged him in the side with her elbow. "No reason they can't be used for wine if you ask me."

He took one and peeked under the base at the price. "If it's antique, why don't you charge more?"

She rolled her eyes. "I don't own the place, and the man who does isn't bothered with it. He buys out a lot of estate sales, but only worries about the larger antiques, complete sets of china and crystal, and the jewelry. Those he sells in a small antique shop two blocks over. The rest he dumps here. He loses a lot of money that way."

No kidding! He handed back the glasses. "I'll take those."

With a smile, she took them to the counter to wrap them up while he stood there, turning and glancing around the store. "I think that's all I'm going to buy here. I don't want to accidentally purchase something she's seen, especially if she was freaked out about the deliveries."

Bingley glanced up from an old beat up chess set. "Probably a good idea. I don't want to have to explain how you might have found this place without following her."

Once Erika had boxed and bagged the glasses, he paid, and the two of them began the walk back to Darcy's house. As soon as their feet hit the sidewalk, Bingley began to chatter endlessly about his bowl game picks, why he'd picked them, and the stats while Darcy's eyes remained glued to the store windows. What else could he get Elizabeth? He had a week still to go and one gift picked out. He needed to find something inexpensive and something that she'd love, but what?

He halted in his tracks and stared at the display in front of him. "Bingley!" His head shot forward to where Bingley stood a few feet ahead.

"Darcy? What are you doing?"

He pointed to the window next to him. "I found another gift."

Before Bingley had a chance to respond, Darcy stepped through the door to the shelf beside the window. An assortment of Christmas ornaments hung on hooks, begging for a shopper's notice, but it was the one ornament he saw on the tree in the window he sought. Scanning back and forth, two rows down the little felt black cat halted his search. He picked it up and started toward the register, but a picture to his right made him veer in that direction instead.

"Clearance from Halloween maybe?" came Bingley's voice from beside him.

"I doubt it. It's a little late for that, and nothing is Halloween themed."

"I don't understand why Lizzy hasn't put two and two together and figured out it's you."

Had he been so obvious? "How would she figure it out?"

"Well, the day after you meet Grunt, you had cat treats sent to her apartment. To me, that would be a clear giveaway."

He paused and turned to Bingley. "I'm the last person she would ever consider as a possibility. In fact, I bet I could deliver one of the gifts myself, and she still wouldn't suspect me."

A lopsided, toothy grin appeared on Bingley's face. "You're on!"

He shook his head with a small laugh. "Besides, she has a picture of her cat on her desk at work. I'd ordered the cat treats on Friday, not after dinner on Saturday."

"I'd forgotten about that picture," said Bingley with wonder. "It's actually a joke between Lizzy and her assistant. Since Lizzy hasn't had a date in forever, Charlotte said she should have a picture on her desk of the only man in her life." Bingley stopped speaking and stared at him for a moment. "How do you remember those little details?"

"Because I've been by her office a number of times with Hurst, and I made the most of each opportunity to get a good look around while he talked to her. It's how I knew she likes snow leopards—she has a calendar of them to the side of her desk, and it's how I knew about her cat."

He took another look at the items in front of him. He'd almost had a theme the first week with the bath supplies, but he'd never considered buying her cat décor. She had a black cat, so she might find some of it a lot of fun. Her apartment also didn't have much decoration. It was well furnished with nice, quality pieces, but lacked adornment.

He picked up a framed vintage postcard and brought it closer. The black cat in the illustration sat tall and gave a rather superior expression to the laughing crescent moon he was perched on. The artwork was probably a replica, but it didn't matter. It was still perfect. The pose of the cat reminded him of Grunt.

"I'm going to get these two things for now. I'll figure the rest out later." He set his purchases with the card on the counter for the sales girl, and as soon as she handed him his bag, they stepped back into the windy cold.

"What amazes me is you have so little hope of her ever liking you back, but you're still trying." Bingley kept his gaze straight ahead while they walked. "I don't know if I could do it if I were in your shoes."

"You've never been in my shoes, Bingley. You have a natural way with people I don't. If you put your foot in your mouth, most people find it funny and let it go. I inevitably shove the foot further down until I gag on it. All I can do is try. Do I think she'll drop everything and fall into my arms when she finds out? No way. But, if I can manage a conversation with her—a real one, I'd say all of this was worth it."

Chapter 8

"Charlotte!"

Elizabeth's assistant hurried into her office with a pen behind her ear and her hair askew. "What's wrong?"

It had been one of those days. Poor Charlotte had run from the first floor to the seventy-fifth, and she was about to do it again.

Elizabeth pulled the document from the printer. "I need you to take these down to finance and have the department head sign off, then run them to Mr. Darcy's office. Mrs. Reynolds indicated he wanted them by four."

They both peered at the clock. Damn! It was three-forty-five. If Charlotte had to wait in finance or if she became stuck waiting for the elevator, she would be late. Elizabeth's foot started to tap out a steady cadence against the floor.

"Don't start that, Lizzy." Charlotte held out her hand, her eyes didn't waver, and her jaw set. "Hand them over. Even if I'm a few minutes late, Mr. Darcy won't call for either of our severed heads on a platter."

When her assistant hurried off, Lizzy collapsed back into her chair, closed her eyes, and rubbed her temples. Was it five o'clock yet? Of course not, she just looked at the clock, but Lord how she wished it was! The weekend couldn't come quick enough!

"Knock, knock."

She opened her eyes and sat up. "Jane? Why are you up here?"

"I came to rescue Charlie. He said all of you have been up to your armpits in paperwork and deadlines today, so I thought I'd drag him away from the office for dinner. Do you want to come?"

Her shoulders slumped as she surveyed her desk. Of course she wanted to come, but how? "I don't see how I can. I just sent Charlotte on an errand. I think I'm done for today, but I'm just not sure yet. If

Mr. Darcy has a problem with the document, then I'm back to square one."

"There won't be a problem," said Mr. Darcy as he walked through the door. "I'm certain it's fine. You should go to dinner with Charlie and Jane." He held up a box, and Elizabeth's eyes zeroed in on the snow scene that adorned the paper. "This was delivered to my office by accident." When he stepped forward and placed it on her desk, she put her hands on either side of it and inhaled to steady herself.

How odd! She'd come to expect these little breaks during the day. When this one didn't appear by one o'clock, she'd been disappointed.

"I wonder what it could be." Jane bounced forward and tapped the top. "Don't just sit there. Open it!"

She pulled the card from the top, tore the wrapping away, and leaned back and stared. It was a crate, covered with a solid lid. She carefully removed the cover. Inside, tucked into a bed of what appeared to be straw, was a bottle of red wine, a claret, and then there was . . . What was that? She picked up the mystery object and started to laugh. "Jane, look! It's a wine stopper."

Her sister giggled. "Oh, that's perfect. Grunt is always spilling drinks if they're left around the apartment. Now, you have a little Grunt to stick his head in your wine bottles." She picked up the bottle of sparkling water on Elizabeth's desk and stuck the silicone plug inside. The cat's feet perched on the rim of the opening with its head wedged inside the spout, its behind stuck up in the air.

It had to be the cutest thing ever. She touched it and smiled. How often did she clean up glasses of spilled water as Grunt grew up? He'd once stuck his head into a jar she'd filled with water then tipped it when he tried to get his head out. Sometimes, he just dipped his paw inside and accidentally pulled the glass with him.

Jane tilted the bottle of wine up so she could see the label. "You should break out the glasses you received earlier this week and drink it this weekend." She looked up at Mr. Darcy. "You should see the glasses. Lizzy texted me a picture Wednesday when she received them. They'd be prettier if they weren't pink, but . . ."

"I happen to like pink."

His forehead crinkled. "Who are the gifts from?"

She shrugged and arranged the stopper back in the box. "A friend."

After giving an incredulous laugh, Jane picked up the card. "Her Secret Santa has been sending her a personalized Advent Calendar. She receives a present every day."

"Jane!" She gave her sister as nasty a glare as she could.

His eyebrows lifted. "This person sounds quite ambitious."

Avoiding his eyes, she nodded. "Definitely, but I do worry about how much this person has spent. All of this couldn't have been less than thirty dollars."

"Perhaps they thought only of you and how much you would enjoy each item."

"Oh, it's not always a present in this sense." Elizabeth motioned toward the box. "I've received a certificate for adopting a snow leopard through a wildlife fund, and this week, I was sent confirmation of a donation made in my name to the Meryton Cat Sanctuary."

Jane placed the wine back in the straw. "He's been on a bit of a cat binge lately."

Thank goodness for Jane. If she kept her focus on her sister, she wouldn't have to meet Mr. Darcy's eye, and that man made her all kinds of uncomfortable. It must be his disapproving stare that made her so uneasy. That was the only way could explain the effect he had on her. What else would cause a fluttering in her stomach and the prickling along her skin? Romance novels might say love, but she certainly didn't love Mr. Darcy. She didn't really know him!

"I suppose he's been on a bit of a theme. I received that framed vintage-looking cat postcard on Monday, the donation confirmation on Tuesday, the wine glasses on Wednesday, and a black cat Christmas ornament on Thursday. Today's is obviously the wine and the stopper."

"Where did you hang the picture?" asked Mr. Darcy.

When their eyes met, Elizabeth's insides gave a jolt, and she swallowed. "I haven't yet." He shoved his hands in his pockets, but his shoulders remained rigid. He always stood stiff as a statue. Didn't it make his shoulders or neck hurt?

"You don't have much decoration in your apartment yet. I would think you'd be eager to hang it."

"I feel guilty keeping all of it."

His brows drew down a bit in the middle. "Why? This person meant for you to have these gifts. What if you hurt their feelings?"

"I don't want to hurt anyone," she said. "My issue is that it's more than what's required and a good deal of money spent, so I've considered returning most of them to my Secret Santa. I can't return the food items, but I can everything else. The food deliveries alone were an amazing gift."

A gasp came from Jane. "Lizzy! I agree with William. You might really cause this person pain. I understand why in a way, but it is something to consider. This person put a lot of time and thought into these gifts. Besides, what would they do with them? Could they even be returned?"

"I hadn't considered that." She nibbled on the inside of her cheek. Was she being incredibly rude to insist on returning them? What if they were stuck with the gifts because they couldn't have their money refunded?

The dip of Mr. Darcy's eyebrows became more severe. "Whoever your Secret Santa is, they sound as though they've made an effort to get to know you and brighten your day."

"I agree, but I'm still allowed to have concerns, aren't I?" Was she completely off her rocker to find this all over-the-top? Mr. Darcy seemed to find it nothing to be concerned about, so why did she?

"I thought my lovely Jane was coming to rescue me, but when she doesn't show, I find her in her sister's office. I've been betrayed." They all startled and turned. Charlie's head poked around the door frame, a large smile on his face. "Is Lizzy coming to dinner with us?"

"I've invited her," said Jane," but I can't get an answer out of her."

Mr. Darcy moved to the side so Bingley could enter. "I told her she's free and clear to leave for the day, but she won't hear of it."

Elizabeth huffed. "I need to make sure those documents all check out before I go. Is it terrible that I want all my work correct and finished before the weekend?"

Without a word, Mr. Darcy picked up the phone on her desk and dialed an extension. "Mrs. Reynolds, has Miss Lucas brought some paperwork to my office?" He looked at her with his eyebrows raised. "She has. Good. Are they correct?" He paused. "Thank you."

When the phone was back on the receiver, he crossed his arms over his chest. "Mrs. Reynolds is placing the documents on my desk. She looked over them first and said they appear perfect, and before you say anything, she types every memo, sees almost every bit of paperwork that crosses my desk, and takes notes on almost all of my meetings. She knows the deal as well as we do."

"There you have it." Charlie's arm wrapped around Jane's shoulders. "I don't know about you, but it's been a hectic day and I'm starving. I want nothing more than to relax with a drink and a medium rare steak."

Elizabeth stood and removed her purse, setting it on the desk while she leaned over to get her case.

"Come on, Lizzy," said her sister. "Giorgio's is just around the corner. We can come back for your bag."

Charlie grabbed Jane's hand and tugged her towards the door. "I called for a reservation earlier. Darcy, you're coming with us, aren't you? I booked a table for four."

He glanced between them. "If it's okay with everyone and there's room. You have a reservation already, and I don't want to intrude."

"Of course, you're not intruding!" Of course, Jane would say that! "Charlie said he booked the table for four."

He was Charlie's friend and they could invite anyone they wished, but a part of her hoped he would say no. After all, he could have work to finish . . . he could need to make a phone call . . . he could need to floss!

"I'd enjoy a steak from Giorgio's. Thank you for asking." His eyes met hers for a moment, and she attempted a small smile.

As they filed out into the corridor, Charlotte approached from the direction of the elevators. "Is everyone heading out?"

Elizabeth shifted her purse to her shoulder. "We're going to dinner, but I need to return for my case and the box on my desk. Why don't you go home a little early? Maybe you and Bill could go out for drinks."

After a peek back at her desk, Charlotte blew out a breath. "I wish I could, but I need to organize my desk. I will not come back Monday to that train wreck. I also need to do my prep work for next week. I wouldn't know what to do with myself if I didn't have everything ready when I came in."

One thing about Charlotte, she'd always been compulsively organized. It was one of the many reasons Elizabeth valued her as an assistant.

"That's too bad," said Jane. "The three of us need to go to lunch together next week. I'll message you with the days I'm available, and you should set something up."

Charlotte waved. "Definitely! I'll look forward to it. You guys have a good time. Lizzy, if I'm not here when you get back, give me a call later."

Once they'd all said good-bye to Charlotte, they made their way outdoors. The weather wasn't poor, but the sun hid behind a sky full of dingy looking clouds and an icy breeze made the temperature feel colder than it really was.

Charlie grabbed Jane's hand and headed toward the restaurant, leaving Elizabeth to walk next to Mr. Darcy. His hand brushed hers, and she sucked in a quick breath when a jolt of heat traveled up her arm.

"Forgive me. I didn't want to run her over." His deep voice was right next to her ear, and she almost slapped her hand to her neck at the tickling sensation that traveled down her back.

She glanced over her shoulder. How had she missed that little old lady with the cane? "It's okay. I was too much in my own head, I suppose. I never saw her."

As soon as they turned the corner, he cleared his throat. "I know I apologized before, but I hope you know that I meant what I said that night in the car. I'm sorry for how your first day went."

She turned her head in his direction, but something prevented her from looking directly at him. She just couldn't.

He cleared his throat again. "I also meant what I said in the coffee shop. I'm pleased with your work for the company so far. Bingley was right to hire you. I hope you're happy at Darcy Holdings?"

Her head shifted enough for their eyes to finally meet, and her heart beat a little faster. Why couldn't she control her own body with this man? Even now, something in his eyes tugged at a place in her chest, holding her gaze captive. "Yes, I'm very happy. Thank you."

"Why are you two lagging behind?" Charlie waved them forward while he and Jane stood in the open door of Giorgio's. "Let's get inside. That wind is cold, and I want that drink!"

He held his breath waiting for something, anything to tell him he was really forgiven until Bingley interrupted, and she gave him an apologetic smile before she hurried to catch up. When he approached them from behind, he reached over Elizabeth's head to hold the door open for her. She glanced back over her shoulder, their eyes barely meeting. "Thank you," she said softly before she turned to follow Jane inside.

A few people waited near the host's podium, but people often sat at the bar while they hoped for a table at Giorgio's. The steak house was one of the best kept secrets in that part of town but the cozy atmosphere invited many back. Because of Bingley's reservation, they were seated right away, their server approached them soon after for their drink order, and they were left to peruse their menus.

Bingley opened his and immediately closed it, placing it on the table. "No point in looking. I know what I want."

After a peek over his menu at Elizabeth, Darcy surveyed the choices and closed his own. "Me too. Have you ladies decided?"

"I want the surf and turf," said Jane. "What are you having, Lizzy?"

He watched her forehead crinkle as she concentrated on the choices, his eyes drawn down to her teeth lightly biting her bottom lip. His hand clenched the arm of his chair. Her full bottom lip bounced back when she released it, and he swallowed—hard. She didn't mean to drive him crazy, but those little things all made him squirm in his seat. He wanted to drag his teeth along that lip himself right before he . . . He cleared his throat and shifted, his eyes returning to her face.

She wasn't wearing much make-up, but she never did. She simply didn't need it. The little bit of gloss she wore gave a perfect accent to her peaches and cream complexion. A sharp pain in his shin made him gasp and jerk in his seat.

"Sorry." The half-smile Bingley sported made him appear not the least bit sorry. Neither did Jane's odd cough. Was it him, or did it sound more like a giggle?

Elizabeth glanced around the table. "What's going on?"

Bingley took Jane's menu and grinned. "Nothing. Have you decided what you want?"

"I'm going to have the grilled shrimp skewers."

Once the server took their orders, they all sat without speaking until Bingley laughed. "We're good company tonight. Lizzy, Jane tells me the color of your bathroom came out well."

"It did. I hadn't thought to put almost a turquoise color with white and black tiles, but I loved the pictures I found online. One place even listed the shade of the paint, so all I had to do was find out where to buy it. Jane helped a lot. It would've taken me all day if I'd done it by myself."

"Now, she needs some new towels and bath mats to match the paint." Jane took a sip of her wine.

"My towels still have some use to them." Elizabeth's eyes held a bit of a spark and her tone became defensive. "I know I've taken my time fixing up my apartment, but it's getting there."

Darcy shifted in his seat. "Jane told me how you moved in with the furniture from the house you shared with some friends at Harvard and that you've built it up a piece at a time."

She shrugged. "I saw no reason to buy nice furniture when the place needed so much work. Uncle Andrew and I knocked a wall out between the kitchen and the living room so it was open and painted it all. Since we were working on the project while I was at Longbourn, it took us several months to complete the job. The kitchen needed new cabinets and countertops. Then I had to save up some money for a new couch and the other furniture. It's been one room at a time."

"What was the most challenging part of the remodel?" He leaned on the arm of his chair. The movement shifted him a little closer to her, but he craved to learn more about her.

"The laundry room," she said without hesitation.

Jane smoothed the pristine white tablecloth in front of her. "Our Uncle Andrew is a plumber, and he's pretty good with all sorts of construction jobs. He's renovated the last few homes he's lived in. He does the work himself, sells it after two or three years, and buys something a little bigger."

"My apartment belonged to my grandparents, and my uncle owns it now. He and my aunt won't take money for rent, but I've covered the cost of fixing it up." With a light touch, Elizabeth's finger traced around the base of her wine glass. "When I moved in, the place had no laundry room, which of course, isn't unusual in the city, but it did have two bathrooms. I talked Uncle Andrew into converting the smaller of the two bathrooms into a laundry room. The only trick was the dryer, but I have a friend from college who lives in England. We were chatting about it one night, and she mentioned how they use a water-filled condenser instead of a vent." She lifted a shoulder in a sort of shrug. "I'd never heard of one before. I found a condenser kit like she described at a local hardware store, so Uncle Andrew ripped out the bathroom and adjusted the plumbing. We did replace the exhaust fan in the ceiling for a new one, so when the dryer is going I turn on the fan. It helps to keep it from getting too muggy."

Bingley tapped out a rhythm on the arms of his chair. "It's a great idea, isn't it?"

Nodding, Darcy sipped his scotch. It was definitely a good idea. Not many apartments in the city had a place for a washer and dryer. If someone was looking for a larger one bedroom, the addition could be an attractive selling point.

"I didn't need two bathrooms for just me, and Uncle Andrew did confess that he didn't like me at the laundromat by myself at night. Once we painted and refinished the floors in the second bedroom, it became a study anyway."

Her commitment to paying for the renovations and purchasing new furniture could be why her apartment still seemed bare. Ripping out the kitchen would've cost a small fortune by itself. The job had been one of the most expensive things he'd done to his house in the last few years. Not that her kitchen was the same size as his, but new cabinets and appliances were never cheap.

Would he ever discover some aspect of Elizabeth or her personality that he didn't like? She knew her way around a contract, she remodeled her own apartment, and she didn't pretend she liked him because of his position or his income. Hell, what wasn't to like?

Chapter 9

"So, he didn't just apologize once. He said it twice," said Charlotte. She relaxed on Elizabeth's sofa while Grunt sat on the cushion beside her, never taking his eyes from the interloper. Charlotte didn't like cats, and whenever she came over, she was like a magnet for Elizabeth's little troublemaker. Every time, he tried to sit in Charlotte's lap, and every time, he was rebuffed. He'd already made three attempts this afternoon, and now, he watched and waited for his next opening.

Elizabeth looked down from the stepladder where she prepped the wall to hang her Christmas cactus. "Yes, but what if he only said he was sorry because Charlie insisted rather than because he wanted to?"

Charlotte raised her eyebrows. "That was months ago. Besides, do you really think Mr. Darcy does anything he doesn't want to do? If he said it once, then I might consider it, but no man apologizes twice unless he means it."

"Everyone has obligations they don't like—even Darcy."

Grunt put a paw on Charlotte's thigh, and she scooted an inch or so over, making him pull it back. "Honestly, I think you're in some serious denial, but I can't force you to like the man."

Elizabeth lifted the stud finder, turned it on, and began to slowly run it across the wall. "I'm not in denial."

"You are. You're so prejudiced against him, you can't see matters clearly. He's complimented your work, and now he's apologized twice for what he said on your first day, but you still think he doesn't like you."

"The apologies were nice, but it doesn't change how he's stared at me when we were in the same room." She'd been surprised to relax and enjoy the conversation at Giorgio's. At least, he didn't look at her like he disapproved for once. He'd actually been . . . nice.

Charlotte opened her mouth like she might say something else, but instead, she grimaced and closed it.

Elizabeth lined up the hanging bracket in the middle of the stud with a small level and marked the screw holes. "What were you going to say?"

"Nothing," said Charlotte.

"I don't believe you."

"Look, you'd go apeshit if I said it, so I'm keeping my mouth shut."

Elizabeth climbed down and stood at the base of the ladder with her hands on her hips. "Now, you have to tell me."

"No, no I don't.

"Charlotte!"

"Lizzy!"

Gah! She hated it when Charlotte went on one of her stubborn streaks! She grabbed the drill, the bracket, and the screws. "Come help me a minute, please."

Before Grunt could try another sneaky leap to her lap, Charlotte stood and held the bracket so Elizabeth could fasten it to the wall. "Why can't you just tell me?"

Her best friend threw her hands in the air. "Because you're being civil to the man at the moment, and I don't want you to freak out on him the next time he looks at you in a meeting."

She gasped and set down the drill with a thud. Oops! That was a little harder than she intended, so she lifted it. Thank goodness, it didn't mar the coffee table!

"You know me better than that, Charlotte."

A strange laugh burst from Charlotte. "It's precisely because I do know you that I'm certain I need to keep my mouth shut." As Elizabeth stepped back onto the ladder, Charlotte handed her the simple plant hanger, which reminded her a little of the macramé ones her grandmother used except the rope was black and rather thin. Once the pink potted Christmas cactus was nestled inside, Elizabeth climbed down.

"I love this. Thanks for the idea."

"Don't look at me." Charlotte plopped back down on the sofa. "You know I live and breathe Pinterest. Did you see the old belts used to hang pots along the wall? I thought of you when I first saw that one. You've said for the last year that you wished you had a place to grow herbs where your cat won't tamper with them."

The idea had been just what she'd been searching for. Three stark white containers, each with an opening on the back, attached to the wall with an old leather belt. It wouldn't make it so Grunt could never get to them, but it made it a lot less likely.

"I loved it. After you sent me the image yesterday, I bought a set of the exact containers on eBay, and the last time I was in the thrift shop, Erika had some neat old leather belts. They've definitely seen better days, but I think it would give a great distressed look to the planters." A loud knock made Grunt trill and abandon his pursuit of Charlotte's lap to race toward the door.

Charlotte laughed. "He likes company."

"Depends. Sometimes he hides, but when he does this, he's usually being nosy."

They followed him to the foyer and Elizabeth peered through the peephole. Wow, that girl stayed busy making deliveries! She opened the door. "Hi, how are you?"

The same delivery girl as the lanterns, the candles that followed, and yesterday's poster grinned widely. "Good morning." She handed the large, flat wrapped package to Elizabeth. "Have a good day!" she called over her shoulder as she walked away.

"You too!"

A gleam lit Charlotte's eye when Elizabeth closed the door. "Is that today's Secret Santa gift?"

She turned it around to the glittery silver twenty. "I think I know what it is."

"How?"

Grunt rubbed along the edge, so she picked it up and started back to the living room. "The package yesterday was exactly the same size. I'd bet anything it's another poster."

Rubbing her hands together, Charlotte perched herself on the edge of the sofa cushion. "Well, let's see it! I haven't even seen yesterday's yet."

Elizabeth bit her lip and shook her head. "I don't think I should."

"Why ever not?" asked Charlotte.

"I don't think it's right to open them when I should be returning them."

Charlotte rolled her eyes. "Then don't give them back." She reached forward, and with a long rip tore the paper down the front and pulled it clear. "It's perfect for you." She cocked her head to the side a little. "Isn't that a reproduction of a work of art?"

Elizabeth looked down at the more ornate variation of the Chat Noir print she received the day before. "It was a design for a cabaret in Paris by an artist named Théophile Steinlen. I'd seen it before but didn't know much about it until yesterday. I researched it online after it was delivered."

"Where's the other one?"

She passed the poster to Charlotte, hurried to the bookshelf, and pulled it from behind. "I had to hide it because I caught Grunt trying to bite it."

The posters had the same illustration of the black cat, but the text differed. The print delivered on Saturday had less information and the red box under the cat and the design behind his head wasn't as vivid as today's.

Charlotte pointed to the wall behind the sofa. "Once they're framed, you should hang them both there. I like the variations on a theme impression they give." She perked up and started to wag her finger at Elizabeth. "You know what? Craft Center is having a frame sale. We should go."

"I'm not framing them yet."

"But why?" Her friend's tone became higher pitched. "You don't have anything but that plant on the wall in here and with the neutral tones of your furniture, these would look amazing and would also add some color."

"I'm serious! I don't feel right accepting all of this, Charlotte! I can't return the snow leopard adoption or the food, but I can give back the rest of it."

Charlotte threw up her hands and dropped back onto the sofa, sending Grunt, who lurked behind her, darting off with a chirp. "You're certifiable."

"Thanks a lot!" Elizabeth put the posters together and slid them back behind the shelf. "Whoever this is has spent entirely too much. I can't in good conscience accept it all."

"Well, I happen to disagree, and I *know* Jane would too."

"I still believe Charlie and Jane know more than they're letting on. I need to have a sit down with my dearest elder sister this week. I'm going to figure out what she's hiding."

"You think Jane knows the identity of your Secret Santa?"

"I can't explain it, but she's too happy when the subject is discussed. I also know that if she were in my position, the gifts would be given back. She'd never accept them all."

A throaty sigh came from Charlotte. "Then both of you need your heads examined."

The house vibrated with the slam of the front door and Darcy winced. Why did Ana always have to do that? Mrs. Hill's high-pitched chatter could be heard, but he couldn't make out what she was saying. Their housekeeper was such a grandmother to them. Now, she would probably bake a couple dozen cookies for Ana to take back to her apartment. Goodness knows Ana had no idea how to bake! He rolled his eyes.

At the tell-tale clomp of her Docs approaching, he put the lid on his pen and walked to the doorway, leaning against the frame. "Why do you always slam the door?"

"Because I love the fuss Mrs. Hill makes when I surprise her."

"Then the repair, when it's needed, can come out of your money. I still don't understand how the plaster isn't crumbling around the frame."

"Okay, I'll try to remember next time." She crossed her arms across her chest. "So, what's this about going through Mom's stuff?"

"One of the charities our mother supported with time and donations is having an auction next month, and I received an email requesting items to sell." His voice started to become scratchy, so he coughed. The lump that steadily formed when he began speaking of his mother remained. "I thought of her scarf collection. I also thought about donating some of Mom's and Dad's clothes to a shelter I learned about recently. They help find jobs for the homeless, particularly those with children. They need appropriate clothing for job interviews and dressing the part once they're first hired."

Ana's eyes shone, and she glanced down for a moment and swallowed. "Why now?"

"Because we've avoided this for too long. Because I think Mom and Dad would like to know that their belongings helped someone else rather than sitting in a closet rotting away. I thought you might want some of Mom's clothes or scarves, so I didn't want to donate them without having you help me sort through them first."

Her breath left her in a whoosh. "I hate this."

He wrapped his arms around her. "I know you do, but as much as we'd like to keep those rooms as a sort of shrine, it's not healthy and it's not realistic. If it wasn't for Mrs. Hill, everything would be coated in dust anyway. We never go in there."

"I know, but I like avoiding things. Makes it so much easier to believe they're simply away somewhere on vacation."

"I wish they were, sweetheart."

After one last squeeze, she pulled back and wiped her cheeks with the heels of her hands. "Let's get this done. You might want to have Mrs. Hill make some coffee. She'll also need to break out the extra boxes of tissue."

"Come on." He took her hand and tugged her toward the stairs. "I'll take you out for pizza when we're done. We can drown our sorrows in meat lovers with extra bacon." She gave a choked chuckle. "I'll even take you out for ice cream after."

"Nah, I don't need ice cream. Wine and chocolates are so much better."

When had she decided wine and chocolate was better than ice cream? This was as tragic as when she moved out last year. She'd so had her heart set on living in an overcrowded apartment with three of her friends. He'd hated it when she left. He didn't live that far from the college, but she craved the independence and the life of a typical college student. In the end, he couldn't say no.

She turned on the light when they entered the room, releasing his hand and trailing her fingers across the cherry stained footboard of the bed as she crossed to the windows and pulled back the curtains. Despite Mrs. Hill's cleaning efforts, flecks of dust caught the light as they floated through the air, giving the room a gloomy feel. Ana picked up a framed picture of the four of them, taken the summer before the crash, when they vacationed in Greece. His sister had just read the first Percy Jackson novel, and his parents took advantage of her excitement over mythology.

She replaced the picture, opened the middle drawer, and handed him a stack of silk. After she took the remaining scarves, they sat on the bed and sorted through them. Ana didn't take many; she didn't wear scarves often. The memories attached to the scarf probably prevailed more than a desire to wear it.

While she went through them a second time, Darcy ran his fingers along one in his lap. It was a blush colored Hermès his mother bought not long before her death. The tags were still attached. She'd never worn it.

"Are you okay?"

He nodded and held the swath of fabric out. "It's brand new."

She fingered the label. "Mom always did love Hermès. Why do you look like you're thinking entirely too hard about something?"

"Do you think it would be weird to give it as a gift?"

A side of her lip curved up. "That depends. Who were you thinking about?"

"Never mind." He folded the swath of silk and put it back in the box they'd found nestled in the middle of the stacks. "It's a long story."

"We don't have anywhere to go since we still have to go through their closet. Anything is better than remembering."

So, he updated where he stood with Elizabeth while they filtered through the closets. When he was done, Ana giggled as she shoved one of her mother's suits down the bar to donate. "I can just see Charlie trying to keep this a secret. I bet he's bursting at the seams." She paused and turned to face him. "You know this could bite you in the ass. She might think you're trying to buy her."

"Charlie said the same thing, but I hope not. If I'd wanted to attract her with money, I would've gone straight to Tiffany's." He rested back against the wall. "She'd love that scarf, but it's way beyond the spending limit I gave for myself."

"But you didn't buy it. Technically, it cost you nothing." Ana's eyebrows lifted on her forehead. "I don't think you'll be breaking some big rule. She could find it creepy, but Mom never wore it. In a way, it's better to give one of Mom's scarves as a gift than have some stranger purchase it at the auction. I say go for it."

He returned to sorting through his father's ties. Should he? Shouldn't he? He could go 'round and 'round for hours deciding.

"What do you have planned for the rest of the gifts?"

Her voice broke through the whirring of his brain while he pulled a striped Hugo Boss aside that he liked. He didn't really need any ties, but something in his heart refused to give all of them away. "I donated money in her name to the Snow Leopard Conservancy. She'll receive the notification tomorrow. I might give her the scarf, and then my surprises for Christmas Eve and Christmas Day."

"You're missing one."

"I know. I keep hoping some idea will fall into my lap. When I've taken a moment to look around instead of stressing, I tend to find something."

"You said her apartment is sparsely decorated. What about a nice throw or a few pillows? I've seen faux fur ones that are super soft. I bet there's a Snow Leopard print. It would be pretty and functional. If she didn't want to drape it over a chair or the back of her couch, she could keep it tucked away and use it when she's watching a movie or reading a book."

It wasn't a bad idea, but would she want a faux fur one? "Mrs. Reynolds did say she liked the shoes we bought to replace hers."

"What shoes?"

"Oh, Elizabeth broke one of her heels on the way into the office from delivering some paperwork. Her assistant had called in sick, and we had an important meeting that afternoon so Mrs. Reynolds called that stylist she uses."

"What did they send over?"

"They were pink and black snakeskin with extremely high heels." He couldn't forget those heels! Her legs had looked amazing when she'd strode into the boardroom with those adorning her feet. He'd had to focus to keep his eyes above her hemline when she'd approached, or he wouldn't have been able to conduct the meeting, and a loss of concentration would have been the least of his problems.

"What designer?"

He snapped out of his memory to Ana leaning into his face. "I don't know, but I do know that she freaked out at the expense."

His little sister looked up at the ceiling and shook her head. "Louboutin, Manolo Blahnik, Jimmy Choos?" When he shrugged, she crossed her arms over her chest. "I swear. You're hopeless."

"That's what you tell me."

"Ha, ha!" She glanced at the large closet of clothes surrounding them. "Do we have to go through everything today?"

"Did you look at Mom's shoes?"

"I have bigger feet than Mom. It would be ridiculous to hold on to shoes I can't wear."

"Then, yeah. Let's get out of here." He'd had enough an hour ago. "I'll notify the charities, and Mr. and Mrs. Hill can help get this moved downstairs for pick up."

Before they left the room, Ana opened their mother's jewelry box and scanned the inside. She shifted a few things around, finally picking up a piece. "Do you mind if I keep this?"

"What is it?" He stepped closer and took a ring from her, turning it around in his hand. Was that a ruby or a garnet?

"Dad bought Mom the ring on my first birthday. I thought about it recently. I've never worn rings much, but I'd like to start wearing this one." Ana's birthday fell in January, so it was a garnet. His mother wore it daily just as she did the pearl ring she wore on her index finger, given to her on his first birthday.

"Of course, you can have it. It should definitely be yours." He set the piece back in her palm. "I'll never sell our mother's jewelry. You can have whatever you want out of it, though I'd rather you not take most of it while you're living with friends at college." He put his hands up, palms out. "Before you get mad at me, I'm not accusing your friends of anything—"

"I know. It's more about who they might bring into the apartment. A friend of mine had a necklace stolen during a party at her place. I would be heartbroken if it was something of Mom's."

She slipped the ring onto the ring finger of her right hand. "I believe you promised me pizza, brother dear, and I definitely intend to make sure you keep your promises."

With a smile, he wrapped an arm around her shoulders. "Pizza it is."

Chapter 10

Elizabeth walked back to her office from the meeting she'd had with Mr. Hurst. One last wrap-up before they took a break for the Christmas holiday. Three days off and the weekend to do what she wished—to sleep in as late as she wanted—it sounded like heaven.

When she stepped through the doorway into her office, it was there on her desk, just as she thought it might be, and in some bizarre way hoped it would be. How weird she now felt that way! She kept saying she was going to give the gifts back, but she looked forward to receiving them—that little surge of excitement she had right before she ripped back the paper. Was that feeling addictive? Must be, or why else would she feel like this?

She walked further into her office. She'd look like an idiot if she did no more than stand and stare from the doorway. After all, the present wouldn't bite.

She dropped her purse and briefcase onto her chair and bit her bottom lip. What would be in the present today? Monday, she'd received a confirmation of a donation in her name to a snow leopard conservation group and yesterday was a faux fur snow leopard throw. It had been all she could do not to toss it over the back of her sofa when she got home. Instead, she stashed it away where Grunt couldn't claim it as his own.

Just who was this person? She really needed to find out. She'd interrogated Jane and Charlie on Sunday. She'd even made a special trip to their apartment to do it, but both of them denied knowing who pulled what name. What bugged her was they never said they didn't know, and Charlie couldn't look her in the eye. She might not be a litigator, but if she were, she'd be all over him if she were cross-examining him as a witness!

"You have another." She looked up to find Charlotte, standing just inside her office, and nodded. "It's not going to bite, you know. Open it. I want to see what it is."

"Charlotte! I can't do this anymore! You know I've never been comfortable with this, and I've tried to figure out who this person is, but I can't get any sort of hint. How can I accept any more gifts? I should've started turning them away weeks ago."

"Oh, come on. I still believe your Secret Santa is of the male persuasion, and he *definitely* has it bad."

She traced her finger along the two in the twenty-three printed on the package. "But you won't tell me who you think it is, and I can't get anything out of Charlie and Jane."

Charlotte leaned against the corner of Elizabeth's desk. "Did Jane behave suspiciously?"

"No, but Charlie did. He wouldn't look me in the eye when he denied it. You know I have a sense about these things. He has some idea, but he won't spill."

"Don't get all crazy when I ask this, but what about the big boss man?" Charlotte spoke softly, probably because the door was still wide open.

"William Darcy?" Elizabeth laughed and shook her head as she moved her belongings and sat in her chair. "I don't see how it could be him. You know how I've caught him staring at me. He looks at me like he's judging me. I doubt he thinks about much more than the company."

"Elizabeth," said Charlotte in that voice, the one that always tried to make Elizabeth see reason. "That man has a little sister, remember? From what I've been told around the office, he's doted on her since before his parents died. He became her guardian as well. You should hear the assistants who've been here for years talk about how he has taken such amazing care of her. Other than the few encounters you've had with him, you really don't know him."

One side of Charlotte's lips curved up in a wicked grin. "I've seen the way the man stares at you, and it's not one of a man looking to find something wrong. He either looks like he's in pain or he wants to throw you on that boardroom table and have his way with you."

Something inside Elizabeth jolted, and she squirmed in her chair. "Are you sure he's not simply constipated?"

With a roll of her eyes, Charlotte closed the office door and resumed her previous spot. "He's not constipated. He appears lovelorn."

"You read too many bodice rippers."

"Think about it! The day after you complained that he was behind you in line at the coffee shop, you get a cup of coffee and a muffin delivered to your desk. Don't forget that you hand delivered those papers that morning. He would've known you either skipped breakfast or would be needing a pick me up."

"That doesn't explain the other gifts, though."

"I know you haven't forgotten that you sometimes have had to sit next to him during meetings. He's probably noticed that you frequently wear lavender perfume."

Elizabeth sat back in her chair. "How would William Darcy know my favorite animal is a snow leopard or that pink is my favorite color?"

"Wow, I've said it before and I'll say it again. *You* are in some serious denial," said Charlotte. "Have you looked at the wallpaper or screensaver on your computer lately? Or perhaps the calendar hanging on the wall. Any idiot could see you have a preference for snow leopards. As for your favorite color, your phone case is pink, you often paint your fingernails pink, your cup is pink, and you have several scarves and a couple of suits in different shades of the same color. That's an obvious clue if I ever saw one." The last was said rather dryly.

"I still don't think it's him. From what you said, it could be anyone in the office who noticed."

"I looked up those bath products you received. Do you know how much they cost?"

Elizabeth put her hands on the armrests and pushed herself straighter in her seat. She'd intentionally not researched most of the gifts. The words "French milled" on the labels had her suspicious as it was. "I really don't want to know."

Charlotte had held out the latest package, so it appeared in front of her face when she turned. "Open it. I'm dying to know what's inside."

Elizabeth frowned and yanked the box away. "It's creepy."

"Ha! I'd love for a man to send me expensive bath products and my favorite things every day for twenty-five days. It's only creepy if he's stalking you, which he's not. No one loiters around your office or follows you home. You're just looking for excuses not to like the man."

"Because I don't know who he is! It's been making me crazy since all this mess started." She took a deep breath and tugged at the paper until it fell away from the box inside. Carefully opening the lid as though something would burst from within, she leaned over to peek inside, that little bubble of anticipation curling in her stomach.

"What is it?"

Elizabeth couldn't see well enough, so she removed the lid and pulled away the tissue to find a neatly folded pink silk scarf. With careful fingers, she lifted one corner and the entire swath of fabric came into view. It was exquisite!

Charlotte's low whistle broke the silence. "Hermès? You're one lucky girl, Elizabeth Bennet."

Her head jerked up to Charlotte holding the tag for her to see while she sank back into her chair. "The rest of the gifts might've added up to be expensive, but this is over the top. I can't accept it. It's entirely too far over the limit."

Charlotte opened the scarf completely and gasped. "It's gorgeous. Wherever he bought this, I doubt he can return it."

"But this is different from the others. It's a small gift if you don't consider the label, but I don't live in a hole. I know what Hermès is and that it's expensive—even if I don't know how much one costs." She reached forward and fingered the soft fabric, letting it slip through her fingers. "It's certainly beautiful."

Before she could react, Charlotte slipped the scarf around Elizabeth's neck and began to arrange it. "If you're determined to give it back, then at least try it on to see how it looks. How often do you get to wear a Hermès scarf?"

Elizabeth stood and looked at her reflection in the framed mirror on the wall while she tucked and arranged the fabric so it suited. "Okay, there, I've tried it on. Happy?" She began pulling to remove it before something happened to ruin it. That would be just her luck. She would attempt to do the right thing, only the scarf had a large coffee stain or lip-gloss smudge.

At a knock on the door, she called, "Yes!"

As she slipped the silk from her neck, William Darcy entered but stopped just inside, standing stiffly and holding a folder in one hand. "I hope I'm not disturbing you?"

"No," she said quickly, folding the length of fabric to put it back in the box. "Charlotte and I were merely speaking of Christmas. I was about to start on the papers you requested."

He dipped his chin in a formal sort of nod. "Good. I look forward to reading through them when you're done." He lifted the folder and held it out for her. "I brought the specifics for the property. I believe you'll also need the property records for the final draft."

When she took the folder, her stomach clenched and her heartbeat quickened. Why did he make her so darned nervous? She moved behind her desk and placed it beside her keyboard. "Thank you for bringing them down, but you could've just emailed the information. You didn't need to go to the trouble of delivering it yourself."

"I assure you, it was no bother." He glanced at Charlotte, who excused herself and hurried out before his eyes darted to the pink silk in Elizabeth's hand. "A Christmas present?"

She started and took the fabric in both hands, the soft material slipping through her fingers. "Yes, but I can't accept it."

His forehead furrowed. "Don't you like it?"

"I do. I do like it. It's probably the loveliest scarf I've ever seen, but it's too expensive. I don't feel right accepting it."

"Perhaps the person who gave it to you didn't consider the cost an issue. Instead, they might've only considered the joy you'd receive from wearing it."

"You believe I should keep it? It's far beyond the Secret Santa limit."

"This person is your Secret Santa, too? I'm paying them entirely too much," he said, holding the tag where he could read the label. A small lift appeared on one side of his lips. Was he making a joke? Before she could respond, he cleared his throat. "I don't expect the permits or the other documentation until after Christmas, so please don't work late. I expect you to enjoy your holiday." After a tight smile, he strode out, leaving her speechless.

William Darcy had made a joke. He'd also told her not to work late. Who was this man and what had he done with her normally uptight, abrupt mannered boss? Could Charlotte be right about there being more in that head of his than Darcy Holdings?

William Darcy strode back to his office. Damn! Elizabeth didn't know where the scarf came from or that he didn't actually pay a dime for it, but would that make a difference when she discovered his identity? Probably not. She would still insist it was too much.

Mrs. Reynolds followed him and closed the door behind her. "Well? Did she open it?"

"She intends to return it to me. It's too expensive."

The older woman smiled in her grandmotherly manner. "I warned you she would."

He dropped into his chair and leaned back. "Other than jewelry, I've had a difficult time coming up with new ideas. Once the bath products were exhausted, some gifts were easier than others, but when I saw that scarf, I knew it should belong to her."

"If she discovers it's vintage, she's going to be all the more adamant you take it back. I can only imagine her reaction to your gifts for Christmas Eve and Christmas Day." She crossed her arms over her chest and looked at him over the rims of her glasses. "You know if you hadn't been such a horse's ass on her first day, you might be dating her rather than admiring her from afar."

"I know," he said, his voice low and grumbling. "You don't have to remind me."

They both turned when the door opened, and Charlie walked in wearing his usual happy expression. "I just stopped by Lizzy's office. If the scarf wasn't so expensive, you know she would be wearing it everywhere."

"How did you know it's from me?"

"Because she told me it's from her Secret Santa and that, my friend, is you."

Darcy glared, which only made Bingley laugh. "Don't give me that look. You put yourself in the dog house without any help from me. If you hadn't been such an ass—"

"Yes, I know. You and Mrs. Reynolds love reminding me of that, don't you?"

Mrs. Reynolds laughed and Bingley rolled his eyes. "'I have a mountain of paperwork on my desk. I can't be expected to take the time to welcome a new company attorney. Especially one who required her sister's boyfriend to get her a job. You hired her, Bingley. You make her feel welcome.'" Bingley's voice was the deep mocking one he always used when he imitated him. That voice was annoying! It always highlighted his worst moments.

"Why do we have to do this again? I hadn't intended for her to overhear me and I apologized—twice!"

Bingley plopped into a chair. "I know. You never do mean it, but this time, you regret it. She's the first woman you've noticed in years, and you screwed it up before you even laid eyes on her."

While Darcy would've loved to deny it, Bingley was right. It hadn't taken long for him to bemoan the stupid and untrue words he'd spoken that day. Her eyes, the way she arched that one eyebrow, usually at him, the sway of her hips when she walked, the way her hair rippled over her shoulder when she concentrated on a document during a meeting, all of these things intrigued him. How many times now had Bingley been forced to clear his throat to redirect Darcy's attention?

"Earth to Darcy!"

He jumped when Bingley's hand waved in front of his face, and Mrs. Reynolds chuckled.

"Stop it. I'll figure it out."

"Don't do anything stupid." Bingley stood and leaned over his desk. "I'm the one who rigged the Secret Santa so you could do this. Need I remind you that if you do anything to hurt Lizzy, Jane will kill me?"

Darcy waved a hand to shoo them from the room and sat back in his seat with a groan. The problem was that Elizabeth Bennet wasn't just another stunning face; she was intelligent and well-spoken. She was also meticulous, thorough, and since her work on the Wickham fiasco, Hurst never stopped singing her praises.

Today, after only several months with the company, Hurst informed him that she should replace him as head of the legal department. Big problem! If this entire Secret Santa thing made her dislike him more, he was screwed! He met with Hurst several times a week. How would he manage the same with Elizabeth?

He opened the bottom drawer and pulled a wrapped package from the back with the number twenty-five on the top. If she thought the scarf was too much, what would she think of his final two gifts?

She'd already mentioned returning the entire lot of presents. Talk about a nightmare come to life! He'd planned all of this to make her happy, and she might just throw it all back in his face. How in the heck did he get into messes like this?

Chapter 11

Elizabeth smoothed the red satin over her stomach and turned, checking her reflection in the full-length mirror while Grunt, as usual, watched from his cozy perch on her bed, his gaze stern.

"Don't sulk. You're a cat. You aren't supposed to give me the stink eye if I leave. Besides, I know that once the door closes behind me, you'll drink the water from the Christmas tree, play with the ornaments, and fall asleep on top of your kitty tower. You won't miss me yelling at you to stop misbehaving."

He'd taken such a liking to so many of the shiny glass baubles, she'd had to move them up the tree and relocate the less destructible plastic and wooden ornaments near the bottom. He was still so much the kitten she'd adopted almost a year ago, always into something. He yawned and she laughed, turned to face him, and held out her arms. "Do you approve?"

He yawned again widely, stretched, and lifted his paw, bestowing a long lick along its edge before dragging it over the top of his head.

Her hands dropped to her sides. "You could've said something. A hiss would've at least been a little helpful. A chirp even? Perhaps a meow?"

Grunt ignored her while he proceeded to thoroughly wash his ears. The doorbell rang and her suddenly silent companion halted his bathing when his head jerked toward the bedroom door.

Grabbing her clutch from beside him, she hurried to the entry and stood on tiptoe to see through the peephole. A man she didn't recognize with gray hair and wearing a black suit, stood in the hallway. She wasn't expecting anyone. "Who is it?"

"Car service, ma'am. I'm here to take you to the Darcy Holdings holiday party."

Car service? She cracked the door enough to speak to the man face to face. "There must be some mistake. I didn't arrange for a car." He held out a small wrapped package with the number twenty-four on the top, and she stiffened at the sight of the glittery, silver number. It was another Secret Santa gift?

"I was told to give you this."

Elizabeth shook her head and sighed as she carefully took the package. "I'm sorry, but I can't accept something so expensive. Can you call whoever hired you for the evening and refund their money?"

"I'm afraid we don't issue refunds, ma'am. Whether I drive you to the party or not, the money is spent." He pointed to the package. "My advice would be to open your gift, grab your purse, and enjoy the ride. The money's wasted otherwise."

Carefully, she pulled back the paper and stared at the flat square box. What if another Hermès scarf lay inside? She had to uncover her Secret Santa's identity at the party! This had gotten out of hand!

When she lifted the lid of the box, no expensive scarf or trinket lay inside—just a card on a bed of silver snowflake printed tissue paper with a neat script that read,

"I hope to dance with you this evening.
SS"

No name? Of course, there was no name! It wouldn't be a Secret Santa if the person revealed their identity.

She read the message again. Her Secret Santa wanted to dance with her, so it looked like Charlotte's intuition was correct—not that she didn't agree with her. Her Secret Santa was definitely a man, but how in blazes was she supposed to dance with him without knowing his name? "I don't suppose *you* know who my Secret Santa is?" she asked.

The man lifted both bushy eyebrows and shrugged. "No, ma'am. I don't know anything about a Secret Santa. I'm just the driver."

She bit her lip and stared at the card for a moment. If she didn't take the car, her Secret Santa had wasted his money. Did she have a choice? Her best option was to take the ride and pay him back once she discovered his identity, regardless of the cost. She certainly wasn't broke, but she didn't splurge on cars and drivers, particularly when she was still remodeling her apartment. Paying the bill for her Juke's tiny parking space under the building was painful enough, which was why she sold her beloved little coupe. In the city, she'd rarely needed it with the subway and she could get to a lot of places outside of the city by train. It was really a frivolous expense.

"I'll be back in a moment." She closed the door, grabbed her coat and clutch, and glanced around the living room. "Why do I feel like I'm forgetting something? Oh! *My* Secret Santa gift!" She grabbed a small silver-wrapped box from under her tree and opened the door. "Okay, I'm ready."

With a friendly smile, the driver waited for her to lock up and led her down to the sidewalk in front of her building, where a classic car she could only identify as a Rolls Royce stood grandly along the curb. The driver opened the door, and she climbed inside, trying not to flinch or squirm at touching the plush creamy leather and mahogany interior.

The driver leaned down into the doorway. "Would you care for a glass of wine?"

She looked at the soft, snow-white leather seats. "Wine?" What if she spilled it?

His eyes crinkled at the edges when he chuckled. "I have red or white. It's your choice."

"I suppose it's also paid for already."

"Yes, ma'am."

After another look at the upholstery, she sighed. "Let's not tempt fate. I'll have a glass of the white, please."

"Prosecco or Chenin Blanc?"

Seriously? She had a choice? She leaned forward and scanned the front seat where an ice chest rested on the passenger side floorboard. "Chenin Blanc, please." She may as well! As he said, it was paid for and something niggling at her gut cried she would need it before the end of the evening.

He took his place in the driver's seat, served her wine, and started the car while she relaxed back and carefully buckled herself in with one hand. Soon, they were moving steadily in the direction of the ballroom the company had hired for the party while she sipped her wine and watched the passing storefronts.

She'd always loved holiday window displays. Every year, she made a point of taking a day to walk around the neighborhood so she could enjoy the glowing lights, the Christmas trees, the quaint snowclad village scenes, and the toy trains adorning the more festive displays, yet tonight, despite the pleasant scenery, a part of her was wound as tight as could be.

What was she going to do about her Secret Santa? Would he be at the party? The big gift exchange was to take place tonight, but her Secret Santa had already given her today's gift.

All she could do was take a gulp of her wine and exhale a long breath in a futile attempt to relax. The ridiculous stressing about this had to end! She was wound up in knots and had been for a couple of weeks!

Regardless of who her Secret Santa was, she would thank them but she'd have to try to return the gifts. If they were friends, it would make things so much simpler, but she was still relatively new to the company. She hadn't really gotten to know everyone yet.

Before she was ready, the car pulled up to the curb at the ballroom, and the driver came around to open her door. When she stepped out, she paused and handed him the glass. "Thank you."

He almost tilted forward, like he was giving a miniscule bow. "I'll be right here when you're ready to leave."

Her body gave a small jerk. He intended to drive her home, too? "This person hired you for the entire evening?"

"Yes, ma'am. My instructions were to convey you to the party and to ensure you arrive safely to your door when the party is over. I know you may prefer not to remain for the entire night, so when you wish to leave, I'll be waiting for you here."

"There you are!" She turned abruptly as Charlotte approached and whistled. "Sweet car. When did you decide not to take the subway?" After a quick "thank you" to the driver, she and Charlotte began climbing the steps.

"I didn't hire a car. He came with a package."

"Is that gift twenty-four? Nice! I wouldn't have minded riding in that! It's certainly better than the smelly taxi I took here."

"I doubt it was that bad," said Elizabeth with a grin.

"It was! I think the person before me must've had a bag full of raw fish they were taking home for dinner."

"You've had a flair for melodrama since we were teenagers. You should've studied acting and gone into theater."

Charlotte's nose crinkled. "You know how much I *love* to perform in front of a group. That's always worked so well for me in the past."

The two of them burst into giggles. Elizabeth would never forget their fourth grade Christmas program. Sister Mary Margaret almost fainted dead away when Charlotte's nerves got the best of her, and she got sick on stage. Charlotte was hailed the hero of the evening by everyone but Lauren Hazelton, who was furious Charlotte's digestive pyrotechnics went off at the beginning of the girl's solo during Silent Night.

They stopped at the coat check. Elizabeth traded her coat for a ticket and waited for Charlotte. "Is Bill joining you?"

"No, he had some last-minute job at de Bourgh's. He wanted to make sure no late shopper left without some expensive piece of jewelry." Charlotte rolled her eyes and looped her arm through Elizabeth's. "Anyway, I don't want to stray too far from you. I can't miss the big reveal! Your Secret Santa is bound to approach you sometime tonight, and I'm dying to see who it is."

Elizabeth gasped when they entered the opulent ballroom decked out in Christmas trees and twinkling lights. "It's incredible."

The same whistle as earlier came from beside her. "Have I thanked you lately for bringing me with you when you started at Darcy Holdings?"

"You know I couldn't leave you behind. Who else would I find to second-guess me and make sarcastic comments?"

Charlotte gave a huge smile. "You know you love me."

Elizabeth looped her arm through her friend's. "Let's grab a glass of wine."

As the two strode straight to the bar, she caught sight of a few children milling around with their parents. "When Mrs. Reynolds sent out the email, I thought it was strange to have a company Christmas party on Christmas Eve, but I hadn't realized people would bring their children."

"From what I've been told, the former Mr. and Mrs. Darcy started the tradition a long time ago. They wanted the ability to bring their children, so it became a family night. There's even childcare somewhere for those who become a handful or babies who might need a nap."

Two little boys decked out in suits bumped Elizabeth when they ran by, but before they could get far, one of the ladies from finance stepped in front of them and began wagging her finger in their faces. She gave Elizabeth and Charlotte an awkward wave and mouthed, "Sorry," her face tinged with red.

"Come on," said Charlotte, tugging her arm. "We've been here five minutes, and I don't have a drink yet." When they reached the bar, Charlotte leaned forward and placed her order while Elizabeth took in everything around her, waiting for her turn. She slowly pivoted to absorb the grandeur of the entire room but almost jumped a foot back at a tall, suit-clad figure who suddenly appeared in her way.

"Good evening, Miss Bennet. I hope you're having a good time."

Her eyes traced up the festive red, green, and silver tie in front of her to the face of none other than Mr. Darcy. He had bent forward slightly when he spoke.

"Well, I just arrived, but everything is beautiful."

A tiny lift appeared to one side of his lips. "I'm glad you approve." His eyes left hers for a moment when Charlotte turned around. "Miss Lucas."

"Mr. Darcy," she said quickly. "You throw a great shindig." She waved off to the side. "Excuse me for a moment. I want to say hi to Cindy from personnel."

Wait! Where was Charlotte going? Elizabeth tried to grab her hand, but she scurried away with an evil hint of a grin, like the little traitorous witch she was.

"Were you waiting to order a drink?"

She turned back to Mr. Darcy and nodded. Why did the ability to speak suddenly vanish? "Yes, I wanted a glass of wine." The words were almost whispered.

He held out a hand over the bar. "Red or white?"

"White, please. Chenin Blanc if they have it?"

He spoke to the bartender, who hurried away, returning a few moments later with a glass. Mr. Darcy handed him a folded bill and passed Elizabeth her wine.

"I thought it was an open bar?"

"It is, but the house Chenin Blanc is only so-so. I thought you'd prefer this one."

She set the gift she carried on the barstool beside her and propped her clutch on top while she attempted to open the clasp. "Then let me pay you back. I don't expect you to buy me drinks." His hand covered hers, and she jumped. His palm was so warm!

"I ordered the upgrade without asking. I don't expect you to pay for it. I'm happy to do it." He almost seemed to shift a little closer, and something inside her chest fluttered. "You look lovely this evening."

Did he just give her a compliment? After a sip—or was it a gulp?—of her wine, she resisted the urge to wipe her sweaty palm down her dress. "Thank you." Was he ever going to move his hand? The heat radiating from that point was slowly spreading up her arm. She'd never had that happen before, and it was unnerving. In a last-ditch effort to preserve her sanity, she shifted her purse off the barstool, and his hand dropped to his side.

"I appreciate the hard work you've put in since you started at Darcy Holdings."

He watched her reaction carefully. She hadn't expected the compliment and he was certain she still didn't like him, but how he wished she would give him a chance! It was impossible to miss her wide eyes and the slight grab at her assistant's hand when Miss Lucas left, not to mention her moving her purse so his hand was no longer touching hers.

She stared into her wine and cleared her throat. "You don't have to say that."

"I wouldn't tell you unless I truly meant it. You should know that I haven't exaggerated when I've complimented your work. It's been exemplary. I'm pleased Charlie insisted on hiring you. You've been an asset these past months, and after New Year's, I hope you'll meet with Hurst and myself to set up the transition of the department from his hands to yours."

When he mentioned the meeting, her eyes darted from what had to be the most interesting drink on the planet directly back to his face, and her mouth opened. She did a fantastic job. She wasn't surprised, was she?

She put her hand to her forehead and closed her gaping mouth. "Does that mean you intend for me to take over as head of the legal department?"

"I hadn't intended to tell you tonight . . . like this . . . but yes."

"I thought Craig Denny was in line for that promotion." Her hand moved from her forehead to her hip; she stared at him as if she were trying to find something on his face—some smudge or mark he didn't know was there.

"Before you started at the company, he was our top choice if we promoted from within. He's a competent corporate lawyer, but we still would've taken applications in the event a more qualified attorney applied. He wasn't guaranteed the position. We just happened to hire a more qualified candidate a few months ago, so there's no reason to search for another. Hurst has also been unofficially familiarizing you with everything our legal department does since you started. He must've had a feeling you were what we needed."

Her eyes searched his, she took a large gulp of wine, and coughed when some of it went down the wrong way. "You want me to head the department." She sounded rather in awe. "Did Hurst insist, or perhaps Charlie? I don't want the position if Charlie's responsible."

He should've known she'd feel that way. Why did she have such a difficult time believing him? "Charlie has had nothing to do with this. He knows you're Hurst's recommendation, but he hasn't had any input in the decision. Hurst and I met a few days ago, and I happened to agree completely with his assessment."

"You did?"

"Miss Bennet, you've completed every project you've had in a timely and thorough manner, and with little guidance from Hurst or any hiccups. You know what needs to be done as well as he does, and you don't miss a beat. Why wouldn't we promote you?"

She blinked, and her chin gave a slight hitch back. "I suppose when you put it like that," she said softly. "Thank you, Mr. Darcy."

"Does that mean you accept?"

"I do. I will certainly attend the meeting. Just have Charlotte add it to my calendar."

With a nod, he held out his glass of scotch. "To new beginnings."

She touched the rim of her glass to his. "To new beginnings." She took a sip of her wine and cleared her throat. "If you'll excuse me, I should join Charlotte."

"Of course."

She took a step but stopped and peered back over her shoulder. "Merry Christmas, Mr. Darcy."

As she hurried off, he couldn't pull his eyes away. She strode up behind Miss Lucas, who stood at the buffet. Elizabeth whispered in her assistant's ear, and Miss Lucas all but dropped her plate, squealed, and hugged her with a wide-eyed happy expression.

When she pulled back, Elizabeth put her hand to her cheek while she spoke animatedly to her assistant. What he wouldn't give for her to be so easy with him! At this rate, he'd be forever in her company but feel as though he was watching from the outside.

The evening dragged by like one of those epic movies that never seemed to get to the point. He couldn't avoid business obligations and tried to ensure he spoke with as many of his employees as he could, yet he could never quite catch up with Elizabeth. He caught glimpses of her here and there—she put the gift she carried on the table with the rest of the Secret Santa gifts, she and Miss Lucas made plates at the buffet, and now, she was dancing with Hurst. The old man sported an enormous grin as he twirled her around the floor while she laughed and giggled just loud enough to be heard over "Rockin' Around the Christmas Tree." As soon as the music ended, Darcy somehow stood much closer to the dance floor than he had a moment ago. His feet must've betrayed him and crept forward without him realizing. She drew him in, and he couldn't resist the pull.

"Darcy!" called Hurst during the break. "I believe this is the best Christmas party yet, and your mother did an excellent job of planning the holiday festivities when your father ran the company."

He gave a brief nod. "Thank you. Now that Mrs. Reynolds has planned the party for a few years, she's become quite good at it." He shifted on his feet and clenched his pocketed hands into fists. "Hurst, if you don't mind, I was hoping to dance with Miss Bennet. If she'll give me the honor of her company."

With a grin, Hurst held Elizabeth's hand in Darcy's direction. "Of course! She doesn't want to be stuck with an old schmuck like me for the entire evening." Before she could open her mouth to argue, he held up his palm. "It was kind of you to dance with me, but you should dance with some men your own age. You'll have much more fun. Besides, if I don't dance with my wife soon, she just might make me sleep with the dog tonight." After a wink at Elizabeth, Hurst wound his way through the dancers toward the opposite side of the room.

Darcy gestured further into the dance floor. "Would you like to dance?"

She glanced between him and those swaying to the slow ballad only a few feet from them. "I . . ."

Good grief! She meant to refuse him. He was as alone as Charlie Brown with his Christmas tree. "We're starting over, aren't we?"

"Well, yes, but you don't *have* to—"

Was he going to have to beg? "I know I don't have to, Elizabeth, but I would like to; however, if you don't want to, *you* don't have to." That had to be the least eloquent statement ever. He'd had to concentrate to keep his tongue from getting in the way.

She placed her hand in his and a frisson of something shot up his arm. Her soft palm pressed against his and the warmth from where their flesh met began traveling through him. She stiffened, but instead of looking at him, she stared at where their hands touched. Did she feel that, too? Was that why she stood as stiff as a board and her eyes bored into his tie? If she had laser vision, she'd have burned a hole through his chest by now.

When her opposite hand rested on his shoulder, a current of sorts seemed to course through him, almost as if someone attached one end of a set of jumper cables to a battery and the other to his hand and the shoulder she touched. How did he feel that spark through his suit coat? He'd never experienced anything like it, but it was like a drug and he wanted more.

She licked her lips, and his gaze settled there. Without lipstick and just a light sheen of gloss, they looked natural yet so soft and inviting. What would it be like to kiss her? His fingers slipped along the silky skin of her hand while he continued to be entranced by her mouth. Would her lips be as soft as her wrist or would they be softer? A groan nearly escaped, but he gave himself a subtle shake instead. He had to get his mind away from that topic but quick! She might slap him if he gave in to temptation and suddenly leaned in for a kiss.

"I understand you'll be at Charlie and Jane's tomorrow."

Thank the Lord! Something to think about other than kissing her. "Yes, my sister's spending the holidays in Maine with her boyfriend's family. By her pictures on Instagram, she appears to be having a wonderful time."

Her teeth appeared as she smiled. "You have an Instagram account?"

"My sister set it up. She insisted Facebook was for old people, and that I *had* to have Instagram to stay in touch with her when she travels." He drawled it out a little just as Ana had said it.

Elizabeth chuckled, and his heartbeat accelerated at the sound. She had a great laugh—warm, bubbly, almost contagious. "How old is your sister?"

"She's twenty-one."

"Does she travel that often?"

"She's studying cello at Julliard. Her advisor has been exceptional at locating study opportunities abroad the past two summers. She spent last June in Paris and the year before she spent July in London."

"You must miss her when she's so far away."

He sighed. "I do. I don't see her nearly as often as I would like."

"Perhaps once she's graduated and settled, you'll see more of her." Her voice was upbeat—optimistic even.

"Perhaps. I hope so."

He continued to savor the feel of her in his arms until the song faded to an unwanted end. Elizabeth drew back with a jerk, as though he'd shocked her, and glanced around them while running her hands down the fabric on her hips. "Thank you," she whispered. Before he could respond, she pivoted on her heel and strode in the direction of the restrooms.

Had he done something wrong? They'd been talking and things seemed to be going well until the song ended. "Elizabeth!" She disappeared into the crowd, but he continued to head in the direction she walked until he reached an empty back hallway. Several doors led off the corridor, one reading the word "ladies." Could she have changed her mind and gone somewhere else or could she already be in the ladies' room?

He slumped against the wall and drew the small package from inside his coat, the silver twenty-five reflecting the multi-colored lights filtering in from the ballroom. He had to find some way to give it to her, some way to tell her he was her Secret Santa. He also would need to convince her to keep the gifts. He had no use for them, and he'd purchased them with her in mind. They belonged to her. He wanted her to have them.

After a glance at the ladies' room door, he shook his head. What was he doing? Stalking her? This wasn't the way to mend things between them. Before the end of the evening, he needed to devise a way to tell her who he was, but not like this. Pushing from the wall, he made to slip the package back in his coat, but instead of sliding into his pocket, it fell to the floor.

He bent to pick it up, but a feminine hand touched it just as he did. "What's this?"

His eyes darted up to Elizabeth, holding the other side of the gift— the Secret Santa gift—her eyes huge as they turned to him. "You? You're my Secret Santa?"

Chapter 12

The moment Elizabeth stepped into William Darcy's arms on the ballroom floor, she struggled—struggled to think about anything but that current that flowed through her when his hand touched hers, struggled to make any sound at all come from her lips, and struggled to ignore how sensitive her skin became to whatever touched her. Every tiny hair on her body stood on end, her dress caressed her legs with every shift of the fabric, and other bits of clothing rubbed . . . well, she wasn't going to go there!

She had to get her mind off of this effect he had on her. Think! Think of anything! Had he seen any good movies lately? But, when would he have gone to the movies? He arrived at work before the rest of the office and left later than all of them. Christmas! That was it! "I understand you'll be at Charlie and Jane's tomorrow to open gifts and for Christmas dinner." The words came out in a rush, but she'd gotten them out.

His eyes lifted to her face. Had he been staring at her lips? No, not William Darcy. He would probably find the quarterly reports more interesting.

"Yes, my sister's spending the holidays in Maine with her boyfriend's family. By her pictures on Instagram, she appears to be having a wonderful time."

Charlie had mentioned Darcy had a sister. They'd seen her the day they bought their Christmas trees, but Instagram? He didn't seem like the type to spend a lot of time on social media.

"You have an Instagram account?"

He smiled—not one of those tense, tight-lipped half-smiles he gave at work, but a real, wide, dimple-revealing one. She pressed her lips together to prevent the gasp that almost escaped. Wow! She wasn't blind. She'd been well aware that the man was good-looking, but when he smiled like that, he was more than just good-looking! Most of the women in the office would shuck their panties rather than cringe at his approach if they saw that smile.

When he'd spoken of his sister, a part of her heart ached just a bit for him. He'd put on a good face, but something in his voice was sad and a little wistful. Charlie had indicated Darcy and his sister were quite close. He must have missed her terribly.

She bit her lip and glanced around. What should they talk about now? They'd discussed work earlier, but she had to be capable of speaking of something that wasn't related to Darcy Holdings. She resituated her hand on his shoulder, inadvertently slipping to his chest and touching more than she'd intended. Was that muscle under the expensive suit coat? He worked out? She trained her eyes on his tie. This was ridiculous! He was William Darcy, her boss, not a freaking Calvin Klein underwear model.

How she heard the song end over the pounding beat in her ears was a mystery, but when the music faded out, she thanked him, turned tail, and made her escape. She had to get away from him and the way he made her feel like she couldn't control her own body.

As she hurried from the floor, a corridor appeared where the crowd thinned, so she walked in that direction as quickly as her heels would allow. A ladies' room door was just inside on the right, and she rushed through, hightailing it into one of the stalls. Once she'd locked the door, she pressed her back against it. With a groan, she covered her face with her hands. "He must think I'm an idiot."

A dance! It was only supposed to be a dance until she groped his chest. Thank goodness she didn't grope anything worse!

What was she doing? This was stupid. So what if the guy worked out, or if he was devastatingly handsome. She needed to keep her distance so she didn't make a fool of herself. "Okay, Elizabeth. Time to suck it up and get back out there. As Aunt Maisie always says, 'You're making a mountain out of a molehill'."

She took a deep breath, unlocked the door, and checked her reflection in the mirror. Once she'd tucked a few stray strands of hair back into place, she made for the exit but stopped in the doorway at the sight of Darcy turning toward the party.

Her hand cushioned the door as it closed behind her while he took a few steps toward the ballroom. The sound of an object hitting the floor echoed down the corridor and made her look down near his feet. She cocked her head to the side. Why did that look familiar? Without thought, she stepped forward, knelt down, and picked the small box up, but met with resistance from the hand on the other side.

"What's this?" When she said the words, the light reflected just so off the silvery glittered numbers on the top. She knew that wrapping! Her eyes hurt like they popped from their sockets as they met his. "You? You're my Secret Santa?"

Somehow, they both ended up standing while still holding the package. Her final Secret Santa gift. Her last Secret Santa gift from . . . William Darcy?

"Elizabeth—"

"*You* are my Secret Santa? *You*? *You* purchased the bath products, the lunch, and the coffee and muffin, and the scarf, and paid for the car tonight?"

He awkwardly scratched the back of his head and nodded. "Yes."

She stared at him for a moment, but when he only watched her with his eyebrows drawn down, she put her hands on her hips, leaving him to hold the present by himself. "Well, I appreciate the time and thought you put into the calendar, but you'll just have to take it all back." Good! Her tone insisted she wouldn't take no for an answer.

His lip twitched on one side. "Take them back? You want me to take back the coffee and muffin?"

"Of course not!" She placed her palm on her forehead and closed her eyes. "The bath products remain unopened, so I will need to return those to you along with the scarf, the cat décor, and the wine. They're lovely gifts, but all of it added up to too much money. In good conscience, I simply can't accept all of it. I'd also like to know how much the car cost you for the evening. I want to reimburse you for it."

"No—"

"No?" Heat unfurled from the deepest portion of her gut and spread throughout her body like a spark takes hold and becomes a fire that engulfs a dry field. She clenched her hands into fists and opened her mouth but started when it wasn't her voice.

"I gave you those gifts because I knew you would take pleasure in them. I wanted you to have them."

"They're too expensive."

"I know the gift exchange had a spending limit, but I never considered the cost an issue."

Why did that not surprise her? He didn't have the same worries most people had when it came to money. He could spend more than the average person and not blink an eye. "Maybe not to you, but what about the rest of your employees, those who didn't have the boss for their Secret Santa? It's hardly fair to them."

He frowned, his eyes shifting to the gift in his hands. "I never considered how others might feel. I only thought of you. I wanted to do something special for you. Mrs. Reynolds keeps an ear out for office gossip. She would've told me if anyone became upset over it, but no one seemed to notice."

She closed her eyes and took a deep breath before opening them again. Why did he not understand how much this bothered her? "Because I didn't advertise the gifts. A few of the other assistants noticed the coffee and muffin and a couple of the bath supplies, but Charlotte and I kept quiet about most of it—especially the scarf, though

Charlotte does have a bet with the assistants who know. They've all wagered about your identity."

She clenched her hands into fists. "You were in my office the morning I opened the scarf. You *knew* how uncomfortable the price of that gift made me, and you still arranged for the car service tonight. Why?"

He held one hand out, palm forward. "It's not what you think. The scarf was my mother's. She'd never worn it, and I knew it would be perfect for you. As for the car, it's one of mine, and Carson is my driver. Mrs. Reynolds needed me for a few last-minute decisions, so I had him drop me off an hour before the party started. He then drove to your apartment and brought you here."

She deflated and covered her eyes with her hand. He may have spent nothing on those gifts, but that was beside the point. "That's not what I asked." How could he stay so calm when she was holding her anger in by a thread?

"You wanted to know why I chose the car?"

"Perhaps before, but not now. Now I just want to know why me? Why do all of this for someone you don't like?"

"I thought I explained earlier that I don't dislike you at all," he said, shifting on his feet.

"You said you were pleased to have me work for you, but do you think I don't notice how you glare at me all of the time? You might approve of my work, but you must find something wrong or you wouldn't behave as you do around me. I don't know what it is, but it's pretty obvious by the looks you send my way."

He let out a long exhale and blinked a couple of times. "Wow, I never realized just how badly I've screwed up with you until now."

Screwed up? "What's that supposed to mean?"

"I don't hate you, Elizabeth."

"You don't?" Her voice had that edge to it. The one that would normally have Charlotte sending out for hard liquor.

"I don't dislike anything about you. I actually . . ." He cleared his throat and shifted on his feet again. "I actually think you're very beautiful—especially your eyes. They sparkle when you're happy and talking and have this fiery quality when you're angry or inspired. I can't explain it, but they draw me in and I can't look away."

As he spoke, her hands, which had moved to her hips, gradually slid down until they hung at her sides. He what?

"At first, I tried to ignore it. You work for me, so I considered you inappropriate. I've never dated an employee." A strangled chuckle faded away. "Not that I've dated anyone in a few years." He glanced at her and then to the package still in his hands. "You've become all I think about. I . . . I've fallen in love with you."

Then, the thread snapped.

"You what?" Her hands had clenched again at her sides, and her tone was rough. Maybe he shouldn't have said anything.

"I've fallen in love with you."

An odd laugh fell from her lips, one that was high-pitched and forced. He'd debated numerous times whether to tell Elizabeth the truth—whether to reveal to her that he was her Secret Santa, whether to tell her of his feelings. He never expected her to rush into his arms, and even though he'd had plenty of fantasies where she had, it wasn't a realistic expectation.

"Was this entire month of gifts meant to buy me? Did you think you'd tell me it was you, and I'd fall into your embrace like some sad, pathetic creature in a sappy romance novel?" Her voice rose with each question until she glanced over his shoulder at the party behind him, and her volume dropped dramatically. "Did I get the promotion because of your feelings?"

"No! You earned that promotion with your determination, your work, and your intelligence. You were Hurst's top recommendation, and I happened to agree with him. My personal feelings had nothing to do with it. I would never base such an important decision on anything but a person's ability to do the job."

She stepped forward, her eyes shooting daggers. "I don't believe you."

A giggle and the click of heels made them quickly step back from one another until Stacy, Charlie's assistant, walked by, looking at them both warily before she went into the ladies' room.

Once the door closed behind her, he ran his fingers through his hair. "I would never lie to you." Oh, Lord! This was going downhill fast, and he had no idea how to keep it from devolving further. "I simply wanted to bring a smile to your face. When I asked Bingley to ensure I was your Secret Santa—" He sucked in a quick breath. Crap! He wasn't supposed to tell her that part!

"You set the whole thing up? Charlie knew?"

"I wasn't supposed to tell you about Bingley. Please don't be angry with him. I threatened to fire him if he didn't go along with my plan."

"You did?" she said, her voice flat.

"Not really." He gave a chuckle that came more from the nerves twisting around in his stomach than amusement. "I hoped to lighten the mood."

They both jumped when Stacy exited the ladies' room and eyed them both. After glancing back and forth two or three times, she shrugged and returned to the party, occasionally glancing over her shoulder until she reached the ballroom. Not a word was spoken until she disappeared into the crowd.

"Do you find all of this funny?"

He turned back to Elizabeth and shook his head. "No." They couldn't go on arguing. Elizabeth needed time to cool off, which meant time away from him, and well, he needed to escape with at least part of his heart intact. "I appreciate your integrity, but the gifts are yours. I would also like you to have this." He held out the final package. "It's for you. I have no use for it. Please."

"No," she said. "I'm your employee, remember? The gifts are as inappropriate as I am."

His heart dropped, and he closed his eyes for a moment. When he opened them, she stood before him, her jaw tense and her lips pressed into a thin line. "Please forgive me. I didn't mean it that way. Perhaps it would be best if I leave you to enjoy the evening before one of us says something we'll regret. Carson will be waiting for you after the party. I hope you'll accept the ride home. I'd like to know you made it safely." He watched the package while he turned it in his hands. It was better than looking at Elizabeth's angry expression. How could something meant to make her happy turn out so wrong? "Merry Christmas, Elizabeth."

Before she could speak, he rotated on his heel and strode in the direction of the party, passing Miss Lucas as she entered the corridor. She took a long look at him then glanced past him at Elizabeth. He didn't stop, but when he joined the crowd, he peered over his shoulder at Elizabeth, who was throwing an arm up in his direction while speaking heatedly to her assistant. Stacy obviously clued in Miss Lucas, but was she also cluing in the rest of his employees? That was all he needed—for Elizabeth to never forgive him.

He shoved Elizabeth's gift into his pocket and put on his game face. He had a few more people to greet before he could leave. He didn't have time to let his personal feelings get in the way of work; however, rather than taking his time, he sought out the remaining three members of the board and handled the last of what was required of him for the evening.

After one final glance around the ballroom, he began making his way to the entrance when Bingley appeared before him. "Sorry I'm late. Caroline had some catastrophe or another that turned out to be nothing more than an attempt to tag along for the party. Jane is searching for Lizzy." He rubbed his hands together with his typical big grin. "So, what've I missed?"

"Elizabeth figured out I'm her Secret Santa." He kept his voice low. If Stacy hadn't informed the entire company already, he didn't want to be the one to do it.

Bingley's eyebrows lifted. "Why does that not sound good?"

"She wasn't happy with me."

His friend gave him a sidelong glance. "You told her you're in love with her." It wasn't a question.

"She questioned whether the promotion was because of my feelings."

His eyes bulged and he gave a bark. "She's worked at Darcy Holdings long enough to know you wouldn't sacrifice the company to ingratiate yourself to a woman. You wouldn't have the reputation you do if you hired and fired women based on your personal feelings."

"She's only worked for the company a few months. She doesn't know me that well, it seems." He pulled the gift from his pocket. "Please put this under your tree for tomorrow. I want Elizabeth to have it."

Bingley's forehead crinkled and his brow drew down. "You can put it under the tree yourself."

He shook his head. "I think it would be better if I didn't come. My presence would only make matters awkward. Elizabeth needs to cool off, and I don't want to ruin her holiday." He coughed in an attempt to loosen the knot in his throat. "Please tell Jane Merry Christmas for me." He patted Bingley on the shoulder and strode away while his friend's mouth hung slightly open.

Bingley needed to understand that he had to do this not only for Elizabeth but also for himself. Fortunately, no one stopped him before he reached the doors. He retrieved his winter coat, and after a few words with Carson, climbed into the first taxi that stopped at his hail and had the driver take him straight home.

Chapter 13

As Darcy strode briskly in the direction of the party, Elizabeth shook worse than a leaf struggling to hold on to its limb in a fierce wind. He loved her? What a load of crap!

His tall frame began to disappear into the throng when Charlotte passed him and hurried to her side. "What happened? Stacy found me at the bar and insisted I needed to check on you."

"What else did she say?"

"Nothing. She said you were back here with Mr. Darcy and appeared upset."

"Upset? Why would I be upset? Darcy is my Secret Santa." Charlotte's eyes never widened or bulged. She didn't gasp. "But you knew that already."

Charlotte bit her lip and nodded. "If you remember, I mentioned him more than once, and I flat out told you. You were the one who insisted he couldn't be. I couldn't force you to see what I thought was so obvious, so I let it go. I wasn't going to beat you over the head with it."

"You should have." Elizabeth covered her face and groaned. This was going to make her job so awkward! Her physical reactions to the man were enough to make matters uncomfortable, but Darcy being in love with her . . . the mere thought made her cringe. "I'm sorry. I shouldn't blame this on you. You tried to tell me, and I wouldn't listen.

"Did he tell you he has feelings for you?"

She stumbled over to the wall, leaned against it for a moment, and lightly bumped her head against the satiny wallpaper. Two hands pulled her away and turned her around.

"I'll take that as a yes," said Charlotte.

"He never even looked at me like he cared. I mean, I thought he hated me. His eyes seemed so cold and hard."

Charlotte giggled and pressed her lips together to stop it. "I'm sorry."

"What's so funny?" Lord, she was tired all of a sudden! Even her voice sounded worn out.

"Lizzy, if you believe that was hatred in Mr. Darcy's eyes, then we need you to take lessons in body language. I've brought you coffee in the meetings, and I've stood in once or twice for Mrs. Reynolds to take notes. I've seen him stare at you, and I remember wondering how you didn't catch on fire. That man didn't look at you with disdain or resentment, he looked like he wanted to lick you from your feet to your head like an ice cream cone."

Elizabeth gasped. "Charlotte!"

"Well, do you want me to lie to you? The man has it bad, and you've refused to see the truth from the beginning. It's worried me how pig-headed and blind you've been. I've never known you to be so intolerant of anyone."

"Because he's an ass!"

"No, he's not." Charlotte crossed her arms over her chest. "An ass doesn't apologize twice for what they said when they were in a bad mood, an ass doesn't go out of his way to give you an amazing Christmas just because he drew your name for a Secret Santa, and an ass wouldn't have worn the dejected expression Mr. Darcy did when he left this hallway." She let out a long breath and shook her head. "I'd ask if you were kind, but I'm somehow certain you shredded his heart, didn't you?"

Elizabeth covered her face with her palms. Lord, her eyes burned. She wouldn't cry! "I don't want to do this. I want to go home."

"You're going to run away? You think that'll make it all better?"

"It's an improvement over this lecture."

"Do you remember when Rob Delaney dumped you in high school? You made yourself miserable for a month because you couldn't face it? Do you think this is any different? Mr. Darcy isn't going anywhere either. We were juniors when Rob ended it, so a year later, you both went in opposite directions for college, but tonight, you accepted Mr. Darcy's promotion. You won't be going anywhere for a long time. You can't avoid this. You can't avoid him. You're going to have to face him and at least make some sort of peace the two of you can live with."

She put her hands up and out at her sides in a sort of shrug. "But that doesn't have to be tonight."

She took three steps back, but just before she turned, Charlotte began to follow. "Where are you going?"

"I need to get a taxi. I'm going home."

"What about the car Mr. Darcy hired for you tonight?"

"He didn't hire it. It's his personal car and driver." She shifted through the crowd, heading for the lobby, with her head down. The last thing she needed was another confrontation with Mr. Darcy.

Thank goodness no one was sitting at their table. She could grab her clutch without anyone asking questions or protesting that she was leaving.

"Lizzy." Charlotte's voice drawled her name when she neared the doors, but Elizabeth kept walking until she reached the coat check. "Why didn't you recognize Mr. Darcy's car and driver? I remember that he insisted on giving you that ride home a few weeks ago?"

"He drove a Mercedes that night. Besides, it was dark, and I couldn't see the driver." She handed the ticket to the girl behind the counter. "I was too surprised by Darcy's apology anyway."

Charlotte glanced behind her. She said something, but it came out as a jumble of sound.

"What did you say?"

"I said, 'Why doesn't that shock me?'"

The girl passed the coat. Elizabeth slipped it on and hugged Charlotte. "Call me when you get a chance. I'm sorry, but I need to be alone and I can't do that here." She tried to leave but a hand to her elbow pulled her back.

"Please take the car. I don't like you rushing off upset and jumping into the first cab that stops, or worse, taking the subway. You know how you are when you're like this. You pay attention to nothing around you because you're so in your own head."

"Charlotte."

"No, promise me, or I'll follow you out without any coat or hat."

Elizabeth's shoulders slumped. "Fine. I'll take the car, but I do so under protest."

"Noted."

She pushed the door with her back and held her mitten up. "Merry Christmas."

"Merry Christmas," said Charlotte.

The door closed, and Elizabeth pivoted to face the darkened street. The Rolls Royce still sat along the curb—exactly where she'd left it. Why did she promise Charlotte? She didn't want to sit in Mr. Darcy's car, or sip his wine, or . . . who knows!

Elizabeth took her time on the steps, but as she approached the back of the car, Mr. Carson jumped out and opened the door. "I hope you had a good evening, miss."

She forced a smile, a part of her fighting the urge to snap at him. He had no control over his employer, so she shouldn't take out her frustrations on him. "Yes, thank you."

She slid into the plush interior and buckled herself, turning down the glass of wine the driver offered when he resumed his place behind the wheel. Her eyes burned and a slight ache behind them threatened to become a full-fledged pounding in her skull. She just needed to hold it together until she reached home! Once the door of her apartment shut behind her, she could cry to her heart's content.

The man made no sense whatsoever. He was in love with her? Charlotte claimed to have seen it all along, so why hadn't she? Was she so blind? Or had her perception flown out of the window? How could she have gotten it so wrong?

It wasn't just being blindsided, though. Why did her body react in such a crazy way around him? She had to work to concentrate in his presence and he rarely touched her, but when he did, it was strange. No one had ever caused the shivers and goosebumps he did.

Her head fell to the back of the car seat. It was almost as if she didn't know herself. She'd never reacted that way to anyone, and the remembrance made the muscles tighten in her shoulders, squeezing through her neck to her head. Oh, there was the mind-numbing pounding.

She closed her eyes and began to envision this fantasy of telling Darcy where he could shove his Advent calendar. The ruder and more drawn out her diatribe, the more cathartic it all became—until he kissed her. She shot up like a light. What was that?

"We're here, miss."

After scanning the backseat, she unbuckled as Mr. Carson opened the door. "Thank you. Merry Christmas."

"Merry Christmas," he said.

She peeked over her shoulder when she walked into the building. The man hadn't driven away yet but stood by his door while he watched her go inside. Normally, she took the stairs, but she got into the elevator and hit the button for the third floor. As the doors closed, Mr. Carson climbed into the car.

Her feet dragged when she left the elevator, and when she reached her apartment, the key stuck in the lock a little. It figures. Nothing was going to go right for her tonight. When she finally managed to open the door, Grunt's furry little face poked around from the hall table to greet her.

She dropped her clutch and picked up Grunt, cuddling him to her chest. "Hello, sweet boy. I'm so glad to see you." Two steps more and she came to an abrupt stop when she looked up at the living room.

"Grunt!" He spooked and jumped from her arms onto the back of the sofa. "Really! You had to do this tonight?"

Her tree. Her beautiful Christmas tree lay across the coffee table. Baubles hung precariously from its branches and a few appeared to have rolled or were batted away since they now resided in various corners of the room.

She peeled off her coat and tossed it across the chair so she could try to stand the tree back up. All she needed was the wood floor to be water damaged. Afraid that the tree sap would be everywhere, she removed her jewelry from her wrists and her hands and placed the pieces on the kitchen island before sticking her arm inside the prickly branches. When she hauled it upright, the tree still stood straight, but ornaments and shards of colored glass littered the floor, and a good-sized puddle soaked part of her area rug. At least the broken ornaments looked like the cheap ones she'd bought rather than the heirlooms her grandmother had given her.

She dug two towels out of the hamper and threw them down to soak up part of the mess then she went to her room, changed from her dress into a pair of pajama pants and a tank top, and gathered more of her old towels from the bathroom.

A rattle came from the living room and she growled. "Grunt!" The little twerp found a tiny glass bauble and was chasing and batting it across the wood floor when she returned. Without warning, she scooped him up and tossed him into her bedroom. She then continued drying the rest of the water.

In the end, it took her almost ten minutes to wipe it all up, including getting under the tree stand and propping part of the area rug so it would dry without marring the wood. Another fifteen was spent sweeping and vacuuming the broken glass, and another five re-hanging the ornaments that had survived.

When she finally shoved her vacuum back in the laundry room, she let Grunt out of his prison. He'd scratched at the door and meowed for the last five minutes, and the sledgehammer now pulverizing her cranium couldn't take the sound another second.

After she kicked off her shoes, she padded barefoot to the kitchen, pulled down one of her cheap, old wine glasses, and felt around the back of a bottom cabinet for that bottle of merlot she was certain was hiding back there. After several blind passes, her hand wrapped around the neck of the bottle, and she pulled it out, pouring a hefty glass the moment it was uncorked.

The oaky vintage rolled over her tongue on her first gulp. This wasn't a nice leisurely glass. This was stress relief, pure and simple. Before she reached the couch, she turned back to the kitchen, grabbed the bottle and took it with her. "Always be prepared" sounded like a pretty good motto all of a sudden.

Something sharp and painful made her hiss and draw up her foot. She sat on the sofa and set the wine on the coffee table so she could take a look. Was it a good idea to be padding around without shoes after the mess she just cleaned up? No, of course not, and now, she was paying the price. A tiny shard of green tinted glass peeked out from the pad of her foot.

The small wound didn't bleed much and didn't require a Band-Aid, so she hobbled to the kitchen and washed the sliver down the sink before she returned to her comfy spot on the sofa. She'd turned the Christmas lights on while she redecorated, so she drank her wine and dimmed the overhead lights so the only illumination came from the tree.

What a night!

What was she going to do about Mr. Darcy? She drank down the remainder of her first glass and refilled it. At least she didn't have to think about it right now.

She pulled a comfy blanket from the drawer in the coffee table and covered her legs. She loved Christmas! She loved Christmas trees! What kind of tree did Mr. Darcy have?

Gah! Stop that! She drank down the rest of her second glass.

Grunt hopped up and stretched himself across her lap and began to purr. She couldn't help but scratch behind his ears while he tilted his head so she hit all the right places.

"You're such trouble. And you know you're too cute for me to stay angry for long."

She continued to pet him while she sipped her wine. Her head started to lighten and her vision became a bit hazy. She blinked a few times. The pounding in her brain was starting to subside, but thoughts kept whirring and whirring around in there. Why couldn't humans have a switch so they could turn that shit off?

It didn't take long before she stared at the bottom of her wine glass. Crap! How did she drink it all so fast? She set it on the table and watched the lights twinkling while Grunt's little motor slowly faded. He was falling asleep.

She rested her head against the back corner of the sofa. What was Mr. Darcy doing? Was he upset about what happened, or had he gone to bed like nothing was wrong? What did the man wear to bed? She'd seen him in jeans that day, but usually, he wore a suit. Maybe he wore a pajama suit to bed? She giggled and pulled the blanket a little higher before everything faded away.

Chapter 14

Elizabeth slipped on her last earring as her eyes met Grunt's golden ones in the mirror. "I know I cuddled with you last night, but I'm still mad at you, you know." She spoke in what almost sounded like a growl, but that didn't intimidate the black fur ball at all. Rather than appear all sad like a dog, he continued to sit primly on the fuzzy throw pillow and stare unblinkingly. He couldn't care less that she came home from the holiday party last night to her pretty Christmas tree sprawled inelegantly across her coffee table, the angel across the room, laying on her side.

This morning, after a pain reliever and a strong cup of coffee, her head wasn't as muddled and no longer ached, but her stomach still rolled. She was going to have to spend the day with William Darcy. William Darcy, her Secret Santa. William Darcy, her boss. She'd have to play nice, too, because Jane wouldn't tolerate any sarcasm or downright ugliness on Christmas. No one was allowed to be Scrooge with the always-smiling Jane Bennet.

When she walked out of the room, the soft tinkle of the little bell on Grunt's collar trailed behind her. She pulled her favorite fuzzy boots from the hall closet and sat on the sofa to put them on. The Bennets never dressed for Christmas, and today, she dressed casually as always, though she wore her best jeans and her favorite red sweater. Not that she wanted to look good for Darcy! She reached for her coat; the little black furry demolition crew had settled himself on top like he owned it.

"Don't look at me like that. I didn't wear this for him." Grunt continued to stare. "Okay, I don't care if you believe me or not. I have to go. I'll be back later, and if the tree is still standing, I'll consider giving you a can of tuna." He made that usual deep little grunt he always did when she lifted him off and placed him on the floor. She slipped on her coat, gloves, and scarf, grabbed the bag of gifts, which contained two bottles of wine, of course, and hurried out the door.

Charlie and Jane's apartment was fortunately not far, so she braced herself against the bitter cold and walked quickly, crossing the street and hurrying through the park. When she reached their building, Charlie buzzed her up and opened the door as she approached.

He bit his bottom lip and shoved his hands in his pockets, looking a lot like a puppy expecting a spanking with a newspaper. "You made it. Jane was worried you would oversleep." Elizabeth had planned to harangue him and Jane when she arrived, but why did she suddenly not have it in her?

"No, I managed to drag myself out of bed this morning."

He took the bag from her, and she took off her coat and other winter gear, hanging them on the hooks inside the hall closet door. "I told Jane that you didn't stay long enough at the party for too late of a morning, but you know your sister, she always worries that things won't be perfect."

"She's always been that way. She wants everyone happy." She followed him into the kitchen where Jane was putting the candied pecan topping on the sweet potatoes with her cell phone propped to her ear.

"Yes, Mom, Lizzy's coming over today. Didn't you get to wish her Merry Christmas this morning?"

Elizabeth began waving her hands back and forth and shaking her head madly. "No!" she mouthed. She hadn't missed her mother's call, she'd simply not answered. She'd speak to her mother later, when she wasn't suffering from a hangover. To deal with her mother now would only drive her to drink more.

When she finally caught Jane's attention, her sister rolled her eyes. "Lizzy isn't here yet, but I'll tell her to call you when she gets the chance." Jane nodded. "Well, I won't sit her down and force her to speak to you. If you don't hear from her by this evening, I'd call back. I'm sure you'll catch her then . . . Okay, I'll do that . . . Yes, I promise . . . Tell Dad I love him. I love you too . . . Bye."

Jane set down the spatula, turned off her phone, and huffed. "Elizabeth Shae Bennet! You shouldn't avoid our mother on Christmas and you know it!"

Charlie chuckled while he dug the wine out of the bag and set it on the island, kissing Jane on the cheek before disappearing into the living room with the gifts.

"I just couldn't this morning, Jane. I woke up with my head throbbing. I would've screamed if I had to listen to any more gossip about Mom and Dad's neighbors. I don't care if Mrs. Long is having an affair with her lawn boy, or that Mr. Goulding has been elected mayor of Naples and his wife wore the ugliest outfit ever to his inauguration. One of the many reasons I don't live in Florida is because I need distance from Mom or she'll make me crazy." She shook her head while Jane pursed her lips in an effort not to laugh. "I'm not kidding."

After covering the dish, Jane wiped her hands on a nearby dishtowel. "I know Mom can be trying, but you should have more patience with her."

"Mom could try the patience of a saint. I promise to call later or send a message."

Jane exhaled and her shoulders gave way as she let the air out. Yes, Jane was disappointed in her, but not everyone had her patience or kindness. "I have everything prepped. Let's go open the presents. I can't wait for you to see what I got you. You're going to love it."

She grabbed Elizabeth's hand and pulled her into the spacious living room where they sat on the floor around the tree. Charlie played Santa and passed out the gifts one at a time, so they could watch each other open their presents. Jane and Elizabeth had always gone searching for the perfect gift for one another, so they always wanted to see the look on the other's face when that gift was opened. Elizabeth couldn't help but grin when Jane opened the periwinkle blue off-the-shoulder cashmere sweater. Jane had talked about wanting a blue sweater for months but never could find just the right one. When

Elizabeth found this one at Bloomingdale's, she didn't hesitate to buy it. It was so Jane.

"I love it!" Jane clutched it to her chest while she hugged Elizabeth. "Open yours." Her sister's eyes sparkled as she sat back on her heels. Charlie handed her the fairly large present, and Elizabeth put her ear next to it while she worked to shake the heavy box gently.

"Stop it, Lizzy! I want to see you open it!"

After a quick giggle, Elizabeth set the package on her lap and slowly began to pull at the tape. She always shook her gift from Jane, who never failed to respond in the same way. With one long rip of paper across the top, Elizabeth gasped at the picture on the box. It was the stand mixer she'd been wanting for the last year. "Where did you find it?"

"I ordered it online. I know you preferred to buy it at a store in case there was an issue, but I know how much you wanted the copper color."

Every time they were near a kitchen store, she dragged Jane in, but they either didn't carry the copper color, they were out of stock, or she didn't have the extra money. She never expected Jane to buy her one. "Thank you."

Charlie laughed. "You know she only bought it so you'll bake for New Year's. Did she tell you about the cherry pie she tried to make last week?" He ducked at the wad of gift wrap Jane tossed at his head. Her sister was an excellent cook, but no matter what she tried, she always ruined desserts. Elizabeth had dropped off an apple cranberry pie and another drunken pecan pie for Charlie on Christmas Eve.

"I don't mind baking. You know that." She hugged Jane and sat back. "Is that everything?" She set the stand mixer to her side, and when she turned back around, a familiar package was held out in front of her, its silver, glittery numbers winking up at her. Oh, no!

"I don't know why you have that, but I told Darcy I couldn't accept it." She hadn't paid attention before—blame it on the hangover—but where was Darcy? "When is he coming, anyway?"

Jane cleared her throat and took her hand. "Lizzy, he's not coming."

He wasn't coming? "Yes, he is. You told me he is, and he confirmed it last night."

"I don't know what you said to him after you discovered that he's your Secret Santa," said Charlie, "but he came to me and gave me your last gift. He said he didn't want to make you uncomfortable on Christmas."

Elizabeth swallowed in an attempt to loosen the lump that formed in her throat. "Did he have somewhere else to go?"

"I don't think so." Jane picked up the scraps of paper around her and began shoving them into a nearby bag. "His sister is—"

"In Maine, with her boyfriend and his family." A part of her wanted to crawl into a hole and hide. Because of her, he was spending Christmas day alone.

When she'd gathered up most of the mess, her sister took the gift from Charlie and set it in Elizabeth's lap. "I know why you're uncomfortable accepting gifts over the limit, but I've gotten to know William a little since I started dating Charlie. In some ways, he's a lot like me. He's not outgoing. In fact, he's very reserved. I've also seen the difference between how he behaves in public versus a small group of friends, and I understand that his reserve is how he deals with how uncomfortable he is."

"Jane, I never thought he was uncomfortable around me. I thought he didn't like me."

"Actually," said Charlie while he shifted to a chair. "Darcy has been awkward in large groups of people since we were boys, and he's not good making conversation with people he doesn't know well."

"He does fine in business meetings with clients he's never met." Elizabeth set the gift back under the tree. "He might be uptight, but he's not rude."

Charlie leaned forward and rested his forearms on his legs. "He's uneasy in meetings, but he has a goal, something he needs to accomplish. He does what he has to for the good of the company. I know he was appallingly rude to you on your first day and I'm not excusing it, but in his defense, he didn't know you were there. He would've never said those things to your face." He took in a long breath. "Believe me. He regrets it more and more every day."

She stared at the gift under the tree. She couldn't take her eyes off of it—like it called to her and she couldn't resist the pull.

"You know you want to see what it is," whispered Jane near her ear. "You've loved every gift he's given you. You may have felt guilty over the cost, but he has never asked me for advice on what to buy. He did all of it on his own."

"Other than have Charlie rig the Secret Santa."

Charlie's laugh broke a little of the tension in the room. "I thought he owed you after you overheard that remark."

She stood and sat on the sofa, so she was directly across from Charlie. "And how do I know that his feelings for me didn't get me the promotion?"

Charlie all but bolted from his chair as he pointed at her. "Stop right there! You will never ever say that again, and I'll tell you why. If someone overhears you, they might believe it's true and tell everyone around the office then *no one* would take you seriously. You also need to remember how long I've known him. He would *never* promote or hire someone based on a personal relationship. He is well aware of his responsibility not only to his employees, but also to his stockholders. He can't afford to hire and fire based on personal feelings and *never* has he even considered dating anyone who works for the company until you."

She crossed her arms over her chest. "Well, that's not going to happen. I've never met a man who makes me more uncomfortable than he does."

Her sister narrowed her eyes at her and tilted her head a little to one side. "How do you mean?"

Elizabeth shifted back and scratched at an invisible mark on her favorite pair of jeans. "It doesn't matter."

Jane kept her eyes trained on Elizabeth. "Yes, it does."

"No, it doesn't."

Charlie looked between them. "I don't get it."

"Lizzy's attracted to him."

"No, I'm not!"

One side of Jane's lips tugged upwards. "By her denial, I'd say big time."

Seriously! She didn't come here for this! Why was she even putting up with it? At Charlie's chuckle, she threw her arms up, stood, and walked into the kitchen, heading straight for the cabinet containing the wine glasses. Jane walked in and leaned her hip on the island while Elizabeth set the glass on the counter.

"It's just the two of us. Tell me what has you so worked up." Jane placed another glass next to hers, along with Darcy's present.

Elizabeth ignored Jane while she concentrated on opening the bottle of wine. Once she poured herself and Jane large glasses, she took a big sip. "Why?"

"Because you've always laughed off most people's comments, but William's really bothered you. You've always taken everything he's said so personally. You also confessed to me a while ago that none of the men you ever dated had that spark. Does William Darcy?"

"How am I supposed to know? I haven't kissed him, you know." She took another gulp of wine, but as she pulled the glass away, Jane took it from her hand.

"Has he ever touched you, even if you simply handed him paperwork and your fingers brushed against each other?"

Her cheeks burned as if she were sitting directly in front of a blazing fire. She took the glass of wine back from Jane and took another sizeable drink.

"Well?"

"He put his hand on mine last night." She wrapped her free arm around herself. The mere mention of it tickled her skin. "I've thought he was good-looking, hot even, but I never thought it was because of an attraction. I convinced myself that he didn't like me at all, and I . . . I thought the way I reacted was because of how much I didn't like him."

"You get goosebumps, a certain heat from his touch, butterflies in your stomach?"

A nod was all she could manage.

"I think you should open this," said Jane softly, pushing the gift closer. "He put so much thought into each and every one of those gifts. He wouldn't go to so much trouble if he didn't care. Charlie even told me that in the past, William had his assistant buy his Secret Santa gift, but he insisted on seeing to each and every one of yours himself. If he wanted to try to buy you, he could've hauled out the big guns and purchased jewelry or a car, but he didn't. His gifts weren't super expensive, but his priority was to find something you'd adore. Don't you think he deserves a fair chance at your heart?"

Elizabeth set down the wine and picked up the thin box. "When we touched, I felt like I lost control of myself."

"But that's not a bad thing. You're always in such control of everything. Sure, you've had crushes or dated, but since you've been an adult, you've never let yourself fall for someone. School and your career came first."

"No man has made me feel that way."

Jane gave a crooked smile. "No man has ever pissed you off so much in the past. I think that was the biggest clue right there. I'm still amazed it never occurred to me."

Her eyes burned and blurred a little. "He really stayed home today because of me?"

With a shrug, Jane swallowed her sip of wine. "That's what he told Charlie."

She sucked in a breath, tore at the end of the package, pulled out the box, and lifted the lid. Once she'd pulled back the tissue paper, she froze, staring at what was inside. How did he know? With shaky fingers, she lifted the single ticket.

A whistle came from Jane. "Before you say anything, I never told him it was your favorite. I don't think I've even told Charlie."

Elizabeth put the lid back on the box and hurried into the hall, grabbing her coat, hat, and gloves. "I need to talk to him. He must hate me after yesterday."

"I doubt it. You might want to ask Charlie where he lives before you run out the door, though."

She stepped around the corner. "Charlie? Where does Darcy live?"

He looked over from the football coverage on television. "On Riverside Drive. Do you remember when you, Jane, and I went walking to the park and you pointed to the large grey stone house on the corner and commented on how much you adore it?"

"The one with the ornate dormer windows?" she squeaked.

Charlie laughed. "That's it."

Maybe she should just bang her head against the wall now. Shit! That house was insanely big and he lived there by himself? She took the present from Jane and kissed her on the cheek. "With any luck, I'll be back with an extra mouth to feed."

Jane opened the door and called, "Good luck!"

She shook the entire walk but it wasn't from the cold. The house wasn't far. She'd passed it often enough when going to Riverside park or for a jog. She loved that house.

Her eyes roved over the exterior when she approached and this fluttery feeling started in her stomach, but before she could chicken out, she climbed the steps and rang the doorbell.

After a few moments, an older lady answered. "Hello?"

"Hi, I need to speak with Mr. Darcy. Is he in by any chance? My name is Elizabeth Bennet."

The woman shook her head. "I'm sorry, but he isn't at home."

Of course, he wasn't. He'd probably made other plans after she'd abused him last night. "Could you please tell him I stopped by? I need to speak with him."

After a nod and a Merry Christmas, the door closed in her face, and Elizabeth's shoulders dropped. She would have to try again later. She really needed to speak to him—apologize to him for being such a blind idiot. While walking back to the sidewalk, she looked back and forth. Maybe she'd go for a walk in the park before she went back to Jane's.

"Miss Bennet!"

She whirled around. It was the driver from the night before who walked up behind her. "Carson? Is that right?"

"Yes, miss. I'm sorry about my wife. She was only doing what Mr. Darcy asked. This morning, he told her he wasn't at home to guests, but I think if he knew it was you, he'd make an exception."

"I don't want to get her into trouble," she said, shaking her head.

With a smile, he motioned her inside. "I'm letting you in. I promise I can take the heat if I've overstepped."

Before she could overthink it, she followed him inside, glancing up at the decorative trim in the entry and the high ceiling and marble floors of the foyer. She followed him down a flight of stairs and around a corner where a clanking sound echoed through the hall. Carson opened a door and stood to the side so she could enter.

"I believe the two of you need to talk." The words were spoken quietly before he left her standing there by herself. What the heck? How much had Darcy told him?

The clanking sound made her turn and—oh my stars and garters! She peeked back down the hallway. Why would he just leave her like that? She turned back and forced herself to clamp shut her lower jaw. Didn't Carson realize that Darcy wore nothing but a pair of workout shorts?

His back to her, Darcy lowered slightly to balance the bar across his shoulders and did several squats while she all but whimpered at the sight of his back muscles shifting and straining, not to mention his butt, which when he was at a full squat, was outlined quite well by those shorts.

She coughed in an attempt to get his attention, but he must not have heard since he put the bar back on the rack and straightened. He reached his hands toward the ceiling in a long stretch, and her eyes rested upon a black ink armband tattoo on his left bicep. Uptight Darcy, head of Darcy Holdings, had a tattoo?

The sudden quiet caused her to startle and look up to the dark eyes now watching her from across the room. He pulled a cord at the base of his neck and a wireless headphone dropped from his ear. Well, that would explain why he didn't hear her.

"You didn't come to Charlie and Jane's." Well, duh! Way to go stating the obvious!

He pulled out the other headphone. "No, I thought it would be better for everyone if I made myself scarce."

She set a foot forward but pulled it back. Perhaps it was better to stay where she was. He wasn't exactly welcoming. "I hope you don't mind. Your driver, Carson, let me in. His wife said you weren't at home."

"It's fine," he said. He picked up his shirt from a nearby bench and slid it over his head, covering those broad shoulders from the eyes she needed to keep on his face rather than the skin buffet in front of her. It wasn't easy. He pointed to the hand that held his gift. "You opened it?"

Her hand lifted and she looked down to the box. "I did. *Phantom of the Opera* has been my favorite since I was a young girl, but what I can't figure out is how you knew?" Her eyes were wide when she turned them back to him.

"You don't remember?"

Her eyebrows drew down in the middle as she gave this adorable little frown. "Until dinner at Giorgio's, I can't remember ever having a conversation with you that wasn't work related."

"We didn't speak of it, but you and Miss Lucas did. I was in the elevator one day when the two of you entered, I think to go to lunch. Once you both said hello, you turned around and proceeded to continue the argument you must've been having before the doors opened."

A small curve appeared to one side of her lips. "Charlotte and I are always having some completely trivial and nonsense conversation. You'll have to remind me on this one."

He picked up his towel and draped it around his neck. "I believe the contested topic on this occasion was whether Josh Groban would make a better Phantom or Raoul. Miss Lucas was of the opinion Groban should be the Phantom, and you—"

"I think his voice is more suited to Raoul." She gazed back down at the ticket. "I'd completely forgotten about that."

"I thought someone with such particular opinions on the subject must be a fan." He grabbed his water bottle and stepped closer, not stopping until he stood directly in front of her. She'd definitely surprised him when he turned around. He hadn't expected her to call him, much less come to his house, but he wasn't upset over it. It made him hope as he hadn't let himself hope before. Her perusal of his backside that he caught when he turned around only fueled that fire.

She gave a tight smile. "You seem to know so much about me, but I know hardly anything about you."

"I'm not that interesting."

"I doubt that," she said softly. If only she would look at him instead of continuing to stare at the ticket.

He held out his arm so she would accompany him back upstairs. "I have the other ticket in my desk. If you'd like to take Jane or perhaps Miss Lucas, I'd be happy to give it to you." His stomach knotted up as he said the words. He had to offer, but he so wanted to be the one beside her if she'd let him.

She paused on the steps and faced him. "You have another ticket?"

"Yes, even though I debated whether or not to tell you the night of the party, my original plan was to find some way to give you the last gift without revealing myself. I wanted to surprise you at the theater. I thought it might give us an opportunity to talk outside of the office. Of course, I didn't know you'd be uncomfortable about the other gifts. Last night, when I was trying to decide whether or not to wait, you discovered me with this."

Her fingers fidgeted at the box. "I owe you an apology for the argument. I don't know why it made me so angry."

"No, I deserved it. I shouldn't have said what I did when you were hired, I completely disregarded the rules for the Secret Santa, and I did put you in an awkward position. I didn't consider how others might perceive the situation." He stepped up and she followed suit until they were again in the foyer and she fell in behind him when he turned and entered his study. He opened a drawer on his desk and picked up an envelope. When he held it in front of her, she eyed it as if it would bite.

Her teeth wore at her lips, and she glanced back at the box in front of her. "I think you should keep it."

"Are you sure?" he asked, withdrawing his hand.

She nodded and finally met his eye. "I am. If you would still like to accompany me, I would . . . well, I think I would like that."

That warmth—the one that settled in his chest when he looked at Elizabeth—spread throughout his body at her shy smile and acceptance. The grin that overspread his face must've been ridiculous, it was so large.

Elizabeth looked around the room—the floor to ceiling dark stained bookshelves, the moldings around the ceiling, and the top of his desk. Was she looking for something or just avoiding his eye? "In the meantime, you should get dressed. We have a Christmas dinner to attend."

He glanced down at his sweaty exercise clothes. "I need to shower first."

Her palm pressed against her stomach, and her cheeks turned a faint pink. "Oh, then I'll see you there when you're ready."

She tried to hurry out of the door, but his hand managed to snag hers before she could escape. His fingers tingled where they gave a slight tug to pull her back into the room. "If you'll wait for me, we can walk over together."

They stood as close now as they did when they danced the night before. He could make out the slight scent of lavender, and when their eyes locked, he resisted the urge to shift closer. Her tongue peeked from between her lips, and without thinking, he leaned in, closing his eyes right as his lips grazed hers. He pulled back a hairsbreadth and almost apologized, but her hand threaded through the back of his sweaty hair and drew him in once again.

This time, her lips barely parted under his, and he laced their fingers together. Was this really happening or would he wake up as he had so many times before to find she'd disappeared with the opening of his eyes? Whether it was a dream or not, he held Elizabeth's hand and was kissing her. He'd live in the now and pray like crazy that it was real. His free hand cupped her cheek as he straightened. "Will you wait for me?" he whispered.

Her eyes opened and searched his. "Yes."

Chapter 15

Elizabeth's vibrant eyes sparkled while she laughed at one of Bingley's terrible jokes, making Darcy's heart beat just a little bit faster. He loved her laugh. He adored a lot of things about her, but when she giggled or chuckled at something, he couldn't help but smile.

He probably looked like an idiot, smiling and staring and appearing completely whipped. Who was he kidding? He was hooked on Elizabeth Bennet, and they hadn't even had a real date.

"Lizzy, I want to show you something in the kitchen." Jane took her sister's hand and led her from the room while Elizabeth glanced at him out of the corner of her eye and bit her lip.

When the door closed behind them, a light kick to his shin distracted him from the disappearance of his favorite view. "So? What happened when Lizzy came to your house?"

He sipped his scotch and shrugged while he avoided Bingley's eye. "We talked some."

Bingley's eyes narrowed. "I call bullshit."

"Excuse me?"

"I call bullshit. You're happier than you were last night and Lizzy isn't exactly comfortable, but it's a different sort of discomfort than before. She's not angry or standoffish now. Instead, she's almost hyper-aware of you, and I don't think she knows what to do with it. So, what happened?"

"It's none of your business. When did you become a gossipy old woman?"

"I don't gossip. I'm curious. Come on, I've talked to you about Jane."

Darcy pointed at Bingley's chest. "You forget that I don't ask about what happens with you and Jane. Most of it you divulge on your own and you don't give intimate details."

His friend's eyes almost burst from their sockets. "Intimate? The two of you got intimate?"

"No! Not that I would tell you if we did. Would you just leave it alone?"

"You know Jane is grilling Lizzy as we speak. She's the one who figured out Lizzy is attracted to you."

He choked while trying to swallow his latest sip. "How do you know that?" The words came out high pitched, and he coughed.

"She told me," said Bingley with a careless shrug. "I was sitting right here when Jane asked her."

"And Elizabeth answered?"

"No, but she walked out of the room and Jane followed. It was pretty obvious the answer was yes."

Darcy pulled himself a little taller; a part of him wanted to beat his chest and do a ridiculous impression of Tarzan. He'd caught her ogling his butt at the house earlier. Just how attracted to him was she, and why had she been so resistant to him if she was? "She's attracted to me?"

Bingley sat forward and leaned on his knees. "Jane's never seen her react so vehemently to an insult before. Most of the time, she'd laugh it off and never think about it again. I don't think Lizzy knew what to do with herself." As he sat back straight, he rubbed his thigh with his free hand and took a sip of his drink. "Just be careful with her."

"What's that supposed to mean? You know I wouldn't intentionally hurt her."

"I know." Bingley glanced towards the kitchen door. "Do you remember the joke about Grunt's picture on Lizzy's desk?"

"She doesn't date, so he's the only man in her life, if I recall correctly."

"Exactly. Lizzy has been driven since she decided she wanted to be a lawyer. She didn't do much partying in college and rarely dated, even once she graduated. I can remember two dates since I've been involved with Jane. Both were when she was at Longbourn, and both sank on the first night out."

Darcy had to admit he was curious. What kind of men had she dated? "Do you know what happened?"

An odd chuckle came from Bingley. "One was a setup. Mrs. Bennet is a loon and thought this distant cousin would be a good match for her. Lizzy thought she was to meet up with family, and by the main course, he was making plans to introduce her to his mother."

This guy sounded more like some of the women he'd dated than a man. Sheesh! "What happened?"

"She left before dessert and I don't think she's forgiven her mother yet. Just don't mention it in front of Lizzy's assistant. She dates him now."

"That's awkward."

Bingley's forehead crinkled. "Lizzy thinks Charlotte is too good for him, but she really doesn't care. She avoids the guy. He's a real kiss ass." He perked up for a minute. "He works for your aunt at de Bourgh."

Laughing, Darcy shook his head. "That doesn't surprise me. My aunt loves a good suck up. What about the other guy?"

"He made it clear he expected her to 'put out' pretty early on." Bingley used air quotes and grinned. "Lizzy poured her red wine in his lap and left."

"Nice." He grinned and crossed his ankle over his knee.

"Anyway, I've done my brotherly duty and warned you. I now have to say I'll kick your ass if you hurt her." He picked up the remote. "Let's check the scores on the bowl games."

"Bingley?" His friend peered back. "Would you have threatened to kick my ass if it were Caroline?"

"God, no! But I might've had your sanity evaluated."

"Lizzy?" Jane's voice drawled out her name. She'd been trying to get information about Darcy since the door swung closed behind them, and the last thing Elizabeth wanted to do was discuss him. She'd tried to change the subject more than once, but Jane refused to let her.

"Why do I have to tell you?"

"I've told you all about Charlie."

She pointed at Jane. "And I've stopped you from telling me some things. I don't need to know about your sex life. You might be a nurse and capable of discussing anything, but I still have some boundaries."

"If you'd become a divorce attorney, you wouldn't."

"Gah! I'd be miserable. I still like to believe in a fairy tale ending, not that Cinderella and Prince Charming end up splitting their assets fifty-fifty or according to some prenup."

Jane's eyes narrowed a tiny bit while Elizabeth tried not to squirm. "Did he kiss you?"

Elizabeth's cheeks burned. They had to be as red as a freaking stop light. She put her glass to her lips and took a gulp of her wine while Jane giggled and clapped. Once she'd swallowed, she set her glass on the granite countertop. "I didn't say a word."

"You didn't have to."

"Why do I feel like I'm being interrogated by Mom?"

Jane huffed and dropped back against the cabinet. "Oh, come on. We've always shared everything."

"We're not sixteen anymore, and I'm not looking to tell you about some miserable date I had. He hasn't picked his teeth with his fork, he hasn't told me he expects me to 'put out,' and he doesn't consider us engaged by the main course. It's different, Jane. I can't explain why, but it is. I'm sorry."

Her sister put down her wine and hugged her. "No, I'm sorry. You're right. I've always wanted to talk about Charlie because I'm so happy with him, but I suppose this is different for you. You didn't recognize that you were attracted to him and it must be awkward to come to terms with."

When Jane drew back, Elizabeth bit her lip. "I tried to explain it earlier, but it's hard to put into words. I've always found him attractive, but I've never thought of the way I felt as an attraction. Until you said it, I was too caught up in being angry with him or finding some reason to avoid him." She glanced at the clock on the oven. "Do you mind if we leave a little early?"

Jane's eyebrows nearly rose to her hairline. "What do you have planned?"

"I think we could stand some time to talk." She put up her hands. "Just talk."

"Charlie and I will survive." This almost wicked grin stole across her face. "I have a couple of presents Charlie hasn't opened yet."

"Jane! Eww! Please remember I have to work with him. The last time you told me something, that I didn't want to know by the way, I almost burst out laughing in the middle of a meeting."

She hurried around the island and through the door. Both men sipped their scotch while the television spouted off recaps or replays of the bowl games. She approached Darcy's chair and started to touch his shoulder but drew back when he turned.

His brows dipped in the center. "Is something wrong?"

"No, but I'm ready to go home and I . . . well, would you walk with me?" Why did she feel like a teenager again?

He stood, and Jane took his empty glass and hugged him. "Thank you for coming."

"Thank you for inviting me." He clapped a hand on Charlie's shoulder. "I'll see you on Monday."

"Definitely!" Charlie raised his glass. "Merry Christmas."

"Merry Christmas." Darcy picked up a bag from near the tree with his presents from Charlie and Jane and followed Elizabeth into the entry. Once they both were decked out for the cold, she reached for her stand mixer.

"Is that one of your presents?"

"Yes, from Jane."

He handed her his bag and picked up the box. "Is that everything?"

She nodded while she finished putting on her gloves. "Yes, Jane and I only buy each other one present. It's become a kind of tradition. We spend all year finding that one perfect gift."

When she opened the door, Jane's voice called from the living room, "Lizzy! Don't forget to call Mom!"

"Okay!"

As they headed down the stairs, he shifted the mixer to one side. "You haven't spoken to your parents yet?"

"No, and I hope I don't sound ungrateful when I say this, but my mother can make me insane. I love her, but she's been texting me constantly the last few weeks with all of the gossip from Florida. Then, a few days ago, she mentioned some boy from my high school she wants me to call. I'm certain it's a setup."

"Does she do that often?"

"Twice, and both times were a nightmare." A deep laugh made her insides flip as she took the last step. When he opened the door, she inhaled deeply in an attempt to quash the fluttery sensation that had taken over her body. He was just a guy walking her home. Nothing more.

What a freaking lie! That kiss had reduced her knees to a wobbly mess, and she'd been tongue-tied around him the rest of the day. Now, as she crossed the street at his side, his energy radiated to her and made her skin pebble into little bumps.

"You don't mind walking through the park tonight?"

A dimple peeked from his cheek. "It's a little warmer this evening, and I'm not particularly ready to say goodnight to you yet. If I called Carson, the evening would be over much sooner than I'd like."

"Unless you want to come up and talk." He paused and faced her, and she forced herself to meet his eye. "I don't have any scotch, but I have wine, amaretto, and coffee."

His lips curved up just a hair on each end as he took a step. "Coffee and amaretto sound good." When she followed, a few of those butterflies in her stomach settled. "Did you do anything special for Grunt this morning?"

"No, the little twerp is in the doghouse at the moment."

"He didn't break something else, did he?"

"Last night, I came home to my Christmas tree sprawled across my living room."

His shoulders shook, but he pressed his lips together. "I shouldn't laugh. I'm sorry."

"No, I know. When I picked it up, he found a glass bauble that wasn't broken and decided it was the best toy ever. I had to shut him in my room while I cleaned up the glass, and I still stepped on a sliver when I was done."

They emerged from the park across from her building, and he shifted the mixer to one arm and put a hand to the small of her back while they checked for cars. When they were moving again, he used that arm for the awkwardly large box he carried, and if he hadn't needed it, she would've hauled it back. Some part of her found comfort in his touch and a certain satisfaction at him adopting such a protective stance.

He opened the door of her building, and this time, instead of the stairs, she punched the button for the elevator. "I won't make you carry that all the way up."

"I wouldn't mind if you did."

She probably grinned like a fool. Her cheeks were oddly warm, kind of like she had a fever, but she was definitely not ill. The ride up didn't last long, and when she turned the key in the lock, an almost galloping like noise came from inside before it suddenly stopped and something knocked against the wall.

"Grunt." She muttered his name under her breath as she opened the door, and sure enough, his little head peeked around the corner. After she set Darcy's bag next to the table, she picked up the troublemaker. Darcy trailed behind her into the kitchen and placed the mixer on the counter while she did the same with the cat.

"Everything appears to be in one piece, so tuna it is." She pulled a can out of the cabinet and spooned it into a bowl. He trilled, diving in as soon as she dished out the last of it. "Merry Christmas." She scratched behind the cat's ears and leaned against the island while looking at the tall, good-looking man standing on the other side of the counter. "Do you want coffee, or I have some wine?"

He unwound the scarf from his neck, pulled off his gloves and coat, and threw them over the back of the chair. He took the three steps needed to stand face to face and tugged at her scarf, tossing it on the barstool once it was free. "Are you cold?"

"No, I just didn't think about it." She pulled off her cap and unzipped her coat. When she returned to the kitchen from hanging their coats, she pulled out the bottle of wine he'd sent her. "Would you like wine, coffee . . .?"

His hand took hers, lacing their fingers as he guided her to face him. "Why are you so nervous?"

"I don't know." Her heart beat a mile a minute, and she shivered at the caress of his breath against her cheek.

His hands rested on the countertop on either side of her, caging her in. "Really?" His eyes searched hers, and a shuddering breath escaped before she could stop it.

"I've never been in this position before." She covered her face with her hands and groaned. What a thing to confess!

His warm hands rested just above her hips, and she gasped and clutched at his shoulders when he lifted her to sit on the countertop.

"Elizabeth." His voice rolled over her, melting her insides and pulling her eyes to his. "I care about you—a lot. I've dated, but what I felt for those women doesn't compare to what you do to me. If you're uneasy for the same reason, don't be. We'll take things one day at a time and figure it out as we go."

His unwavering gaze whispered that he spoke the truth and a part of her relaxed. She still had a slight tremor, but it was nothing a shot of amaretto wouldn't cure! She definitely didn't need coffee.

"Elizabeth?"

Before she could second guess herself, she pressed forward but paused when their noses were side by side, her lips hovering just over his. His eyes had closed, and his shoulders tensed under her fingers. Could he be just as nervous? He didn't behave like he was, but it was possible.

His fingers caressed her cheek, and his eyes fluttered open. The gentle expression in them provided the courage she needed to move that last little bit and brush her lips across his. He made no move to deepen the embrace but allowed her to set the tone with soft touches of their lips that made her ache for more. Before she took matters into her own hands, she dropped a quick kiss to the tip of his nose. He chuckled, lifted her up, and she slid down the strong column of his body until her toes touched the floor.

"I'd love some water."

She allowed her hand to trail from his shoulder as she turned. "Just water?"

When she peeked over her shoulder, he nodded. "Just water."

Once she poured him a glass, she took out the amaretto. "Do you mind if I have some?"

"No, of course not. I would if I hadn't been drinking scotch. I doubt the two would mix well."

She topped off a small glass, took a sip, and set the drink on the counter to put the bottle away. When she straightened, he pressed his lips against hers and licked his lips. "I might have a little that way though."

She bit her lip. "Okay."

He took her hand and led her to the sofa, but before he sat down, he scanned the room. "What did you do with your Secret Santa gifts?"

"Oh, they're mostly in my study. I hid the posters behind the bookcase so Grunt wouldn't bite on them. Why?"

"Do you mind if I grab something out of them?"

"No, it's the closed door off the hall."

"Get comfy, I'll be right back." He kissed her forehead and disappeared for a moment before returning with a package he unwrapped while he walked. The faux fur throw unfurled when he shook it out and draped it over her legs. While he tossed the packaging in the trash, she took off her fuzzy boots and curled her legs under her.

He took the seat next to her and angled towards her. "Merry Christmas, Elizabeth."

Chapter 16

A hand shifted down her hip and clutched her to him while her hands traced the well-defined muscles of his chest, his abs, and began to follow that little trail of hair on his lower stomach. A suckling kiss to the point where her neck and shoulder met set her insides on fire and distracted her from her study of his amazing body. His fingers kneaded her rear and pressed her to him as she moaned and pressed her palms to his lower back.

"Elizabeth," he whispered near her ear. His breath fanned against the sensitive flesh of her neck, and she shifted in an attempt to get closer. She needed to get as close to him as possible.

She turned her head to press her lips against his chest, but instead of taut, smooth skin, something rubbed and wrinkled under the movement of her nose. Wait! What was that? Her eyes blinked open and stared at the forest green, cotton Henley in front of her. Oh, God!

"Good morning." Darcy's voice rumbled lower than usual. His chest shook under her.

Her eyes snapped shut, and she put a hand over her face. This had to be the most horrifying moment of her life! He kissed the top of her head and pulled her up his chest until she had no choice but to meet his eye. "For the record, the sound of you moaning my name in your sleep is the best Christmas present you could've ever given me."

She tried to bury her face in his neck, but he wouldn't allow it. Instead, he sat up and shifted her more onto his lap, so her legs straddled him. "You have nothing to be embarrassed about."

"Did I . . ." She cleared her throat. "Did I try to grope you?" Please say no! Please say no!

A wide grin broke out on his face. "No, you mostly clenched and opened your hands. Unfortunately, they didn't wander."

She slapped his arm, but the impossible tightness in her shoulders gave way. "I hope you slept okay. I don't even remember falling asleep."

"It was right after you told me about adopting Grunt. I meant to carry you to bed, but I wanted to hold you for a few more minutes. It was such a great night. I didn't want it to end. I guess I fell asleep."

Both of her hands slid along his neck, and she pressed her lips to his. As much as she'd fought it, she belonged in his arms, kissing him. She couldn't explain it if someone asked, but she'd quickly learned it was a place she never wanted to leave.

He leaned in like he was going to break out the tongue, and she pulled back. "I need to brush my teeth before you get any ideas."

His fingers kneaded her thighs while he chuckled and dropped his forehead to her shoulder. "That's a good idea. I'm not thinking too much with the brain in my head right now, anyway." He lifted his face, which was an adorable reddish tint. "It's morning."

"Oh." She traced his stubble covered jaw with her thumbs.

"I need to shave."

"I rather like it. It's a side of you not everyone gets to see. You look so relaxed like this."

He trailed his fingers down her temple, brushing a lock of hair behind her ear. "I'm more relaxed than I can remember being in a long time." He ran his hand along her forearm and brought her palm to his mouth where he deposited a lingering kiss. "Do you have plans for today?"

"I need to call my mother. Other than that, I had a date with a book or a movie, which would progress to a book or a movie with a glass of wine tonight." She glanced to the side and did a double take at the coffee table where Grunt sat, posed in a rather regal position, staring unblinkingly at the two of them.

"He's been watching us since I woke up. By the looks he's been giving me, I'd say he feels I've taken his spot."

"He usually sleeps beside me, so that's possible."

He entwined his fingers with hers. "Do you want to spend the day with me?" She lifted her eyebrows, and his eyes dropped to the charm on her necklace. "Unless you'd rather not. You don't have to."

She traced the line of the buttons on his shirt. "Spending the day together sounds nice. I'm sorry if you thought otherwise, but you surprised me."

William pressed one more kiss to her lips before guiding her off his lap and standing himself. "We should brush our teeth then. Do you have a spare toothbrush, or do I need to wait until I go home to change?"

She grabbed his hand and started down the hall. "I have a spare. Come on."

He trailed behind Elizabeth, through her bedroom, to her bathroom. As awkward as their interactions were at times, she'd become more open with him since yesterday, and he wanted to shout from the rooftops he was so happy.

She opened a drawer and rummaged through several packages containing toothbrushes. Finally, pulling one from the bottom and handing it to him. He stuck his hand in and shifted the toothbrushes she'd left behind, shaking while he silently laughed. All of them were a shade of pink.

"Why do you have one grey toothbrush?"

"It was a freebie from the dentist." She lifted the tube of toothpaste, so he popped the new brush out of the package and held it out.

"You haven't been saving it for a male caller?"

Her bubbly giggle made him smile. "That sounds like a line out of a Regency bodice ripper."

"Are those what you read when you're not at work?" He could just envision her curled up on her sofa, the faux fur throw draped over her, her attention glued to a book in her hands.

"I read a lot of different types of books." She squeezed a dollop onto his toothbrush, gave him a flirty smile, and turned to brush her teeth. Her eyes darted to his several times in the mirror while they couldn't speak. Once they'd rinsed and dried their faces, he tugged her by her top so she slid into his arms and pressed his lips against hers.

Her fingers threaded through the hair at the nape of his neck as he tentatively deepened the kiss. The swift inhale from her caused his fingers to dig into the fabric of her jeans until her palms moved to his chest and pushed him back.

"What's wrong?"

"Nothing. I just need a minute alone. You know, in the bathroom."

"Oh!" He allowed her to turn him around and push him out of the door before it shut behind his back.

He scanned the room, taking in every little detail from the pale grey and white area rug on the wood floors, to the grey and white bedding, and lastly, the blush colored chunky knit throw on her bed. She didn't seem to have one favorite shade of pink but liked a variety of hues. Somehow, he'd always envisioned the walls of her room a Pepto-Bismol pink, but instead, they were almost a light cloud grey. He stepped closer to her bedside table and picked up a frame. Jane, Elizabeth, and an older man, presumably their father, smiled while they stood in front of Widener Library at Harvard.

Grunt jumped onto the bed, sat on a fluffy pink throw pillow, and stared at him as though he were an intruder. Darcy put out his hand, but the door opening made him turn around.

"That was when my parents dropped me off for my first year. My father loves libraries and books, and desperately wanted to see inside Widener."

"Are you more like your mother or father?"

"That's a dangerous question." She laughed and took the frame, glancing at it before setting it back in its place. "In looks, my mother always claims I look like my paternal grandmother, but I think I'm more like my father in some ways. We have a similar sense of humor, and I refuse to gossip like my Mom." She placed a hand on his arm, and her nose crinkled in the cutest way. "She'll love everything about you, which is why you won't meet her for a very long time."

A long time. A warmth bloomed in his chest when she said that. She may not have done it consciously, but if even a small part of her thought of him as permanent or long-term, he couldn't complain.

"What did you want to do with your lanterns?" He pointed to where they stood next to the dresser.

"Jane and I thought they would be nice in the bathroom, but when I decided to give everything back, I left them there."

He peeked back into her bathroom. "If you had some stands, they could go next to the bathtub rather than the floor. The light would be better from them, too."

"That's a good idea." With a slight tip of her head towards the hall, she gestured for him to follow. "Would you like some coffee? We can start by making breakfast, then I'll get dressed and we can go to your house after so you can change."

Darcy trailed behind to the kitchen. "What do you want to do today?"

While she filled a stovetop espresso maker, she furrowed her brow. "I don't know. It's really too cold to go to the park, and a number of places are closed."

"Why don't we see if we can get your prints framed, then look for some pedestals for the lanterns?"

She stopped pouring milk into a small saucepan and turned to him. "Today is one of the biggest shopping days of the year. Do you really want to brave those crowds?"

"I go to a small frame shop near my house. Their work is excellent, and if they're open, they're unlikely to have a crowd. As for the pedestals, I'm not thinking of going to Macy's or Saks."

The small pan went on the stove, and she put her hands on his cheeks. "I don't want you buying me more gifts. I didn't even have a Christmas present for you."

He couldn't help but grin wickedly. "I told you this morning that you moaning my name was the best present ever."

Her cheeks turned a brilliant shade of red as she returned to working on their coffee. "You're enjoying that entirely too much."

His arms snaked around her waist. "I'm simply enjoying my time with you." The cat hopped onto the island and leveled him with a discerning stare. "Why do you call him Grunt?"

"You petted him while he slept last night. Didn't you notice the noises he makes?" She picked up the cat, and he almost groaned before she set him back down. "He does it all the time." She turned in his arms and gave him a smacking kiss. "Now, if I'm going to cook, you need to sit here." He stepped backward as she steered him to a barstool. "I can't move around with you holding me like that."

"Forgive me. A part of this all still seems like a dream. I know I'm really here with you if I touch you in some way."

Her cheek brushed his. "I'm here."

A sharp pain on his ribs made him flinch. "Hey! Why did you have to pinch me?"

One side of her mouth turned up in an impish grin. "I just wanted to prove that you're awake."

Before she could react, he grabbed her around the waist with one arm as his other hand dug into her ribs. A loud squeal and uncontrollable laughter filled the room while she squirmed. "No, please."

He stopped the tickling but wrapped a leg and his arm around her to hold her still. "I must have my revenge for that pinch."

"What if I beg for forgiveness?"

"What did you have in mind?"

He held his breath when her face shifted towards his neck. Would he regret not stopping her? She could do a number of mischievous things to him in that position. When her lips met his pulse point in a suckling kiss, it sent out a shot that tugged through his abdomen to his groin. Her teeth grazed his earlobe, and he turned his head to capture her lips. The temptation to let his hands wander and let things progress overwhelmed him, but he softened his kisses until he drew back. When his eyes opened, her teeth tugged at her bottom lip, but with his thumb, he gently pulled it free.

"I should make breakfast." Her voice was thick and a bit husky, which did nothing to help the fight he was having with his own body. It only made her more appealing. How he wanted to spread her out on her grey and white bedcovers and kiss and touch her until she moaned his name in that voice—just like she had earlier that morning. He shook his head and stretched. He couldn't and wouldn't rush her. Breakfast! Breakfast was good. He needed to think about anything but the erotic images their kisses and innocent touching produced in his imagination.

They talked and laughed while she made them eggs and toast. He pitched in where he could, but mostly touched her hand or brushed her hair from her face when he had the opportunity and thoroughly had the best time of his life. Then, he straightened the kitchen while she changed clothes so they could go to his house.

Carson met them at the curb of Elizabeth's building and drove them home where he rushed upstairs to get cleaned up and changed, while Mrs. Hill gushed over Elizabeth and served her more coffee and whatever home-baked muffins or cookies she'd made in the last day or two.

Once he'd showered and put on clean clothes, Carson dropped them at the frame shop with the posters. Even though it was a small place, the owner opened for the day in the hopes a few people might stop by.

They picked out matting and frames, but when he reached for his wallet, Elizabeth put a hand to his wrist. "Don't you dare."

"Consider the frames part of the gift."

"No." Her hand squeezed his wrist. "I can afford to frame them. I don't need you to spend so much money on me."

His fingers twitched when she took her credit card from her purse, but he let her do what she felt necessary, even though it wasn't.

The weather still held a lot of chill, so Carson had waited for them and ushered them back into the heated car when they were done. Darcy buckled himself in and rubbed the palm of his hand with his thumb until Elizabeth laced her fingers into his.

"Why is it so important to you to buy me everything?" Her tone wasn't angry or disappointed, only quiet.

"I've always wanted to take care of those I love. Georgiana has her own money, but for some things, she comes home and we shop together. I tend to pay when Bingley and I go out for beers or lunch."

"But that would be a working lunch. Technically, the company pays for it."

"True, but I don't consider it at the time. I think because you don't expect it, it makes me want to do it more." He shrugged and traced the fingers of his free hand over hers as he held it. "I like making you smile."

She leaned her head back on the seat. "I don't need presents on a daily basis to make me smile. The advent calendar was nice, but if you do it year 'round, the gifts lose significance. Does that make sense?"

"They're more special if you receive them less."

"Exactly."

"It makes sense. I only want to make you happy."

Her eyes held his and wouldn't let go. "Right now, in this moment, I'm happier than I've been in a long time. I don't need anything more."

He couldn't help but kiss her when she said something he needed to hear so badly. It was no more than a touch to her lips and then her nose, but the wide smile she wore when he straightened, made his chest swell. When she rested her head against his shoulder, he couldn't imagine a more perfect moment.

The car pulled to a stop along the curb, and Elizabeth propped herself on his leg to look through the window on his side of the car. "How do you know about this place?"

"Bingley told me." He opened the car door and helped her out to the sidewalk. "I needed ideas for more gifts. Your pink glasses came from here."

Her eyes almost flashed. "How did you find something I'd never noticed?"

"I had an accomplice," he whispered near her ear.

The bell on the door announced their entrance, and Erika stepped out of the small office to one side of the store and clasped her hands. "Looks like Santa Claus has been playing cupid." She moved from around the counter and hugged them both. "You missed our last shipment, Lizzy. It came in the week before Christmas, so take a good gander around. I'd hate for you to miss anything." She winked at him, and Elizabeth glanced back and forth between them.

"Do I have competition?" Her lips were pressed together but her cheeks quivered. The silly woman was trying not to laugh. His fingers found that particularly ticklish spot on her ribs, but he didn't even need to dig them in at all. "William!"

"You're teasing me."

That irresistible tongue peeked out from her lips before she turned and trotted to the back of the shop, her girlish giggle trailing in her wake.

He followed but had a difficult time keeping his attention on the items on the mismatched furniture and shelves with Elizabeth only a foot or two ahead of him.

"William?"

He stepped behind her and looked over her shoulder to the two white wooden pedestals in a corner. "Those would work for the lanterns."

"Do you like them?"

"Yes, let's get those, and then I need to go buy new towels for my bathroom. I've let it go too long, and the money my father sent me for Christmas is burning a hole in my pocket."

They paid Erika, and Carson met them on the sidewalk to open the trunk when they emerged from the store. The trip for towels was quicker than the time they spent in the old thrift shop. Elizabeth picked out bath towels to match her newly painted walls as well as a white basket before they returned to her apartment.

He helped her set up the pedestals with the lanterns, with the basket on the floor in front. Her towels would be rolled inside once they were washed and dried. He also hung the cat postcard in a small spot in the hall while she supervised. Afterward, she called her parents as they waited for take-out from the Chinese place down the block.

He'd felt more settled and content that day than he had in years. Until it was time to kiss her goodnight and head home—alone. A good workout looked better and better. He'd need to exhaust himself so he could sleep without yearning for her beside him.

Chapter 17

Elizabeth typed a note into the schedule on her computer and closed the program. She pivoted her chair around to retrieve a file from the drawer behind her, but her eyes landed upon Grunt's picture and she stopped and smiled. It wasn't the same photo as when she started at Darcy Holdings. Though William wasn't in the picture, he'd taken this one not long after they began dating.

A month had passed since Christmas, since she stopped behaving like an immature child and faced her feelings for William. As much as she hated to admit it, Jane had been right. They'd been good for one another. He smiled more than before, something most of the women working at Darcy Holdings had noticed. She was more centered and not as quick to jump to conclusions. She never thought of herself as lonely before, but now, she was happier.

With her promotion looming, they'd decided to keep their budding relationship out of the office. They would be outed in some form or fashion eventually, but for the moment, the secret didn't bother her because it wasn't like he hid her out of shame. On warmer days, they walked in the park, they went to the movies last weekend, and they could often be found in the grocery store or the market, shopping for dinner. They simply hadn't bumped into anyone who would tell the world . . . yet.

After a quick knock, Charlotte walked in and rolled her eyes while she pressed the door shut behind her. "You're making that moony face again. You might want to nip that in the bud before the meeting. Otherwise, everyone will know you're knocking boots with someone after working hours."

Charlie, Charlotte, and Mrs. Reynolds remained the only employees at the company who knew of the relationship. She'd hated to hide such a significant part of her life from one of her best friends, but in hindsight, she probably should have. She lifted an eyebrow at Charlotte. "Really?"

"Well, you won't tell me, so I have to fish for my information. I just don't understand how he could still be so happy if you aren't. I mean the man would have to be turning blue."

Elizabeth crossed her arms over her chest. She wouldn't dignify that with a confirmation or denial. Charlotte would just have to live vicariously through someone else. "I have the department head meeting in ten minutes. Did you need something?"

"Oh! Grumpy! Maybe you aren't getting any." Elizabeth just glared until Charlotte's hands slid from her hips. "Oh, fine. I need the Kympton file. Mrs. Reynolds called down to ask that you have copies for everyone at the meeting."

The filing system had their most current projects near the front, so it only took a second to remove it from the drawer and pass it to her assistant.

"By the way, I dumped Bill last night."

Elizabeth stood but didn't hug Charlotte even though it was her first impulse. She didn't appear brittle but almost had this air of strength Elizabeth had never seen before. "Are you okay?"

"Oddly, I'm fine. I think I was with him because I didn't want to be alone. I didn't love him and watching you be so happy since you started seeing Mr. Darcy made me want something real instead. Now, I just need to find Mr. Right, if he exists."

"I'm sure he does."

Charlotte cleared her throat and held up the file. "I should get to the copy room. I'll deliver them as soon as I get them together along with your coffee. Don't wait for me."

"Okay." Charlotte hurried out of the door while Elizabeth gathered her tablet, a pen, and several more files she might need.

When she reached the boardroom, she took her usual seat as the rest of the department heads slowly filed in. Mr. Hurst entered and took the seat to her left. Instead of handing the entire job over at once, she was heading up the new business and slowly running more of the show. The department met once a week to update them both on current projects, but Elizabeth oversaw the meetings and made the decisions with Mr. Hurst present for advice if it was required. Some might have resented his continued presence, but she'd already learned so much from the man and appreciated any insights or information that would make her life easier.

"Did Denny complete those documents on time?" He'd leaned closer and spoke lower. Denny hadn't been thrilled to find his hoped-for spot was going to the newest hire and had challenged her recently. When William had found out, he'd wanted to fire the man, but she'd held him off, insisting she needed to earn the respect of the department herself. If Denny didn't come around, he could find employment elsewhere.

"It was on Charlotte's desk first thing this morning."

"Good girl."

Her breath caught in her lungs when William took the seat on her opposite side. "What was on Miss Lucas' desk this morning?"

"The paperwork for Kympton. I checked it over and it's all in order."

"Good," he said in almost a growl. "He knows better than to challenge a department head. He's lucky I didn't put him out on his ass."

"He's always been a good employee, or you wouldn't have considered him a possibility for my position. You can't terminate him for a first-time offense. With the exception of Mr. Hurst, he's the company attorney who's been here the longest. He might have thought the length of his employment made him a shoo-in."

"We've never promoted that way." Mr. Hurst shook his head. "Don't make excuses for him. He's competent, but he prefers to stay within his specialty and has never tried to learn each aspect of the department. That's a must for the job and no one had put forth any effort until you, and you'd already been doing the same at Longbourn. Denny will have to accept that he's the only person to blame for not getting the promotion. He may have been the top choice from within, but someone better qualified and more knowledgeable would've applied. He never had a chance."

"Hurst is correct." William dipped his chin down just a bit—just enough to level that no-nonsense look he used when he wanted to convince someone of his point of view.

"I understand. I promise I won't take any of his crap. Will that make the both of you happy?"

The two men glanced at one another and nodded. "Yes," they answered almost in unison.

The last department head entered, and the door closed behind her as William started the meeting. Elizabeth took notes and listened, trying not to be distracted by the man sitting to her right. The scent of his cologne proved enough to make her resist squirming in her seat, but she had to fight to keep her mind on topic—not the feel of his lips on hers, the way his muscles felt through his t-shirt. That designer suit hid one hell of a body. He was toned, but not big like a bodybuilder.

Five minutes into matters, Charlotte discreetly let herself in, set the copies in front of Elizabeth with her coffee, and departed without disrupting.

Elizabeth listened to the head of accounting's report when something brushed against her leg. She stiffened and straightened in her seat. Was that what she thought it was? The distinct form of a trouser leg pressed against her bare calf, and she swallowed the gasp. He'd never done that in a meeting before. Was he insane? What if someone noticed?

He removed it when she had to speak, but when she finished, his leg pressed right back against hers. She was going to kill him. Concentrating with him sitting beside her was difficult enough as it was without him trying to sneak a touch. When he finally adjourned the meeting, she pushed her chair back from the table and rose without a word.

It was William's voice that made her pause and turn. "Miss Bennet, I've had notification that your new office has been cleaned and is ready for you to move in. I believe Miss Lucas has been called and is prepping your files and belongings. I hoped to discuss the Kympton matter further once you're mostly settled. Perhaps lunch would be a good idea?"

Mr. Hurst stood behind her and one or two other department heads milled about waiting for William's ear, so she plastered a smile on her face. "Of course. Please set up the time and place with my assistant. If you'll excuse me."

Her former boss chuckled as they left the room, and she stopped and pivoted on her heel to face him. "What's so funny?"

"Why don't I show you your new office?"

She followed him to the same corridor where he worked but to the end of the hall where it opened into a small outer office. Charlotte stood behind her desk, unloading a box onto its surface. "Have you seen it yet? It's big."

"What? It can't be that big."

Charlotte led them into the next room, which wasn't nearly as spacious as William's office, but larger than Mr. Hurst's.

Hurst stepped around her and turned in a circle. "I worked as the assistant before I was promoted, but I never swapped offices. I didn't see the point. The last thing I wanted to do was move fifteen years' worth of files and books. I also never had a true assistant until you. I was told to notify personnel that I wished to interview for a replacement, but I delegated and never saw the need for one. After a number of years, the position was taken out of the budget and the money allocated elsewhere."

Several men from building maintenance entered, setting down a few boxes and her large mirror. She'd need more artwork for the walls in here. There was significantly more wall space.

"Miss, I'll hang that mirror for you later today." The older of the men pointed to the good-sized framed piece.

"Thank you." She smiled before he departed.

The box on top didn't weigh much, so she carried it to her desk and opened it. Her framed picture of Grunt was just inside, so she took it out and put it to one corner of her much grander desk. She set out her pen cup and the little bowls for her paper clips and other small items when Mr. Hurst leaned against her desk.

"How long have you and Darcy been seeing one another?"

She choked on her own spit, coughing until Charlotte hurried in with a bottle of water. "They put your mini-fridge in that cabinet. There was a place for electronics that happened to fit it perfectly. If you need more, it's in there."

"Thank you." She swallowed another gulp. "Charlotte, please close the door on your way out."

When she and Mr. Hurst had privacy, she kept her eyes on the contents of the box while she continued to set up her desk. "How did you find out?"

He crossed his arms over his chest. "People are morons if they don't sense the attraction from the two of you. I noticed it not long after you started, but you didn't seem to like Darcy. It was all I could do not to burst out laughing when you broke your mug glaring at him."

Her eyes darted up to meet his. "You knew?"

"Not until that day. I intended to keep an eye on the two of you, but I knew Darcy was fighting his feelings. I'm glad that the two of you worked things out, and I'm even happier that I didn't have to threaten him with a sexual harassment lawsuit."

"We're not telling people in the office."

"Given your recent promotion, that's smart. It will come out eventually, and some people will still question your position. You won't be able to prevent it." She blew out a long breath while the old man patted her shoulder. "Don't worry about it. It will all work out." He stood and scanned the desk like he'd forgotten something. "In the meantime, I have some files to sort so they can be moved into those enormous cabinets in the outer office, and you need to finish setting up your new desk. You know where I am if you need me."

"Mr. Hurst." He turned around while she fumbled with the stapler she'd removed from the box. "Thank you."

He winked and departed, allowing Charlotte back in when he opened the door. "Mrs. Reynolds called down. She said Mr. Darcy has reservations at Le Jardin at noon. You might want to head up to his office soon."

She emptied the last item from the box, her snow leopard calendar, which seemed out of place in such lofty surroundings. "Don't hang this. I think I'll bring it home." She looked down to where her purse normally was stowed under her desk.

"I'll need to go grab my purse."

Charlotte opened a cabinet behind her desk and pulled her purse from the shelf and then her coat from a small closet hidden behind the door. "You might want to go to that shop you like so much for some decoration. This place is pretty plain."

"I'll figure it out. Thanks." She glanced around Charlotte. "Is that my own bathroom? Why didn't Mr. Hurst want this office?"

"Who knows? It's great, though. That chair out there is the most comfortable one I've ever had. Seriously! I think it must have memory foam. It's amazing."

"You crack me up, Charlotte."

Her friend only waved with her fingers and grinned. "Have fun at lunch with the big boss man."

Elizabeth rolled her eyes while she walked down the much shorter route to the elevators, but took the stairs rather than wait.

Mrs. Reynolds didn't stand when Elizabeth reached the office, but did give a warm smile. "He's waiting for you."

She thanked the woman and continued through, closing the door behind her. He looked up from his work, and both dimples peeked out as he grinned while she set her belongings on the table. "What did you think you were doing during the meeting?"

"I couldn't resist touching you somehow." He rose and walked around his desk. "I've told you what those shoes do to me. What am I supposed to do when you intentionally provoke me?"

He'd caught her. She did know, but she loved those pink and black Jimmy Choo's. The way he admired her legs when she wore them was an added bonus.

His arm snaked around her waist, and he pulled her flush to him. "I did move when you needed to speak."

She cocked her eyebrow and pursed her lips. "I do need to think the rest of the time."

His cheek pressed to hers. "Touching you helped me concentrate." His breath elicited goosebumps down her neck. She shuddered.

"But were you thinking about work?"

A low chuckle vibrated along her spine. "You caught me." His lips trailed to that spot just under her ear, the one that made her shiver, and he kissed her there, ever so softly. "I'm sorry I distracted you. I won't do it again." He placed another searing kiss along her jawline before claiming her mouth. Her hands slid up his chest until one hand clenched his shoulder, and the fingers of the other were woven into his hair.

She lifted to her tiptoes to press herself closer as he deepened the kiss. She followed suit and flicked her tongue against his, which made him cup her rear and pull her to him as tightly as possible. They couldn't keep going like this. The door remained unlocked, and lately, they'd both been holding on by a thread. Elizabeth wanted to take things slowly, but that resolution slipped whenever he kissed her. Unless they were in public, a kiss was never the end of it. Her heart beat furiously, and her breath became more and more uneven when he began exploring the curve of her neck.

Her behind shifted along a solid surface, and she put a hand back to keep from falling. When had he set her on the table? Warm fingers caressed up her thigh until nothing stood between his palms and her panties. He pressed her against him, and one of her legs shifted up to hook on his hip.

"William." She sounded raspy and breathless. "William, we need to stop."

His lips returned to hers in a hard kiss while his hands shifted and clenched the flesh of her thighs. When he ended the kiss, he pressed his forehead against hers. "This is getting harder and harder."

"I'm sure it is." She bit her cheek to keep from laughing.

"I can show you exactly how hard." He growled the words into her ear, but she kissed his cheek and pushed him back so she could stand. With a giggle, she placed her hands on his face, wiping his lips with her thumbs. "Mrs. Reynolds is going to know what we've been up to in here."

He brushed a soft kiss to her fingertip. "She likes you, so she won't care. She'd have a problem if she walked in and caught us, though. I'd never hear the end of a lecture on locking the door."

"We should go to lunch before we get ourselves into trouble."

He fetched his coat and picked up hers before opening the door. "Trouble doesn't sound like such a bad thing," he said softly as she passed.

"Mrs. Reynolds, Miss Bennet and I are going, but I'll return before my two o'clock. Would you like me to bring something back for you?"

His assistant lifted her eyebrows and tapped her pen on the desk. "No, thank you. I brought lunch from home, but you two enjoy yourselves."

When they were in the elevator, William helped her with her coat before he put on his. The city had another cold snap move in, so the wind had a bite it hadn't possessed in the last week. As they exited the building, she put on her gloves and followed William down the block. Once they rounded the corner, he took her hand.

"Do you like your office?"

"I feel strange taking it with Mr. Hurst still working."

He stopped at the crosswalk to wait for the light. "Don't. He never wanted it. Besides, it makes it easier for you to have the office while he's still there."

"Has he said how much longer he intends to stay?"

The light turned green and they hurried across the street. Le Jardin was right on the corner, so he opened the door and ushered her inside. "I'm not sure. He originally told us March, then April, and lately, he's been saying May. His wife joked that he wouldn't know how to quit when the time came and it looks like she might be right. He's worked for the company for as long as I can remember, so I won't push him out. Are you ready for him to retire?"

"No, the team knows who their supervisor is on which projects, and I run the meetings and have learned about the projects he's finishing up. He's still teaching me a lot."

"Good."

When the maître d' showed them to their table, William's hand rested on the small of her back until she was seated. Their table was only for two, so he sat opposite her and stared for a moment. How did she ever think that was a look of dislike? He could set her on fire with the look in his eyes.

"William," she said in a sort of drawled out manner.

"Elizabeth." He grinned and relaxed back in his seat.

So much for the work discussion!

Chapter 18

Darcy unbuttoned his heavy coat with his free hand and pressed the doorbell. As soon as the chime rang through Elizabeth's apartment, the sound of something galloping followed by the tell-tale knock of the hall table against the wall followed, making him laugh under his breath. He'd never been much of a cat person, but Grunt was making him reconsider his position completely. The little guy definitely entertained him more than any dog he'd ever met.

The door opened, but Elizabeth wasn't standing on the other side when he pushed it wide enough to enter. "Elizabeth?"

"I'm not ready yet! I just need another couple of minutes."

Grunt looked up at him from his usual perch just inside the door, so Darcy scratched behind his ears, and the cat made the little groan he usually did before breaking out into purrs.

"Let's put these flowers in some water." He closed the door behind him, and Grunt hopped down from the table to follow him into the kitchen where Darcy threw his coat on a barstool and pulled down a cut-glass vase from the cabinet. The cat tried to stick his face inside while Darcy filled it, but only sniffed until he set it on the counter.

Once the bouquet of red, pink, and white roses filled the container, he set it on the middle of the island while Grunt smelled the rim. The twerp was more than likely trying to figure out how to get around the stems to the water inside.

"What did you do?"

He froze in his spot when his eyes rested upon her. The midnight blue velvet dress hugged her hips before it draped around her amazing legs, the slit up one side giving a tantalizing peek of what was hidden beneath. The wide off the shoulder collar showed barely a hint of cleavage with a sparkling sapphire snowflake pendant drawing the eye just above the neckline. She'd pulled her hair into a bun that rested behind her ear on one side with tendrils of curls falling from the arrangement. "You look incredible."

Her face pinked, and her hand brushed over her stomach. "Thank you. I know it's more wintery than Valentine's, but I fell in love with the dress when I found it. Erika helped with the pendant. It's a broach, but we added a chain so I could wear it like a necklace."

"Blue is my favorite color." He shifted around the island and stepped closer, fingering her dangling sapphire colored earring.

That giggle he adored burst from her lips. "I thought your favorite color was red."

He kissed her cheek right next to her ear. "My favorite color is whatever you happen to be wearing."

"My grandmother would call you a sweet talker. You didn't need to buy me flowers."

"I haven't bought you a present since Christmas. I think I'm due for Valentine's Day. I didn't buy you jewelry or a car, after all."

"Thank goodness for that! But I think there's more than a dozen there."

"I'm not telling," he said. "Roses are also safe in the event Grunt decides to take a nibble."

Her head gave a slight hitch back. "You looked it up?"

"I did."

She grazed her teeth along her bottom lip. "We might want to put the vase in the sink while we're gone. Just in case he decides to get too curious."

After the roses were mostly Grunt-proof, they put on their coats and made their way down to the Rolls Royce parked along the curb. He'd warned Carson in advance that he wanted to open the door for Elizabeth, so his driver remained in his seat.

They settled themselves in, and Darcy entwined his fingers with hers. "Did you bring your ticket?"

"I did. Are you going to tell me what you have planned for afterward?"

He smiled and shook his head. "No, you're just going to have to wait to find out."

She held his gaze for a moment, then brought his hand to her lap where she stared, quiet.

"Is something wrong?"

"No." Her whisper was so soft, he had to lean in to hear it. She looked up and her eyes were glassy.

"Something is wrong. Why are you upset? Whatever it is, I'll either fix it or kick their ass."

A laugh burst from her, and she reached up to place her palm on his cheek. "I'm not upset. Nothing is wrong. I'm simply overwhelmed by how right things have been since we began seeing each other."

He pressed a kiss to her fingers, but when he opened his mouth to speak, she put a finger over his lips.

"I know you said it first, but I wanted to be certain before I said it back." She leaned over and brushed a kiss across his lips. "I love you." The words were whispered, but their effect was anything but quiet. His entire body stiffened, every nerve fired, and his heart began to beat frantically against his ribs. She watched him for a moment, but all he could do was look at her. Had she really just said what he thought she said?

"William, say something. I'm starting to feel a little self-conscious."

"Did you say 'I love you'?" He wrapped his arms around her while she nodded. "I love you too. I'm sorry I didn't respond right away. I guess I didn't expect it so soon. You surprised me."

"I suppose seven weeks is soon for some."

"For others, it can be a lifetime." He caressed her cheek with his thumb. "The more time I spend with you, the further I fall. I don't know if I'll ever find an end. I'm not sure one exists."

She pulled him closer by the lapel, and he lost himself in the sweet pressure of her lips as her breathing gradually quickened. When she pushed him away, she glanced toward the front seat. "I don't want to make Carson uncomfortable."

One side of his lips tugged upward. "Carson is paid not to watch."

"Ha, ha. He still has ears. He can hear what we're doing back here."

"Actually, he keeps a headphone in one ear to listen to his own music. He always has. You can't see it in the dark, but it's usually the one to the middle of the car. He keeps the other free for safety purposes."

She leaned against his side, and he wrapped his arm around her shoulders. "I'll make it up to you. I promise to kiss you for as long as you like when we get home."

The word home stirred something in his stomach. How he wished he could really take her home! Not to a small apartment a few blocks away but to his house. They could cuddle up on the sofa while they watched television or worked in the evening, they could cook dinner together, and he could wake up to the sight of her sleeping beside him every morning, her face buried near his neck and her breath blowing against his skin in little puffs.

He'd spent the night at her place more and more since Christmas, though they never moved past sleeping. She'd wanted to take things slowly, and he wanted nothing more than her happiness which made it more than reasonable to wait. He hadn't dated in two years. He'd been celibate this long—what was a few more months?

When they reached the theater, Carson opened the door, and Darcy handed Elizabeth from the car, placing his hand on the small of her back as he steered her inside. An usher showed them to their seats, and once they were settled, Elizabeth scanned the interior with eager eyes.

He leaned closer, the scent of her perfume tickling his nostrils. "Have you ever seen *Phantom of the Opera?*"

"Once, when I was sixteen. My father took me for my birthday. I'd loved the music before, but it was amazing in person." She gave that impish grin he loved. "The Phantom was terrible, though."

"How so?"

"He breathed by giving a great heaving gasp at the end of every line he sang. I had a hard time not giggling when he was on stage. My father and I still make jokes about it."

"But you enjoyed it?"

"Definitely. The effects were still fantastic, as well as the dancing and the rest of the performers, but we didn't have such great seats." She pointed to one side of the balcony. "We sat up there. My father didn't own opera glasses, so he brought a pair of binoculars. I refused to use them. I was sixteen and embarrassed because they weren't like what everyone else had."

"Did that upset him?"

"No, he rolled his eyes and laughed. He enjoys human idiosyncrasies. I was just one more thing to find interesting while he watched the room instead of the show. He's not a fan of musicals, but he knew my mother would make me crazy by the end of the night. She doesn't know how to whisper softly."

He smiled. Since they'd been dating, Elizabeth had spoken to her mother on more than one occasion, and he'd heard every last bit—her mother's side of the conversation as well.

The lights dimmed, and she sat straighter in her seat as the actors took the stage. He tried to watch the play, but too many distractions pulled him away: Elizabeth's arm pressed against his during parts of the performance, the soft flesh of her hand as he caressed it with his fingers, and, at times, her rapt attention at the stage during the intense moments.

He offered her a glass of wine during the intermission, but she refused it, afraid she'd be bouncing in her seat with the need for the restroom before the finale if she did.

When the play ended, Carson waited with the car along the curb. How he'd managed to squeeze in with the taxis was a mystery, but they didn't question it. As soon as the door closed behind them, Elizabeth opened her mouth to speak, but Darcy covered it with his own. He'd wanted to kiss her for the last two hours and didn't want to wait another minute!

She didn't argue or push him away, but let him continue. Lips teased, tongues tangled, and her little panting breaths against his cheek drove him crazy—crazy enough to slide his hand up her leg until his thumb grazed her panties. Good Lord, were those lace?

Her hands clenched at the shoulders of his coat as a small noise came from her throat, which only made him more desperate. His fingers slipped under the lace to the velvet soft skin he hadn't laid eyes on yet.

A strange sound permeated the lust induced fog that had taken over his brain and he paused. What was that? Then it happened again. Carson cleared his throat, so Darcy kissed Elizabeth's nose while he withdrew his hand from her skirt. "What is it, Carson?"

"I beg your pardon, sir, but we've arrived and you do have reservations."

"Thank you." His voice was rough, but Carson didn't comment, particularly considering how carried away they'd become. Even in the minimal amount of light coming in through the windows, Elizabeth's complexion was a brilliant shade of red.

Carson got out and opened the door while Darcy watched Elizabeth touch her lips. He took several deep breaths, trying to calm himself enough to emerge from the car. When he finally stood, he helped Elizabeth out, but before he could lead her inside, she dragged him over to a dark window.

"What are you doing?"

"I don't want to go in looking like we've been making out in the back of a car."

He couldn't help the grin that looked absolutely ridiculous in the blackened window. "But we have been making out in the backseat of a car." She slapped his arm and pressed her stomach. "I can't believe we did that. I forgot Carson was even there. I'm so embarrassed."

"Sweetheart, all we did was kiss."

She leaned closer, the scent of her perfume doing nothing to help him forget how she felt in his arms. "You had your hand in my panties."

"It was dark, he didn't see, and all I did was touch your hip. I didn't touch anything more private."

"I suppose I should be grateful for that. What if I moaned or made some horrifying noise?"

Darcy laughed and wrapped an arm around her lower back. "God, I would have lost my mind. I was holding on by a thread as it was."

She gave herself one last glance in the window. "My lips might be a little swollen, but there's not much I can do about that."

He drew her towards the entrance of the restaurant. "Let's go inside. I don't want to spend all evening looking in a store window." He held the door open for her, but his hand found its way back to the small of her back once they were inside. The entry was dimly lit, romantic. Just like he'd wanted.

"Do I look okay?"

He gazed down into her eyes and lifted his eyebrows.

"Do I look like you've been sucking on my lips?" She spoke right next to his ear in a low tone. Her breath grazing the sensitive skin did nothing to help settle him. In fact, the mention of what they'd just been doing did the opposite.

His thumb traced over her pouty bottom lip. "They might be a little pink, but I wouldn't worry about it. I doubt anyone will notice."

The hostess approached, and they were quickly seated in the far corner of the dining room. He'd reserved the booth specifically since it was partially secluded from the rest of the diners. He hadn't wanted to spend the night surrounded by people. He'd only wanted to spend it with Elizabeth.

Their waiter appeared for their drink order, they settled on a bottle of wine, and he hurried off to put the order in while Darcy watched her read the menu.

She glanced up. "Do you know what you want already?"

"No, I became distracted. You look beautiful."

Her cheeks colored to match her lips. "And you're very handsome, but decide what you want. I'm hungry." He laughed and made a quick perusal of the menu, closing it and setting it next to his plate when he'd decided.

"William?"

The familiar voice drew his gaze from Elizabeth, and he stood to hug his little sister. "What are you doing here?"

"Well, you know, it is Valentine's Day. I guess Jacob had the same idea as you."

When Ana peeked around him, he shifted to the side so she could see Elizabeth. "Ana Darcy, I'd like you to meet Elizabeth Bennet."

Ana smiled and nodded. "I've heard so much about you. It's nice to finally meet you in person."

"Well, that's rather frightening." Elizabeth laughed. "I hope he hasn't told you anything too bad. If he has, I might have to accuse him of lying."

Georgiana's eyebrows rose on her forehead as he chuckled and shook his head. "Don't believe her. She enjoys teasing me."

"See, now he's telling you not to trust me." Elizabeth crossed her arms over her chest and quirked that eyebrow.

Ana giggled. "I can tell you're doing wonders for my brother. He jokes with me or Charlie but rarely anyone else. I hope we can get together for coffee sometime? I'd love to get to know you better."

"I'd love that," said Elizabeth. "Your brother has my cell phone number, or if anything else, you know where I work."

Ana laughed and motioned to a table on the other side of the restaurant. "I have to get back to Jacob. It's good to finally meet you, Elizabeth. I'll call you about that coffee." Ana gave him a crooked grin as she turned to him and kissed his cheek. "Don't do anything I wouldn't do."

Elizabeth watched Ana as she walked away. "Your sister seems sweet."

He took his seat while he turned to watch Jacob steer Ana from the restaurant. "She is. She can be pretty silly once you get to know her, but she's not too open with people she's just met."

The waiter returned to pour their wine and left just as swiftly as he arrived, leaving them to their conversation about the play and Elizabeth's comparison of the Phantom from when she was sixteen to tonight's performance. When they'd exhausted the subject, they turned to books and movies, which managed to carry them through dinner.

By the time they returned to the car, every cell and nerve ending in his body was on edge. Each evening they spent together made saying goodnight more difficult, especially on those nights he returned to his own home. He held her hand on the ride back, but they were both quiet. Why was that? It had been a wonderful evening. They hadn't lacked for conversation at the theater or at dinner, but now, Elizabeth stared out of the window.

When the car pulled to the curb in front of her building, Carson opened the door on her side, and she looked over her shoulder. "You're coming in for coffee, right?"

He scooted across the seat and followed her out. "Carson, I'll message you if I need you. If it becomes too late, I can always take a cab."

"Very good, sir."

Darcy trailed behind her into the elevator, but once the doors closed, she put both hands on his chest and stood on her tiptoes.

"What are you doing?"

She didn't answer, only grinned as she ducked down to brush her lips just above the collar of his shirt. His hands found her waist under the wool of her coat and gripped while she grazed her teeth along his jawline and suckled his earlobe.

The doors opened and she backed out, her eyes imploring him to follow and his feet didn't hesitate to move. She unlocked her door and peered over her shoulder as she walked inside, dropping her keys onto the table, completely ignoring Grunt, who stood on his usual perch.

Her shoes landed near the wall, he wasn't sure where since he was too preoccupied with her face. She hadn't said a word, but did she know what that expression screamed to his already sex-deprived brain?

Her coat slipped from her shoulders, and when she reached behind her, he cleared his throat. "Elizabeth? I know what this looks like, but I just want to be certain."

Her husky laugh burned through him like a swallow of fine scotch. "I hope it looks like me seducing you."

The gorgeous midnight blue velvet loosened around her chest before it dropped to her feet. "Good Lord, are you trying to kill me?" He'd known that when this moment came he would fight for control, but he hadn't counted on sheer lace in the nearly the same color as her dress.

Elizabeth stepped forward and removed his coat and suit coat, letting them fall to his feet with her clothes. "I hope not. I have plans for you tonight." While she worked out the knot in his tie, his hands slipped around her trim waist. "You aren't just going to stand there, are you?" Her voice was low and had a breathy quality she didn't normally possess. The sound drew him closer. He needed to feel her against him, skin on skin.

His heart stuttered into a quicker rhythm while he toed off his shoes and bent down to kiss her jawline. "Are you sure?" His lips trailed along the column of her neck to her collarbone. She shivered as he lightly bit her.

"Positive." His tie came loose, and she pulled it from his collar before going to work on the buttons. Before he knew it, his shirt was wide open and her hands trailed along his sides to his back. His lips attacked hers, his tongue finding its way to touch hers while his arms pressed her as close as he could to his body.

Lord, she molded to him like she was made to be there. The scent of lavender filling his nostrils only made her more real, more tangible somehow, and he grasped the flesh of her buttocks, clasping her tightly to him. His mind was on overload and he couldn't think of anything more than Elizabeth's toned body crushed against him and how to draw her closer, so close they might never come apart.

A high-pitched breath escaped when she pulled her mouth from his and began to yank the shirt from his arms. He released her so she could pull the sleeves over his hands, but they became stuck. "Cufflinks." The words came out mumbled while he fumbled to reach them. They were easily removed, and his shirt joined the rest of their clothing while the cufflinks were put on the table next to a staring Grunt.

"Maybe we should move this where we don't have an audience." He lifted her, and she wrapped her legs around his waist, taking possession of his lips and making it dreadfully difficult to find his way. After one stumble and subsequent bump into the wall, he made it to the bedroom. His legs hit the edge of the mattress, so he lowered them onto the bed, lifting up from her so he could see her more clearly. "I hope I get more than one chance at this."

A chuckle bubbled from her lips. "Why wouldn't you?"

"Because I'm not going to last very long. I'm already hanging on by a string."

She sat up and began to unbuckle his belt, spreading tiny pecks along his waistline while she unzipped the fly. He was going to burst from his skin if she kept it up. Her assertiveness was sexy as hell and each additional thing she did to move things along only turned him on more. Before she could take things further, he dragged her up so he could kiss her properly as he pressed her back onto the bed.

For a breather, he lifted himself from her again to remove his pants and socks. When he settled on top of her, he propped himself on his elbows, relieving her of some of his weight. They had done so little, but already he was breathing hard, his heart beat a mile a minute . . . and wait . . . when had she removed her bra?

From there, it was a blur. Somehow the last of their clothing was removed, and they managed to get under the covers. His lips wandered so he could taste and suckle all those bits that had been so cruelly hidden away while his hand slid down to places he'd never ventured, places that made her writhe and make these noises in the back of her throat—noises that promised she enjoyed what he was doing as much as he did. It had to have been the hottest thing he'd ever seen, her half-open eyes, struggling to watch him until the very last second when her back arched off the mattress, she shuddered, and went limp. He'd never tire of seeing it. She was so beautiful.

He'd been correct, however. Once he'd given in to temptation and buried himself deep into her warmth, no more than five minutes passed before he roared and dropped on top of her, apologizing.

She brushed his hair back from his face. "Stop it. We talked about how long it had been for both of us. I didn't expect you to go for hours, you know."

"You expect me to go for hours?" His voice was breathless. "You have great expectations of my abilities." Her tiny laugh made his heart feel like it would burst.

"I love you." He brushed his lips against hers tenderly.

"I love you too. You can make it up to me next time." She gave a wicked grin. "And the time after that, and the time after that."

"Then we aren't sleeping tonight?"

She looked toward the ceiling and screwed up her face like she was thinking. "Maybe, but I doubt it."

His fingers attacked her sides, and she giggled uproariously.

"Stop! Please! I can't take it anymore."

He propped his head on his hand, content to stay right there and watch her. He loved her so much and being here in this moment with her was perfect. "Move in with me." The words had popped out, and he stiffened. Would she reject the idea outright? Would she feel he was pushing? They might have only just slept together but that didn't mean he hadn't thought about her moving into his house more and more the last two weeks. They were consenting adults. Why shouldn't they live together?

She bit her lip, and her eyes studied his. "Isn't it too soon?"

"Maybe to some, but not for me. We can work up to it, or if you need to wait, I'll understand."

"Yes."

"Yes?"

She nodded and laughed. "Yes."

He lunged down and claimed her lips. He hadn't meant for it to lead to anything quite so soon, but well, who was he to argue when it did?

Chapter 19

Light slowly penetrated his eyelids and he groaned. They hadn't closed the blinds before they'd fallen asleep. What time was it anyway? And what was that on his chest? It couldn't be Elizabeth because her body wasn't curled alongside his, and her head wasn't on his shoulder. He blinked and looked straight into the golden eyes of Grunt, who sat like a Sphinx on the middle of his chest.

"What are you doing?" The cat didn't blink but continued to stare. "Are you going to kill me in my sleep?" He scratched behind Grunt's ears, and the little black monster began to purr. After a minute or two, Grunt stood, arched his back with a yawn, and hopped off the bed.

Darcy scanned the room. Where had Elizabeth gone? He pushed himself up from the mattress and ran a hand through his hair while he glanced around for an article of clothing. Part of a pant leg peeked out from beneath the bed, so he threw the covers off, sat on the edge, and bent over to pull them out, his boxer briefs tagging along for the ride. Once he'd slipped on his underwear, he made a quick trip to the bathroom and brushed his teeth before venturing into the living room.

A metal clank came from the direction of the kitchen, so he headed that way. Right before he rounded the corner into the living room, he halted in his tracks. What was that? Leaning against the wall, he stayed where he was, his ears trained on the sound he'd never heard before in his life. Was that Elizabeth singing?

She'd never made an attempt in front of him before, and he could certainly understand why! He pressed his lips together to stifle a laugh. Her voice was dreadful! She crooned *Music of the Night* along with a recording of Michael Crawford, but she was way off key and likely gasped as badly as the Phantom from when she was sixteen!

He peered around the wall. Her back was turned, so he tiptoed up behind her and wrapped his arms around her. "I didn't know you liked to sing."

"Oh no." The words came out in a groan as she covered her face with her hands.

His shoulders shook while he turned her around. "Let me tell you a secret." Her fingers parted, so one eye peeked out. "I didn't fall in love with you for your singing."

"Ow!" He flinched at the sharp pain of her fingers delivering a nasty pinch to his side. "I love you." He grabbed her wrist and shifted his hand up to lace their fingers together. "Are you really going to move in with me?"

"Unless you've changed your mind since last night. But, if you continue to make fun of my singing, I might have to reconsider."

"I love your singing." He nuzzled that part of her neck just behind her ear. "I want to hear you sing in my shower." He kissed the shell of her ear. "I want to hear you sing in my kitchen." He kissed her nose, wiggling his eyebrows. "But most of all, I want to hear you sing in my bed."

She chuckled and backed away, checking on something in the oven. "When do you want me to move in?"

"Tonight." No pause happened between her question and his answer. Was that definite enough?

"We can't just move everything today. I've lived here for years. I also have to put my furniture into storage and talk to my uncle. I know he won't sell it, but his oldest daughter starts college this year. She might want to live here." She pulled what looked like a coffee cake from the oven and set it on the island.

"Elizabeth, we don't have to rush to empty your apartment—especially if it makes you uneasy. Whenever you decide you can live with my bad habits permanently, we'll talk about moving your furniture into the house. We have plenty of room. You can use some of your décor for your office if you want. I can even help you bring some of it on Monday. Carson can drive us here first to pick a few things up."

"It's not simply a matter of me packing a bag and coming over. There's Grunt to consider."

"So, pack up his food, his bowls, and a litter box. He'll love having so much to explore."

She rested her forehead against his chest. "You're certain this is what you want?"

"I wouldn't have asked if I had doubts, but if you're not sure, we can wait."

"I suppose I'm nervous, but I'm happy about it. I've always liked it when you stayed with me, and I don't sleep as well when you aren't here." She kissed him on the lips and went back to the stove, turning on the burner for the espresso maker.

"What makes you nervous?"

"Just the change of it all. You also have a housekeeper who does your laundry and cooks for you. I don't know how she'll feel about me sharing her kitchen, and I can't imagine her washing my unmentionables."

"You have unmentionables?"

"Lingerie, like what I wore last night. What if I buy more? She's going to think I'm some easy tramp."

He pressed his lips together to keep from laughing, walked up behind her, and wrapped his arms around her. "Mrs. Hill is married. I'm sure she has a few unmentionables of her own, though I don't want to dwell on it. If it makes you that uneasy, you can go down when she isn't using the washer and run a load yourself. It's not a big deal."

He kissed the point where her neck and shoulder met. "As for the kitchen, Mrs. Hill would never keep you from cooking when you feel the urge. She'd probably offer to help you and would definitely clean the mess. The two of you will have to figure that out. It's not like I eat a gourmet meal every night when I'm home. Some nights, I merely want a salad or a sandwich, so I message her and let her know so she won't go to any trouble."

"I suppose that makes sense."

"I can't wait to see you in my kitchen, dressed just as you are now, singing and making us breakfast." His hand slipped under the soft, long-sleeved top she wore and caressed her belly.

"Even my ratty pajama bottoms."

"Even the ratty pajama bottoms." He closed his eyes and inhaled the scent that would always be her, be Elizabeth.

"Would you get me the milk, please?"

He pressed one more kiss to her head. "Of course."

When she had their coffees prepped, they sat side-by-side at the island but facing one another while they shared a plate of gooey pecan coffee cake, Elizabeth's legs resting across his lap. He was more content than he could ever remember, and they were doing nothing more than eating breakfast.

"Why don't we take a trip to the pet store for some things for Grunt later?"

"What do you think he needs?"

He gave a lopsided shrug. "My house is much bigger. We might have more than one litter box to be on the safe side. He also might like having a kitty tower in several rooms. I've noticed he's pretty good about sharpening his claws on them, and it might keep him from ruining the furniture. I don't think the leather sofas in the media room will tolerate it."

"You're probably right. It might be better to close off most of the house at first, too. We can introduce him to more rooms as time goes by and we see how he does." While they spoke of the feline fur ball, Grunt finished his own meal and plopped down on the island to groom himself.

"Mrs. Hill won't be too fond of this."

"I wipe down my counters a lot. I thought I could keep him off of them at first, but he never cared whether I wanted him there or not. He knows I have food and he's bent on discovering whether or not he wants to eat it."

He grinned and sighed. He loved this, spending time with her without demands on his time and presence and wanted to do it every day. Work would undoubtedly get in the way on occasion, but maybe on weekends?

They finished their meal while discussing how the day would go, he helped her wash dishes, and they decided to conserve water by showering together. As much as he wanted to do more than just shower, he kept it clean despite how much certain parts of his body protested.

They packed Elizabeth's largest suitcase, a garment bag with her winter clothes and necessities, and a smaller bag for her bathroom supplies. As they finished, Carson arrived with an ice chest and several boxes that they used to pack up her groceries while he took the luggage down to a van on the curb.

Grunt was the last to be packed up. He'd stuck his nose into everything while they bagged up his food, extra litter, and his toys before he reluctantly went into his carrier.

When they exited the building, she looked over her shoulder. "Where did you get the van?"

"It belongs to the company. Carson drove over and picked it up before he came here. We can make as many trips as you like today or we can move things a bit at a time. It's completely up to you." They buckled into the second row since the remaining benches had been removed for her belongings.

She bit her bottom lip and held his hand a little tighter. "Do you have room for my clothes or should I wait until we get everything figured out?"

"I thought we might move into my parents' room. Ana and I finally cleaned it out a few months ago. It needs to be redecorated and we need to pick out a new mattress, but it's substantially bigger than my room and has more closet space."

"Maybe as we find room for things, we can bring them over," she said. Her hand rested on the top of Grunt's carrier where he pressed his head against the zipper and Velcro closure trying to bust out.

When they arrived at the house, Carson and Mrs. Hill helped them unload what was in the van before Carson took it around the corner to be parked. Since they might need it for some of their errands, they didn't want to return the large vehicle before the trip to the pet store.

Once they were inside, Mrs. Hill bustled down to the kitchen to put away the groceries while Darcy took Elizabeth and Grunt to the laundry room in the basement. They set up his litter box, then took him out of his carrier for him to explore. He sniffed around for a while before he decided the laundry room wasn't exciting enough for his tastes and ventured out.

Darcy walked ahead of him, shutting doors so Grunt was contained to certain rooms for the time being. When he trotted up the stairs to the main floor, the formal dining room and living rooms were shut off, along with the media room, the study, and the spare bedrooms upstairs.

Elizabeth paused in the family room and glanced around. "Do you mind if I put the kitty tower near the window? With the small courtyard and the bird feeders, he'll want to spend a lot of time staring outside."

"I'll go get it."

Before Darcy could turn around, she grabbed his arm. "I can carry it around, you know."

"You keep an eye on him. Let the man do the heavy lifting." He flexed his bicep and she chuckled. "Don't laugh. That won't help my ego."

"I wasn't laughing at the muscle. I was laughing at what you said. Besides, I don't think your ego has suffered."

He gave her a smacking kiss on the lips and headed to the foyer.

Elizabeth grinned as he walked out. He had one heck of an ass! A chirrup made her turn to Grunt, who now sat in between the open curtains, staring into the garden. Hopefully, he wouldn't try to attack the birds through the glass when spring came.

When William put the kitty tower in its new home, Grunt hopped to the top and sat, becoming perfectly still while he watched outside. In her apartment, he'd always been up rather high, so being so much lower to the ground must have been fascinating for him.

She leaned against the arm of the sofa. "I doubt he'll go far. We'll need to decide where to put his food and water and show him when he finally decides to pay us attention again."

William grabbed her hand and tugged her towards the stairs. "We should unpack your clothes."

She swallowed down the fluttering in her stomach. Yes, she was nervous, but she wanted this. She couldn't explain why, but she did. They'd managed to take things slow for a time, but they'd suddenly accelerated from thirty miles per hour to one hundred overnight. That alone was enough to discombobulate anyone.

When they turned down the first hallway, William opened the first set of doors. The interior was dark, but light filtered in between the closed draperies. He pulled them open and stood to face her, putting his hands in his pockets.

"This was my parents' room. I haven't redecorated it yet. Unless you feel it doesn't suit, I'd like to keep the bedroom furniture. Other than that, the walls need to be painted or papered, the bed needs a new mattress and bedding, and the bathroom needs to be repainted. I love the way you decorated your apartment, so I'm not worried about what you choose. You don't need to ask my approval if you find something you like."

She looked around, running her fingers along the foot of the cherry finish sleigh bed. The room was enormous and between the bedroom area and the small sitting room, her entire apartment could probably fit inside. Matching end tables, a dresser, a chest of drawers, and an armoire all could've made the space feel tiny but didn't.

She walked over to the sitting area. The sofa and chairs were obviously older, though taken care of. They only appeared slightly faded in places. When she moved to the bathroom, she paused in the door. "The tile is black and white like mine." She turned excitedly. "Do you mind if I paint it the same color as my bathroom at the apartment?"

"Of course not. I complimented how well it all went together. Do you remember?"

"I do, but my apartment isn't as grand as this house. I didn't know if you'd want it to a certain aesthetic."

He wrapped his arms around her from behind. "My parents kept the formal dining room and living room a certain way for entertaining business associates, but I never invited any here after their death. I always found it easier to have dinner at a restaurant. I love how comfortable your apartment is so I wouldn't mind if our room ended up resembling your place."

"You do realize that all we need is the mattress, the bedding, and the paint? I love the bedroom set and we could use my sofa, chairs, and coffee table in the sitting area. We could buy a mattress while we're out, as well as sheets and quilts. We could even pick out paint. Jane and I could set to work next weekend."

"No, I'll pay someone to paint during the week. I don't want to wait. I also don't want to lose you to a day of manual labor." She turned in his arms and wrapped her arms around his neck. He wore a soft expression, his lips turned up a bit at the ends. "Do you think you could be happy here?"

Elizabeth ran her hands through the back of his thick hair. "I don't need a huge house to be happy. Lately, all I've needed is you."

His hands framed her face as he pulled her in to claim her lips, pressing his forehead to hers when he was done. "I love you."

"I love you too." She curled her fingers into a few of his locks. "I do have one request."

"What's that?"

She pointed to a painting on the wall over the bed. "Is that a painting of your parents?"

"Yes."

"Can we find it a new home? I don't want to seem insensitive by asking, but I don't think I can be intimate with you while your mom watches. There are just some things a mother should never see her little boy do—even if it is just a painting." His head dropped against her neck, and his shoulders shook.

"Please tell me you're laughing."

He nodded. "Mm-hm."

"Okay, good. You had me worried for a second."

Still laughing, he lifted his head, both dimples showing. "If you hadn't suggested it, I probably would've moved it the first time I noticed it. I'm honestly glad you thought of it." He brushed his lips against hers. "We should probably get out and shop rather than unpack your bags. We have a lot to take care of."

Several hours passed while Carson drove them from store to store. When they returned, Mrs. Hill had dinner waiting for them so they could eat before they sorted out her belongings in their new room. They unpacked the most important items and left the rest, putting it all downstairs in storage until their room was finished. By the end of the evening, they made love and promptly fell asleep in William's room, leaving the door cracked so Grunt could find his way in and out during the night. They wanted to wait until the new mattress arrived and the room was painted to really make the room theirs.

Elizabeth groaned and shifted closer to William. Why was someone making that racket? She cracked her eyes enough to see light filtering in through the curtains. Was it morning already? Just a few more minutes and she would get out of bed.

The noise happened again. "William?"

The voice was familiar. It wasn't William's sister, was it? She'd barely pulled the sheet over her breasts before whoever it was walked in, stopped short, and covered her eyes with her hands. "My eyes!"

William jumped and sat up. "Ana?"

"Yes, it's me! Why in the world would you leave the door open?"

"Because of the cat."

"What cat?"

Almost as if on cue, Grunt stood from his place at Elizabeth's feet, arched his back in a huge stretch, and chirruped before he dropped to the floor and trotted to stand in front of Ana. He sat and stared.

"That cat," said William, dryly while Elizabeth burst into giggles.

"It isn't funny!" The statement came from William and Ana at the same time, which only made Elizabeth laugh harder.

Chapter 20

Christmas Eve one year later . . .

Two hands snaked around Elizabeth's waist as she put on her earrings. "Happy Anniversary Eve." She gazed down to a familiarly wrapped package held in William's left hand.

"Anniversary Eve?"

"Yes, the day before our anniversary. Tomorrow, we'll have been seeing each other for one year."

She turned in his arms. "I know that, but does it really warrant a gift? Tomorrow *is* Christmas after all and, after the way you shopped for my birthday, I'm kind of worried about how many presents will be under the tree in the morning."

He kissed her nose. "That's because I thoroughly expect to spoil you rotten tomorrow, too. You should know that by now—and you can't argue either, because it's Christmas." He pressed his forehead to hers. "I wanted to do this tonight. I guess to sort of replace the remembrance of last year with a better memory."

"Attending the company holiday party with me isn't enough? I've also told you that you should only remember the good parts of the past and leave the negative behind."

One shoulder shrugged upward. "I know, but this is a guaranteed improvement."

"Guaranteed?" She couldn't help but smile when she looked back at the gift. The wrapping paper had the same holiday scene, like one from a Regency print, and was a similar size to the familiar boxes from last year's Advent calendar.

She took the present and moved to sit on the side of the bed, putting the gift in her lap, while William stood before her, his hands stuffed inside his pockets. He didn't say a word but waited for her to open it. She peeled back the paper to the white box and set the wrapping aside.

With two hands she removed the lid, but as she pulled out tufts of tissue, William dropped to one knee in front of her.

Her heart began pumping furiously, pounding in her ears as she looked back down to the contents of the box. Sure enough, a small black case sat inside with an HW on the logo. "What? No Tiffany's?"

He laughed that low rich chuckle that made her insides melt. "No, anyone can get Tiffany's. I decided you needed Harry Winston."

"Harry Winston?" The words squeaked from her lips as he reached inside and pulled it out. He opened the flaps and held out the most exquisite round cut diamond engagement ring she'd ever seen. It wasn't so big it would engulf her finger, but it wasn't a chip either. The setting was simple and elegant, which is what she preferred. Her head began to swim and she put a hand on the bed. She couldn't faint! William would never let her hear the end of it if she did!

William cleared his throat. "You know I'm not the best when it comes to flowery words, but here it goes. Elizabeth Bennet, I think I fell in love with you the moment I first laid eyes on you, and since then, I haven't been able to look away. You're everything I need. You make me laugh, you make my heart beat faster, and you inspire me to be better than I am. When I see you, I see my future—the mother of my children and the woman I want to grow old with. You mean the world to me, and I intend to prove that to you every day we're together. Will you marry me?"

At some point while he spoke, her eyes burned and flooded with tears. One dropped to her cheek and forged a warm trail to her chin where he brushed it away with his thumb. "I hope those are happy tears."

All she could manage to do was nod. She took his face in her hands and pulled him up so she could kiss him. Her lips claimed his, and she quickly deepened the kiss, their tongues tangling as she became heated and needy, wanting him with everything in her. Impatient to feel him, she pulled him between her legs, and her skirt parted at the slit, riding up to her hips while she poured everything she had into the embrace.

One of his hands grasped her rear, and she shifted in an attempt to get closer. God, she wanted him right now! Hips began to move, hers without conscious thought, but when he drew back with his eyes closed, she groaned in protest.

His forehead rested against hers while his breath came out in pants. "While I don't have any objection to where this is going, does this mean yes?"

She nodded, unbuttoning his pants and shucking them down his hips. "Yes! Definitely, yes!"

Before she could slip her hands into his boxer briefs, he grabbed her left hand. "Not so fast." He took the ring from its package and slipped it on her finger. "Before I drop the box and lose this, I want to put it where it belongs. I'm having a hard time not letting go so I can touch you."

As soon as he saw the ring settled on her finger, he slipped off her panties and filled her with himself and all the love he had to give. The interlude may have been quick, but he made sure she found satisfaction before he collapsed on top of her, his weight anchoring her to the mattress. She loved that feeling. She never wanted it to end.

"I love you so much."

He lifted himself on an elbow, wiping the tears from her cheeks with his thumb. "I love you too. More every day." His lips caressed hers. "Definitely a better memory than last year. See? I told you it was guaranteed."

She grinned and lifted to kiss him hard. "You're a silly, sentimental man. I'm glad I'm the only one who gets to see this side of you."

After one last brush of the lips, he carefully lifted himself. "I hope we don't have to change clothes. We'll be late." She followed him to the bathroom where he helped her remove her dress so they both could clean up. Thanks to the slit up the side, the dress wasn't wrinkled, but William's shirt needed to be replaced.

By the time he changed and Elizabeth touched up the light dusting of make-up she wore, they wouldn't make it for the start of the party, but fortunately, Carson didn't have any traffic to contend with during the drive to the ballroom. When they entered, no one paid any mind to their late arrival, or even their arrival together. Their relationship had become public knowledge a while back—in April to be exact, when one of the secretaries from finance saw William and Elizabeth hand-in-hand at the grocery store, picking out dinner for one of the evenings Mrs. Hill was off-duty.

Word spread like wildfire through the company, but William and Elizabeth behaved just as they always had. Of course, a few small people whispered questions of Elizabeth's promotion, but most of the employees refused to believe it and refused to spread the tale. After all, he put too much into the company to let someone into such an important role based on sex, and she worked too hard and was too brilliant at her job to have slept her way into the position.

"Lizzy!" Charlotte waved from where she stood at the bar with Jane. "Come get a glass of wine. I need someone to drink with me since Jane can't."

One of the members of the board had grabbed William when they walked in, so after a squeeze to his hand, Elizabeth joined Charlotte and Jane. She looked at Jane's bubbly drink.

"Soda with lime," said Jane. "What are you having?"

The bartender leaned closer, and she held out a bill. "Chenin Blanc."

Jane scooted up on the barstool, her slightly rounded belly poking out more seated than it did standing. She and Charlie had married in July, and the next thing everyone knew, she was pregnant. Jane and Charlie were over the moon, and ever since, Jane had been bugging Elizabeth to get pregnant so their children could grow up together.

When the bartender set down her drink, Elizabeth lifted it to take a sip but almost dropped it at Charlotte's loud "Holy shit!"

Charlotte took the wine from Elizabeth's hand, set it on the bar, and held her fingers out. "Jane! Did you know about this?"

Her sister tugged her hand away from Charlotte. "It's bigger than mine. Tiffany?"

"Harry Winston." Elizabeth mumbled it and bit her lip as Charlotte grabbed her hand back. Her eyes met William's, and he smiled while he nodded at something he was being told.

"When did he propose?"

"This evening, before we left for the party." Elizabeth picked up the wine with her unoccupied hand and took a sizeable swallow.

"Were you surprised?"

"What's that supposed to mean, Jane?" asked Charlotte. "She's been living with him for nearly a year. Everyone knew it was only a matter of time before Darcy popped the question. I mean, he still looks at her like a moony-eyed teenager."

Jane rolled her eyes. "They could've lived together for years. Some people do. I thought Lizzy might because she was trying to avoid Mom organizing a wedding."

Elizabeth gulped another mouthful of wine. "Jane Bennet-Bingley, you tell Mom about this before I'm ready, and I'll tell her your due date."

Her sister gasped and placed a hand on her belly. "You wouldn't!"

"Oh, I definitely would. Let William and me decide what we want before we tell Mom. You know that she scared the crap out of him when we visited this summer."

A fit of giggles erupted from Jane. "I'm sorry, but his face when she grabbed his butt was priceless. Didn't Charlie tell him that she did the same to him?"

"Apparently not."

Charlotte snickered, finally letting go of Elizabeth's hand. "I'd elope. That would be the best way to keep your mom out of the loop. Otherwise, you know she's going to stick her nose so far in, you'll have to have it surgically removed."

Jane began laughing, a snort coming out somewhere in the middle. "Charlotte, you're terrible."

"But I'm right, and you know it."

Before Elizabeth could take another sip of her wine, Ana bounded up with Jacob trailing along behind her. "Lizzy, I'm so glad you're here." William's sister hugged her and grabbed her hand. "I'm so excited! He really did it!"

It was all Elizabeth could do to keep her jaw from hitting the floor. "How did you know?"

"Who do you think went ring shopping with him? For what it's worth, the one I tried to get him to buy had diamonds all around the band and was a carat larger, but *he* insisted you'd prefer something simpler."

Thank goodness William had gone with his own instincts! She studied her beautiful ring. Even without seeing the alternative, she definitely preferred this one. She didn't want diamonds on the inside of the band. That part of her every day rings always bumped against the side of her desk and took more abuse than the settings. What if she knocked all the diamonds out?

"I'm glad he chose this one, Ana. It's certainly more me than the one you described. It does sound pretty, but more than what I'd want. Thanks for helping him, though."

She'd gotten to know Ana quite well in the last year. The girl sometimes came across somewhat impulsive once you got to know her, but her heart was definitely in the right place.

"Don't forget that I get to be a bridesmaid," Ana said. Her hand hitched up on her hip while she lifted her eyebrows.

Elizabeth grinned. "William and I haven't spoken of it yet, but once, he did mention you would be his best man. Don't worry, you'd wear a dress, but you'd be his witness. We just have to figure out what kind of wedding we'd like to have first. I want it as simple as possible."

Jane lifted her glass. "And to keep Mom as much out of the planning as possible."

"Amen." Charlotte and Elizabeth clinked glasses with her.

"I hadn't considered that." Ana cringed. "Just the thought of her having a hand in the planning gives me flashes of pink tulle and powder blue tuxes."

Elizabeth leaned back against the bar and sighed. "I'm glad she's not that bad. I always imagined a black and white wedding with red roses."

Her sister's eyes closed and she crinkled her nose. "Great, if you get married while I'm pregnant, I'll look like an orca standing beside you."

"You'll be just as beautiful as you always are, Jane, and Mom won't hesitate to tell everyone." Elizabeth took a sip of her wine while Jane rolled her eyes.

"We'll have to talk Dad into buying her a muzzle."

While Jameson prattled on and on about the company and the next board meeting, Darcy let his eyes wander back to Elizabeth frequently while he listened. Heck, he stood at an angle to make it easier since Jameson could find himself interesting for hours. He didn't need Darcy's input at all.

He'd been looking when Charlotte noticed Elizabeth's ring and when Ana became a part of the group. Poor Jacob stood behind her but not really taking part in the ladies' discussion. He didn't know anyone else at the party so he was stranded wherever Ana led.

After a half-hour of Jameson, he clapped the man on the shoulder. "Jameson, I'm looking forward to the presentation at the next board meeting. In the meantime, it's Christmas, it's a party, and I have a stunning date drinking wine at the bar without me." He glanced behind the man to see Jameson's wife seated at a nearby table, watching him with her chin resting in her hand. "Perhaps your wife would like to dance? Merry Christmas!"

Before the man could stop him, he shifted away and around a nearby group of people, giving them a wave and saying Merry Christmas. This year, he intended to spend as much of the evening with his newly minted fiancée as possible.

He walked up behind Ana and leaned over her shoulder. "Jacob looks bored to tears. Perhaps you should dance with the guy."

She jumped and whirled around to hug him. "I'm so happy for you! I had to come tonight just to make sure you proposed."

"Of course, I proposed. But we're not discussing weddings all night long. I intend to dance with my fiancée." He held out his hand. "May I?"

Her empty glass found its way to the bar behind her as she placed her free hand in his. He gave Jane a quick kiss on the cheek, then led Elizabeth to the dance floor, pulling her close and touching his cheek to her temple. "Don't let me get cornered by anyone again tonight."

Her shoulders shook while her thumb grazed up and down his upper back, the sensation penetrating through his suit coat and shirt. How was that even possible?

"Agreed."

His lips brushed the smallest of kisses to her hairline. Before Elizabeth, he couldn't imagine finding happiness. He kept busy with work and exercise, trying not to dwell on what he didn't have, but women were never simple for him—either they were like Caroline Bingley and wanted to marry a wealthy man or they eventually complained that he took them for granted. He'd never found a woman that made him want to leave work on time or even take his vacation until Elizabeth. Obviously, they weren't the right ones. Thankfully, he'd never tried marrying one of them!

Her head tilted back. "What are you thinking?"

He brushed the curled tendrils of hair back from her face. "How perfect everything is. How much I love you. How I can't wait to start a life with you."

"We already have a life together, but we're getting married—making our relationship permanent. I don't want to trivialize it, but I feel like I joined my life with yours when I cleaned the last of my belongings out of my apartment. Marrying you makes us forever. It makes what we have that much more special."

It hadn't taken long for them to find places for her belongings in the house. She now had her own study with her own furniture, and Ana had needed a new bed for her apartment. Elizabeth's was perfect. The lanterns he'd bought her for Christmas last year stood on their pedestals next to the claw foot tub in their bathroom while the artwork all went to her office. In the end, her apartment had been easy to empty. Mr. Gardiner even bought her washer and dryer for when his daughter started college in August.

She was right. They'd been sharing a life since Valentine's Day. They talked about their days over dinner and watched television or a movie together when they felt like it. They planned their weekends and even talked about what they wanted for the future—this future, the one they were starting now.

The music faded, and when he turned to the small stage area, Bingley held a microphone with an enormous grin on his face.

"Oh, no," said Darcy.

"What?"

"Who gave him a microphone?"

Bingley put up a hand, and everyone quieted down while he searched the dance floor. When he found Darcy, his grin became wider. "Sorry to interrupt the party, but my wife just gave me a piece of news about our illustrious leader. Tonight, he finally proposed to our dedicated head of the legal department and was accepted. So, if you don't have your glass, please grab it, because I would like to propose a toast! To William Darcy and Elizabeth Bennet and many happy years together! To the future Mr. and Mrs. Darcy!"

The End

Acknowledgements

First and foremost, I'd my first thank you is to the loyal readers at Austen Variations. I wrote this simply for some fun during an Advent calendar Christmas theme and next thing I knew, I was fleshing out a full-length story. I believe I have a list of shorts that our wonderful followers have requested longer versions. We'll see if I can ever write it all!

For my family, I always give my love and appreciation for their unwavering support. My husband listens to all my frustrations. Poor guy! By the time this book is released, he'll be half-way around the world—without us—and I'll be doing my best to pull everything together wherever I am. At the time that I am writing this, that's still so far up in the air, I can't see it. What makes it worse is to know that it's coming. All those little and big things overwhelm the both of us and make things terribly difficult, but we've always muddled through in the past and somehow, we will again. I love you, Brandon!

My oldest has started as one of my proof-readers and the other two love to tell people I write books. It's amazing to me that they take pride in what I've accomplished. They are always a part of it because I couldn't do this without them!

I've had a wonderful group of friends and fans from Meryton.com and DarcyandLizzy.com since I started in JAFF. They're always good for an ego boost and are a great sounding board for a new story. I always look forward to sharing something new with them.

I've had a number of betas along the way, but Lisa Toth and Suzan Lauder have stuck with me from the beginning, or nearly the beginning. They have become amazing friends and are always a willing ear or eyes when I need an opinion on anything from a book to a blog post. I have learnt so much from them both, and I owe them so much. A huge thanks to Kristi, who has beta'd several of my books, including this one.

My editor, Brynn, was a lucky find. Who knew a cup of coffee and discussion on editing would lead here? She adds the multitude of question marks that I forget, fixes my complements, and keeps me consistent. I'm just thrilled she could take the time between diaper changes, awesome baby giggles, and yoga classes to edit this book as well.

One last thank you to Brenna for proofreading! I am terrible about changing things as I read over and over. I really appreciate the help. It saves my sanity.

JAFF is a relatively small and tight-knit community, and I love that. The support of other authors in the genre is lovely as is the support and devotion of our fan base. Thank you to everyone who has purchased my books, left me wonderful messages, and followed me after reading one of my stories. I wouldn't be able to have this much fun without your support and encouragement.

About the Author

L.L. Diamond is more commonly known as Leslie to her friends and Mom to her three kids. A native of Louisiana, she spent the majority of her life living within an hour of New Orleans before following her husband all over as a military wife. Louisiana, Mississippi, California, Texas, New Mexico, Nebraska, and now England have all been called home along the way.

After watching *Sense and Sensibility* with her mother, Leslie became a fan of Jane Austen, reading her collected works over the next few years. *Pride and Prejudice* stood out as a favourite and has dominated her writing since finding Jane Austen Fan Fiction.

Aside from mother and writer, Leslie considers herself a perpetual student. She has degrees in biology and studio art but will devour any subject of interest simply for the knowledge. Her most recent endeavours have included certifications to coach swimming as well as a fitness instructor. As an artist, her concentration is in graphic design, but watercolour is her medium of choice with one of her watercolours featured on the cover of her second book, *A Matter of Chance*. She is also a member of the Jane Austen Society of North America. Leslie also plays flute and piano, but much like Elizabeth Bennet, she is always in need of practice!

Leslie's books include: *Rain and Retribution, A Matter of Chance, An Unwavering Trust, The Earl's Conquest, Particular Intentions, Particular Attachments,* and *Unwrapping Mr. Darcy.*